PRAISE FOR

When the Stars Lead to You

"*When the Stars Lead to You* is lovely, so lovely. A diverse story full of heart and hope, truth and acceptance, that tackles the tough stuff even as it leaves you breathless. As one of the characters says, **'there's so much love here,' and I didn't want it to end.**" —Jennifer Niven, *New York Times* bestselling author of *All the Bright Places*

"This debut explores all the beauty and ache of first love with so much compassion. Devon and Ashton, both on their own and as a couple, tread a rocky, soul-nourishing path to acceptance and healing. **A book to be savored.**"
—Rachel Lynn Solomon, author of *Our Year of Maybe*

"Debut author Davis provides a new take on the archetypal first-love novel by tackling the impact of mental health, race, and class wars. **A moving love story**, timely given the pervasiveness of mental health crises."
—*Kirkus Reviews*

"Fans of Sarah Dessen and Nicholas Sparks need look no further than Davis's debut for their next **book crush**."
—*Booklist*

"Filled with passion and conflict, Davis's debut novel, [is] **a modern Romeo and Juliet tale**." —*Publishers Weekly*

"Readers who love **a good soapy drama-romance** may find their hearts aflutter from the twists and turns of Devon and Ashton's love." —*The Bulletin*

"A unique look at love and depression."
—*School Library Journal*

When the STARS Lead to YOU

RONNI DAVIS

Little, Brown Young Readers
New York Boston

To Mommy
for teaching me to love books
and
to Ms. Wheeler
for encouraging me to write them

Little, Brown and Company
Hachette Book Group
1290 Avenue of the Americas, New York, NY 10104
Visit us at LBYR.com

Originally published in hardcover and ebook by Little, Brown and Company in November 2019
First Trade Paperback Edition: April 2021

Little, Brown and Company is a division of Hachette Book Group, Inc.
The Little, Brown name and logo are trademarks of Hachette Book Group, Inc.
The publisher is not responsible for websites (or their content) that are not owned by the publisher.

The Library of Congress has cataloged the hardcover edition as follows:
Names: Davis, Ronni, author.
Title: When the stars lead to you / Ronni Davis.
Description: First edition. | New York ; Boston : Little, Brown Young Readers, 2019. |
Summary: After Ashton broke Devon's heart, she focused on preparing for her future as an astrophysicist but Ashton's appearance on the first day of her senior year forces her to revisit their magical summer together.
Identifiers: LCCN 2018057312 | ISBN 9780316490702 (hardcover) | ISBN 9780316490696 (pbk.) | ISBN 9780316490689 (ebk.)
Subjects: | CYAC: Love—Fiction. | High schools—Fiction. | Schools—Fiction. | Depression, Mental—Fiction. | Racially mixed people—Fiction.
Classification: LCC PZ7.1.D3837 Whe 2019 | DDC [Fic]—dc23
LC record available at https://lccn.loc.gov/2018057312

ISBNs: 978-0-316-49069-6 (pbk.), 978-0-316-49068-9 (ebook)

Printed in the United States of America

LSC-C

Printing 1, 2021

BEFORE

-Then-

You'd think someone who wanted to study the stars would know better than to wish on them. There was no logical reason for me to put so much hope in exploding balls of hydrogen and helium, especially since they were millions of light-years away. But it didn't matter. Every single night, I turned my head toward the sky, closed my eyes, and dreamed.

Like right now, sitting on the beach during the summer solstice, watching Arcturus rise. The red giant, twenty-five times bigger than the sun, burning brighter than every star in the northern hemisphere, both awed and terrified me. But it also somehow comforted me. Made me feel safe. So I gave him one simple wish: that I'd have the best summer ever.

My cousin Stephanie and her family lived at the beach year-round. Her parents owned one of the souvenir shops and

a restaurant here. It was just a few hours' drive north from my hometown, so I visited every year while my parents did non-church-affiliated (they really wanted everyone to know that part) missionary work in Honduras. If they knew the things Stephanie and I got up to (boys! parties! kissing!), they probably wouldn't have been so quick to let me go every summer.

I loved these quiet nights before the tourists took over. The tide rolling in, the cool Atlantic waves splashing over my ankles and making me shiver. Pretty soon, they'd be splashing over my knees, then my thighs. I buried my toes in the sand. I liked the way it tickled when the surf carried the grains from under my feet. And I loved the stars scattering all over the sky like diamonds against blue velvet.

This was the dream life.

"Yo, Devon," Stephanie called. "Come here. I want you to meet someone."

And then there was reality.

My cousin fancied herself a matchmaker, but she had no clue about the type of guys I liked. *I* barely had a clue about the type of guys I liked, because I got attracted to so many different kinds. Tall and skinny with pale skin, dark hair, and hazel eyes. Dark-brown skin, deep brown eyes, and locs. Tan skin, dimples, blue eyes, and blond hair.

Two things I did know: He had to be kind, and he had to be a gentleman.

Because honestly? I was sick of kissing a guy only to have him dragging my hand to his pants ten seconds later.

The firelight threw shadows over Stephanie's silvery-blond

hair, making her look almost unearthly. Two boys stood with her, both in silhouette, both holding plastic red cups.

"Devon! Get your booty over here," she commanded.

I groaned, but I trudged over anyway. "Hey, Steph."

"About time." She thrust a red cup into my hand, then threw her arm around me and grinned. Her cheeks were already flushed, her breath warm and boozy. "This is Todd and his cousin Ashton."

"Nice to meet you," Todd said. Polite, but clearly way more interested in Stephanie. I couldn't even blame him. She was adorable; short and curvy with dark-green eyes and a tiny button nose. Completely opposite of Todd, the epitome of tall, dark, and handsome, with piercing blue eyes and jet-black hair. They looked good standing together.

Then I turned to Ashton.

Sweet six-pound, five-ounce baby Jesus.

It's so clichéd, but there was a reason those clichés existed.

Ashton.

Was.

Gorgeous. With a capital *G*.

I had never, ever seen anyone like him. Straight nose, wide mouth, full lips that were slightly pouty. Impossibly clear skin with the tiniest hint of sunburn coloring his cheeks. His short bronze-colored hair was wavy and thick, and my fingers tingled with longing to get tangled up in it. Everything on his face was in proportion, and yet he wasn't shiny-perfect. His ears stuck out a little too much and he was a little too skinny. But that was okay. I didn't mind thin guys. Plus, there was something different about Ashton. A stillness—major contrast to the whooping and hollering around us. And his eyes. So intense. So mysterious. A deep, deep brown that invited me to dive in and get lost.

So I got lost.

Falling, falling, spinning somewhere I'd never been before, but a place I knew I wanted to be. I tried not to stare, but he was staring at me. The world melted away, leaving only me and him and the crashing waves.

"Hey," he said with a gentle smile. His teeth were perfectly white and straight, the result of either amazing genetics or thousands of dollars of orthodontia. With his track record so far, I was betting on the former.

"Hi," I said breathlessly. *Breathlessly*. I was breathless. What was going on?

"So... Devon?"

"Yes," I managed to get out. Seriously? His voice was smooth with a touch of gravel, like how velvet would sound if you rubbed it against the grain. Oh my God. Chills. Everywhere.

"I'm Ashton. Nice to meet you."

I had a weakness for perfect handshakes, and Ashton's was just right. Not so hard it crushed my hand, but not one of those limp noodle ones, either.

"Todd and I are going to get refills," Stephanie said, finally breaking Ashton's hold on me. Yeah... forgot she was even there. "You guys want?"

"I'm good." Ashton raised his cup, which was almost full.

He was still looking at me.

"So am I," I said.

I was still looking at him.

"We'll leave you to it," Stephanie said, then she and Todd were gone.

I raised my eyebrow when Ashton poured his beer into the sand. He blinked at me and blushed.

"I don't drink," he explained. "Your cousin poured it for me, and I didn't want to be rude."

"No worries." I shrugged and poured my own beer into the sand. "I don't drink much, either. She never remembers that."

His eyes scanned the entire length of my body, then met mine head-on. This boy was *so* checking me out…and I could tell by the way his lips parted that he liked what he saw. I'm sure I was looking at him the same way. Because oh yes, I definitely liked what I saw. He must have had terrible-smelling feet or something because there was no way this guy was this perfect.

"So, Devon," he said again. "Hi."

I grinned. "Hi."

He covered his eyes and scrunched up his nose. "Oh my God. We did this already." He peeked at me through his fingers. "Sorry."

Adorable. "Your first time here?"

He shook his head. "My family first brought me when I was five, but I barely remember it. So I have no idea what people do around here. Besides the obvious stuff, I mean."

I shrugged. "Not much, to be honest. I like to walk on the boardwalk or go swimming. Lots of parties, if you're into that sort of thing."

"More into video games or taking pictures," he said. "Sometimes I go horseback riding."

"You have a horse?"

"His name's Leander. I've had him since I was eleven. So, five years."

Ashton was sixteen. Like me.

He pulled out his phone and started scrolling. *Really?* Minus ten points for that. I hated when people couldn't stay off their phones for five stinking minutes. Weren't we having a conversation?

But then he said, "This is him," and held his phone out to me. Immediate guilt for going off in my head.

"He's incredible. Is he an Arabian?"

Ashton smiled at his phone. "Yeah. He's great. Do you have a horse?"

"I like them. But no."

"Oh. That's too bad." He dropped the phone into one of the pockets on his cargo shorts.

"Plus, my cousin says I keep to myself too much," I said. "I have a best friend...but if I had a horse I'd never hang out with people." I buried my pink toenails in the sand. "She likes to tease me."

He looked perplexed. "Why?"

"Why do I keep to myself or why does Steph tease me?"

"Both."

"I'm a big nerd. It's why she's always introducing me to people."

His gaze was steady. "I'm glad she introduced us."

I shivered all over. "Me too."

He looked down at the sand, then caught my eye again. "Do you wanna come with me to get some ice cream?"

A warm, fuzzy feeling spread through my entire being. "I'd love to."

His face broke into a slow grin that made me want to melt right into the sand. Then *I* grinned. We stood there grinning at each other like goofballs until my stomach growled.

Laughing, he held out his hand. "Come on, let's go handle that monster."

I let my fingers intertwine with his.

My summer was already looking promising.

—Then—

THE FIRST WEEKEND OF THE SUMMER SEASON—ONCE THE tourists were good and ingratiated—was always epic. You couldn't walk two feet without bumping into a rip-roaring party. But pick the wrong one and it could ruin your entire summer. Too much beer, people vomiting at your feet, hooking up with the wrong person, STDs. Terrible decisions all around.

Lucky for us, Stephanie always managed to find the right parties. The ones on private beaches with a full bar instead of just a keg. The ones with actual DJs instead of someone's random playlist that always had a Chicago song on it for some reason. The ones where the hosts actually served food like hamburgers and crudités instead of just chips…or nothing at all.

Tonight, we strolled—fashionably late—into an enormous beach house blasting music so loudly the wicker furniture jumped to the beat. There were people everywhere, not that we could see them very well. The only lighting came from the twinkle lights and LED candles and a fancy show from the DJ booth.

"You made it!" Tall, Dark, and Handsome was back, pulling Stephanie and me into a group hug. He was damp, smelling like chlorine. Cold droplets from his hair dripped onto my back, making me shiver.

"We made it," Stephanie said, then turned to me. "You remember Todd?"

"Of course I remember," I said. But I remembered his cousin more. Had it just been last night that we met?

"This is my buddy Justin's place, but I'm the official host. Because Justin's a bitch-ass bitch who doesn't even have a fake ID." Todd turned to me. "Make yourself at home, help yourself to anything." To Stephanie, he said, "*You* come with me."

And great. Now I was alone.

The best and worst part about tourist season was that the faces changed constantly. Meeting new people was always cool. And if a hookup was disappointing, chances were high I'd never see the dude again. Bad because if you did find someone you liked hanging out with, they'd likely be gone in a week. Then you'd have to start all over.

But I loved the possibilities. Anything that happened could be life changing. And tonight, everyone was new.

I grabbed a soda and wandered around, letting the beats soak into my bones and make my body sway. Sweat dripped down my neck as the house heated up from the warm bodies getting caught up in the music.

I made my way out to the pool, where the air was only slightly cooler. A heat wave had kicked off this morning, and the humidity soaked my hair and made the curls shrink into tight spirals. I pulled my hair up into a big pouf, letting the slight sea breeze cool my back.

I was watching a game of beer pong gear up when a voice came from behind me. "You *are* here." My heart sped up at the sound of the low, gravelly rumble that had played nonstop in my brain for the last twenty-four hours.

I whirled around and there he was. An oasis in the midst of noise, sweat, and cigarettes. "Hi."

Ashton smiled, the corners of his eyes crinkling. "I thought Todd was bullshitting me. So when you said you were busy tonight... it was this?"

"*I* never said anything. Steph hijacked my phone, telling me something about making you wait three days." Even though she hadn't made Todd wait three days. But whatever. No way was I going to admit to Ashton that I kinda hoped I'd run into him here.

He frowned and shook his head. "I don't get those rules. Seems like if you want to see someone, just see them."

My knees weakened. "You wanted to see me again?"

His gaze was solemn. "Wasn't it obvious?"

"Ashton!" A girl popped up beside him and shook out her long blond hair. "I can't believe you're actually here!"

He gave her a closemouthed smile. "Here I am."

"You should come sit with me." She licked her pink glossy lips. "Over there."

She didn't even acknowledge my presence.

"I'm good." Ashton stroked my thumb, sending flutters clear up my arm.

With hard eyes, the blonde gave me a once-over that almost canceled the goose bumps from Ashton's touch. Then she turned back to him, all warmth and smiles. "Next time."

My skin prickled as she sauntered off. Then I glanced at Ashton. "Who's she?"

"I met her yesterday. I think she's staying a couple houses down from us."

"Do girls always act like that around you?"

"*You* were going to make me wait three days."

I tilted my head. "Would you have waited?"

He looked me up and down, then his gaze met mine head-on. "Without question."

Holy shit.

We sat on a patio love seat and watched guys toss girls into the pool. People stumbled in and out of the hot tub, holding red cups full of God knows what.

"The people-watching." Ashton shook his head.

"I know."

He leaned back and stretched, slipping his arm around my shoulders. I laughed so hard I almost dropped my soda. "Seriously?"

His broad smile made his entire being light up. "You're not pulling away."

I snuggled into his shoulder. *Mmm*, he smelled so good—cool and clean, like a fresh waterfall. "I guess not."

We watched a group of girls take selfies in front of the pool. A guy to the left of us offered a hit off his bong, which Ashton refused. Then he squirmed. "I always feel so out of place at these things."

I nodded. "I used to love parties. But now? Give me Netflix and junk food, please."

"Exactly! Okay. If we were watching Netflix right now, what would be on the screen?"

"Hold on. Is this a Netflix-and-chill situation, or are we actually watching something?"

"It's a legit binge session."

"Hmm." I twirled a stray curl, thinking. "What do you watch with your friends?"

"My best friend and I like totally different things," he said. "He likes to watch people eating weird shit. I watch sitcoms. What about you? What do you watch with your friends?"

"Romantic comedies," I said without missing a beat. "But what would I watch with you?" I tapped my lip. "Since we don't know each other that well yet, I'll say something funny, like stand-up. But not raunchy stand-up. Because that could get awkward."

"Makes sense. I like it. And we'd have popcorn and M&M's and chocolate chip cookies."

"Yes! Perfect!" I snuggled closer and intertwined my hand with his. "I wish…"

I could smell the mint on his breath. Could practically taste the saltiness of his skin. "What do you wish?" he whispered.

I never got to finish that thought. A loud crash came from just inside the door, followed by a lot of yelling. Then the beer pong game got louder, the splashing in the pool got rowdier...

"...and someone just puked in the hot tub." Ashton frowned, his face a slight green.

"I think that's our cue."

He squeezed my hand. "Let's get out of here."

We left the party and headed down to the public beach. It was empty and dark, except for a few red lights bobbing farther down the shore. We found a quiet spot right in front of the dunes. I kicked off my sandals and stretched my legs. Arcturus had long set by now, but there were still so many other stars.

The cool sea breeze felt good on my warm skin. My entire body flushed because Ashton and I were alone. Even if nothing else came out of tonight, I wanted to kiss him. So much.

"I have to know all about you," he said to me.

"Ask me anything."

"I'll start small. What's your favorite color?"

"Purple. But not any purple. More like a mix between lilac and lavender silk with sunlight shining through it."

He scrunched his nose. "That is oddly specific."

"What's yours?"

"Changes with my mood, I guess. Green or blue when I'm calm, red when I'm pissed."

"So if I see you wearing red, I should steer clear?"

He laughed, showing off those perfect teeth. "I don't know if it's that deep. What music do you listen to?"

I traced swirls in the sand with my toes. "My best friend turned me on to classical, but I also like R & B and pop. And sometimes I listen to show tunes."

His face lit up. "Like Broadway?"

"My dad plays the cast albums all the time. *Rent* is my favorite."

"*Hamilton* for me. It's so good. But I like *Rent*, too." He started humming the melody to "One Song Glory."

"You have a good humming voice," I said. "Do you sing?"

"All the time." He gave me a pointed look. "When I'm alone."

"One day you're going to sing for me," I said, "and you're going to like it."

He bopped my nose. "We'll see about that."

"What other music do you like?" I asked.

"Hip-hop."

"What is it with white boys loving hip-hop? You don't rap, do you?"

"God, no. Rapping is not my lane. I just listen and learn."

I nodded in appreciation. "Okay."

He grew serious, his eyes still on mine. "Tell me more."

This time the words came easier. I told him about how I visited my cousin here at the beach every year. I told him my favorite foods (sushi and sub sandwiches), that I loved burning incense, and that I hated the sound of people chewing. That I earned the money for my first telescope by doing odd jobs for my neighbors, and that I loved being an only child. I told him how I cried every morning my first week of kindergarten, and about the time I wet myself in second grade because mean old Miss Bradley refused to give me the hall pass.

"I've never told anyone half this stuff," I admitted.

He brushed a curl behind my ear. "I'm glad I was the first."

It was silly and weird and a bit scary how the words flew out of me like butterflies, even when I was recounting my most embarrassing moments. How he seemed interested in getting to know me instead of only interested in getting off.

"I want to ask you one more thing," he said.

"Go for it."

"Say we're watching Netflix, but now we know each other way better. What would you binge with me?"

"Documentaries."

He paused. "Seriously?"

"The ones about the universe and space."

He nodded slowly. "I get it. That stuff's cool."

I picked up some sand and let it fall through my fingers. "You think so? Because I want to tell you something else about me."

Ashton leaned back on his elbows. Totally relaxed. "Go for it."

I took a deep breath. "I love the stars."

He sat up again and fully fixed his attention on me. So I kept going. "I *live* for the stars. And one day, I'm going to be an astrophysicist."

He smiled in wonder. "Wow. You're beaming. I love it. So is astrophysics like astronomy?"

"It's a part of it. It deals more with the nature of heavenly bodies. Things like what galaxies, red giants, and black holes are made of. How long they've been out there, and what they mean for us, as humans. Or I can go all theoretical and focus on things like time travel." I wrapped my arms around myself. "I want to solve the mysteries of deep space. And I want to discover new worlds."

His mouth shaped into an O. "This has got to be the coolest thing I've ever heard."

"I can go on and on," I warned him. "You might not think it's so cool then."

"Try me."

So I did. I talked about the stars and physics and deep space. I talked about all the things I'd have to study, like geometry, calculus, and physics. "I want to get my doctorate," I said.

Ashton's expression was steady. As if he actually gave a damn about what I dreamed about. Most people glazed over when I got too into it. But *he listened*.

He nodded, his eyes still on me. "Dr. Devon."

"Kearney. Dr. Devon Kearney," I said.

"Devon Kearney, PhD," he said, smiling. "Has the perfect ring to it. I can't wait till you get there."

"If I get there."

"You will. I believe in you."

That's when my physical attraction shifted into something more: I wanted to be his friend, too.

I lightly poked his shoulder. "If I'm spilling all my secrets, it's only fair you tell me all yours."

"But you know that means we'll have to spend more time together," he said. Then he got really quiet. "I'd like that. A lot. Would you?"

I didn't even hesitate. "I would."

—Then—

Most people probably think waking up at the crack of dawn during summer vacation is plain nonsense, but I wouldn't have had it any other way. Every morning, I let the lightening sky kiss my eyelids until they fluttered open, then I bounced out of bed, ready to embrace the day.

The kitchen was quiet while I poured hot tea into a to-go cup. Then I grabbed my beach bag and headed down. The sea breeze blew curls around my face, and the rising sun warmed my skin while showing me a sky full of pastel swirls.

Morning yoga, in my opinion, was the very best yoga, and I loved doing Sun Salutations while dawn bloomed.

Every day, once my practice was over, my stomach would announce itself in the most obnoxious way, so I'd head back for breakfast. By now, the household would be up. Uncle Steven already off to the restaurant to fire things up for the morning rush. Aunt Susan hopping onto her bike to start her day at the souvenir shop. Stephanie frying bacon and scrambling eggs, grumbling about having to be up so early (to help in her mom's souvenir shop) even though by now it was already 8:00 AM.

Except today, she was smirking when I walked in the door. "Someone's here for you."

"What? Oh!"

"Hi," Ashton said. He was sitting at the kitchen table, flipping a fork through his fingers. "Sorry for randomly showing up like this. I couldn't sleep, so I took a walk, and..."

"You just *happened* to end up here?" Stephanie's eyes flashed with mirth.

"Something like that," he murmured, then turned to me. "Do you wanna hang out?"

My breath quickened and I tingled all over.

Because, um. Hell yes.

"I need to grab a shower, if you don't mind waiting a bit," I said.

Stephanie set a plate of food in front of him. "This should keep him busy."

Quick shower. Brush teeth. Hair in ponytail. Throw on bathing suit with sundress on top. Comfortable sandals. And...go.

Ashton had just put his clean dish in the rack when I came back out. I grabbed a muffin, then turned to him. "Ready?"

He took my hand. "Let's go."

★ · ● · ✕

"It just occurred to me," I said as we strolled along the boardwalk, "the only things I know about you are your favorite color, you have a horse, and you like *Hamilton*."

Ashton frowned thoughtfully. "Honestly, you're not missing much. I'm not that fascinating."

"I don't believe that. Plus, turnabout is fair play."

He stopped walking. "Turna-who what now?"

"You had a turn to learn about me. It's my turn to learn about you."

A slow nod. "What do you want to know?"

We sat on a bench. I pulled out my muffin and inhaled deeply. *Mmm*, strawberry. "Tell me the weird things," I said. "Do you have terrible handwriting? Do you pick your nose and eat it? That sort of thing."

His forehead wrinkled. "What the hell?"

"It's important."

"It's gross."

I raised my eyebrows. "Are you going to answer the question, though?"

"I don't pick my nose and eat it, Devon. Where did you even come up with that?"

"I always wonder random things about people. For instance." I pointed to a blond woman bouncing a chubby blond baby. "Do you think she snores? Or eats onions?"

He tilted his head sideways. "I'm going to say she snores when she's got a cold, and she only eats Vidalia onions."

I turned to him, eyebrows raised. "Wow. You're better at this than I expected."

"I mean, it's kind of fun," he said. "What about that guy over there? Do you think he's ever slipped on a banana peel?"

"Totally. And he's the type to fart and blame the dog. But. We are getting off topic. Do *you* snore? Or eat onions?"

"I'll pretty much eat whatever you put in front of me, and I don't snore. I've tripped over shoelaces, but never a banana peel."

"How do you know you don't snore?"

"It's just a feeling I have," he said with a cocky grin.

Here is something else I learned about Ashton that day: He was kind of musical. There was always change or keys jangling in his pocket as he walked. He constantly bopped his head to some tune only he could hear. He drummed his fingers on his thighs when he was concentrating. Sometimes he drummed his fingers on me—my arm when he wanted to show me something. Or just while he was looking at me, before breaking into a slow smile.

He couldn't keep his hands still. Either it was the drumming or he was flipping a pen or a toothpick or a straw between his fingers. Almost like a meditation.

Because he drifted away. Often. His eyes focused on something I couldn't see. Like now, at dinner. I watched him as he sat, myriad pensive expressions dancing across his face.

"Dollar for your thoughts," I said.

Those brown eyes swung toward me. "A dollar? You know the phrase is 'penny,' right? They aren't even worth that much."

I reached over and touched his hand. "I don't believe that."

He looked at me, his expression curious, but I didn't get a chance to read too much into it before the waiter brought us our food.

"Okay. Here's something weird about me," Ashton said while we were eating. Sitting on the same side of the table in a diner booth because we were already somehow becoming *that couple*. "I like the sound of paper crumpling. Right by my ear. It relaxes me."

Without thinking, I reached up and stroked his earlobe. "What else do you do to relax?"

He sighed and leaned into my hand. "I play video games. A super-violent one when I'm mad. Sometimes I play one where I control virtual people, but that one's a total time suck." He paused, then let out a deep breath. "Right now, my favorite is one I don't tell anyone about because it's a cute game, and my friends and I don't *do* cute games."

"What? That's ridiculous. You like what you like."

"Yeah, doesn't quite work that way."

Then he got really quiet.

The minutes ticked by as he picked at his chicken strips.

"Where do you go?" I asked him.

"What do you mean?"

"When you get quiet like that."

"Oh." He stole one of my tater tots and popped it into his mouth. "I'm right here with you. The only place I want to be."

-Then-

After four weeks, our routine had become familiar, and I wondered how I'd ever filled my summer days before Ashton came along. Most mornings, he'd show up for breakfast, and then, hand in hand, we'd stroll down the boardwalk. Or we'd run down to the beach and swim in the ocean for hours. By now, his hair had lightened from all the sun, and my skin had darkened to a deep tawny.

Some days, Ashton was animated, and he went on a mile a minute about anything and everything. His favorite video game, which he now played on his phone in front of me with zero shame. The latest dumpster fire on Twitter. Some messed-up thing Todd had said to him or tried to rope him into. On our best days, we sang lyrics from *Rent* to each other.

Other times, he was quiet. Subdued. Content to listen to

the surf crashing as the tide rose, to take deep breaths of the crisp salty air. I'd reach over and tweak his nose, and he'd turn to me with the gentlest smile before lightly planting a kiss on my temple.

He'd been busy today, doing something with his family that he didn't seem to want to share much about. By the time he picked me up, he was reflective, but he didn't seem too far away as he held out his hand. "Let's walk."

Right before sunset, we made our way down to a quiet part of the beach. "Be careful where you step," he said. "There might be jellyfish."

We found a safe spot far away from the surf. I pulled a beach blanket from my bag, and then Ashton and I cuddled close, watching the fiery dusk descend and a full moon rise. The temperature had dropped, and I shivered as the sea breeze cut through my shawl.

He slid his arms around me, and with a happy sigh, I settled against him. I loved this. His fingertips stroking my shoulder. The rise and fall of his chest with his breath. Being so close to him.

Pure heaven.

It had been four weeks since we'd first laid eyes on each other, and I was falling for him.

I should've been cautious. But I didn't want to be. Because *I was falling for him*.

"Hey, Dev?"

I smiled. Weirdly enough, no one had ever shortened my name like that, and I loved the way he sounded when he did it. There was a tenderness in his voice that made me shiver all over.

"What do you think we'd be watching on Netflix now?" he asked.

"Baking shows."

He stared at me in disbelief. "What?"

I nodded. "Yes. We'd be watching people make fancy cakes and try not to drop them. Or we'd be watching that show about all the people trying to make stuff and epically failing. Or *House Hunters*. Why? What would you choose?"

He blinked several times. "You'd pick *House Hunters*?"

"Without hesitation."

"But that's not even *on* Netflix."

I pointed to him. "Aha! Only someone looking for it would know that!"

"Look, I'm not ashamed to say I enjoy watching people get all bent out of shape over stupid shit like pedestal sinks and space for entertaining."

And out of nowhere, my brain decided to pop in an image of Ashton and me, looking for our own place. What silly things would we squabble over? What would be the one dramatic hard line one or both of us would have to take, just so there'd be drama?

What the *hell* was I thinking about this for?

To cover my thoughts, I snatched his phone. "How do you even play this game you love so much?"

"You meet neighbors, stock materials, grow things. Do cute little quests."

I squinted at the screen. "Is this *FarmVille*?"

He stared at me as if I'd grown two heads. "It's *Harvest Dreams*."

"Oh," I said. "It *is* cute."

"Let me set up a profile for you."

While he did that, I stared up at the sky. Clouds were rolling in and the sea was getting choppy. A storm was coming.

Two failed quests later, I was done for the night. I handed him back his phone, which he dropped into the pocket of his shorts. "You're new," he said. "We can try again tomorrow."

"No thanks. My special talent is being defeated by every single video game ever created."

"That's because you have better things to focus on. Like becoming Dr. Devon Kearney."

"God. It seems so far off."

"Will you be sitting on a beach like this, studying your stars?"

"Yes. Or maybe a lab. Hopefully in Paris."

He raised his eyebrows. "Why Paris?"

"They have one of the best observatories in the world."

"When you're there I'll have to call you *Docteur* Devon Kearney."

I loved how he talked like he was still going to be in my life all those years from now. I poked his shoulder. "Tell me *your* dreams."

"*My* dreams." He thought while the wind whipped our hair. Then he gazed at me in his soft, special way. "Feels like I'm living them right now."

"Yeah?"

"It's summer. I'm on the beach." He paused. "I'm here with you."

"Me?" I looked down. "Never thought I'd be part of someone's dreams."

"Well, I don't know if *you* noticed, but we've been spending a lot of time together." His voice was light, but the way my heart sped up showed me there was something serious under his joking tone.

Thunder rumbled in the distance. "Yeah. We have."

"I don't want to spend time with anyone but you," he said.

I sat up and stared at him. "So you mean..."

His gaze was fully focused on me. Steady. Sure. "I want to make this a thing. Me and you."

"Us." *Breathless.* This boy was constantly taking my breath away.

"Yeah." His lips curved slightly. "Us. I want to officially watch Netflix with you."

The laughter burst out of me. "What?"

He brushed a golden spiral from my forehead. "I want you to be my girlfriend."

The storm was coming. And I should have been cautious.

But that went out the window a long time ago.

"I'm in."

-Then-

"I HAVE SOMETHING FOR YOU."

"Really?" I grinned at Ashton and clapped my hands. I loved getting presents.

"Close your eyes."

I let my eyelids flutter shut, the impression of the night sky still swirling in my mind. Some nights, the stars were shy, hiding behind fluffy clouds. Tonight, they'd put on a show. There were so many of them, some so densely packed together they looked like blobs of smoke.

Absolutely breathtaking.

I felt Ashton move behind me, then lift my hair.

I shivered all over. "That tickles."

He laughed softly in my ear. "Stand still. I'll be done in a second."

A deep breath. "Okay."

His fingers trembled as he fixed a clasp at the back of my neck. At the same time, I felt the weight of a pendant settle on my chest. "Now you can open them."

I gasped as I lifted the silver key. Smooth and shiny. The top a hollow heart, the shaft a thin cylinder, with a T perpendicular to the tip. "Oh my God, Ashton."

"I know we only became official yesterday," he said. "But I wanted to get you something to show you how much I like you. I guess it's like a key to my heart."

A pause. Then we burst out laughing. "I'm sorry—that was so cheesy," he said.

"*So* cheesy."

"But true," he said, growing serious. "It's yours, Dev. I'm yours."

"You are a romantic."

"Only with you. And I don't care if it is cheesy."

"I love it, Ash." I stroked his cheek. "I won't ever take it off."

–Then–

THE LAST DAYS OF SUMMER ALWAYS CHURNED MY EMOtions. I loved playing in the ocean, burying my feet in the sand, gazing at the sky every night. But the long lazy days eventually got to me, and I became eager to get back into my routine of school and hanging with my best friend and sleeping in my own bed.

Still. I was going to miss my morning yoga routine on the beach, inhaling the sea's briny scent with every deep breath. I was going to miss the oceanfront view out my bedroom window. I'd miss Stephanie and her schemes to draw me out of my shell.

Most of all, I was going to miss the adorable boy who'd managed to sneak away with my heart this summer. Thank God for this one last day with him.

The sun wasn't up yet, but the heat was already heavy and thick. I sat on the porch in my light, pink sundress and straw sun hat, staring at the walkway to Stephanie's house. Listening for the jingle of keys or coins that signaled Ashton's appearance. He should've been here fifteen minutes ago. It wasn't like him to be late. The sun was coming up soon, and I didn't want to watch it without him. We'd been talking all summer about catching the sunrise together, but with us both leaving tomorrow, this was our last chance.

Our plans were literally from dawn until dusk, and then beyond. I couldn't wait for our day to start, even though I'd hate when it ended.

Where was he?

-Then-

THE SUN ROSE IN A SWIRL OF PINK AND YELLOW COTTON candy clouds.

I watched it alone.

-Then-

I TEXTED HIM.

I called him.

I left messages.

Then I started all over again.

-Then-

My skin turned hot and red. Gnats hovered around my forehead, but I couldn't find the strength to brush them away.

He and I should've been sitting down for lunch now. Instead, I was staring at my phone. Where my texts remained unread.

-Then-

Every time my phone buzzed, I jumped. But it was always something else. An email from my school. A reminder to drink water. A text from my mom, finalizing details for my trip home tomorrow.

It was never him.

-Then-

I LEFT VOICE MAILS UNTIL THE BOX WAS FULL.

I sent more texts.

They stayed unread.

What the hell?

-Then-

Mosquitoes feasted on my ankles, and still, I couldn't... wouldn't move from the porch. I just sat there. Even as the moon rose and the stars began to shine, twinkling at me like so much laughter.

We were supposed to be kissing under those stars. Right now. Letting the night take us wherever. Giving in to doing... whatever.

"Oh my God, Devon. Are you okay?" Stephanie asked.

I blinked cobwebs from my eyes. "I'm fine. Go have fun with your friends."

"Devon—"

I hid my face so she couldn't see I was about to lose it. "No. Really!"

Still, she hesitated. “Should I stay with you?”

“Your friends are waiting. Get out of here.”

I must have sounded convincing enough, because eventually, she did leave.

Why was *I* still here?

I needed to go. *Now.*

I grabbed a bike and headed to his beach house.

-Then-

There were no cars in the driveway.

There were no lights in the enormous dining room.

There was no sign of life anywhere.

He was gone.

And he'd never said good-bye.

SUPERNOVA

Chapter 1

I TOOK A DEEP BREATH, INHALING THE RICH LEATHER SCENT of Blair's cherry-red Mercedes. I clutched my pendant as Bishop Hall—Preston Academy's main building—loomed ahead. Ready or not, there was no turning back once I stepped through those tall wooden doors.

I couldn't see the stars right now, but I still made a wish: to have the perfect senior year.

Then I turned to my best friend. "It's bittersweet, isn't it?"

"Sure." Blair switched off the ignition. "Just take away the bitter part."

The sudden absence of Léo Delibes's "Sylvia, Act III: Cortege de Bacchus" made my ears ring. Something about blasting those violins and flutes usually fortified me for the day better than caffeine ever could. But today, the music only made me shaky and anxious.

Blair's forehead wrinkled. "Are you okay?"

I wiped my palms on my green plaid skirt. "I'm nervous. Why am I so nervous?"

"Girl," she said, wrinkles gone, sapphire eyes dancing. "It's the first day of senior year. And you, in all your nerdilicious glory, are already freaking out about getting into your dream college. Aren't you?"

The corner of my mouth lifted in a small smile. "Pretty much."

"Devon," she said, turning serious. "You got this. You know that, right?"

I didn't, really. But she looked so hopeful, I didn't want to let her down. We hooked pinkies. "Let's do this."

I climbed out of the car and stared at what had been my second home for the past three years. People gathered on the stairs, scrolling through their phones or embracing one another, squealing choruses of "How was your summer?" and "Oh my God, you look great!" People called to us, and I waved back, feeling more and more at home with every step. A light breeze rustled oak and maple leaves as Blair and I crossed the courtyard, but it didn't do anything to break up the humidity in the air.

Bishop Hall looked like a medieval cathedral, with sweeping arches and twisting chimeras, its focal point an impressive clock tower of gray stone rising to the sky. As the bells struck eight, the sound resonated throughout the grounds, echoing off classroom buildings and dormitories. Three years ago, this place had been intimidating. Now it felt majestic. Powerful. Blair and I were silent, almost reverent, until the last *bong*.

That never got old.

"We need to go in," I said. "Don't want to be late for Assembly."

"Only"—she tilted her head—"thirty-three more left."

My mouth fell open. "You actually counted how many Assemblies we have left?"

"Sure did. Because now the end to this oppressive high school regime is in sight. And we only have to sing that dreadful school song thirty-three more times."

Only she would consider a cushy private school oppressive. But then, she'd been at Preston since kindergarten, while I didn't start until my freshman year. I loved it here. The uniforms. The way our teachers were called professors. The way everyone took their studies seriously. I even liked the food in the dining hall.

Preston Academy: a school nestled in the midst of golf courses and polo fields. A school where I got graded for things like properly riding a horse. A school full of kids whose parents were Fortune 500 CEOs, international luminaries, Broadway actors. I've heard more than my fair share of talk about inner-city kids being thugs, but I'd seen a politician's kid start a fight on the third day of sophomore year. And who would give a sixteen-year-old a Lamborghini (that he crashed a week later)? A movie star would, that was who.

Every single day I wondered how the hell I'd gotten here.

I mean, I *knew* how it came to be. My grades were extraordinarily good, and it was no secret that the private schools in the area had been recruiting for diversity. Apparently, I was the perfect match: diversity points for being both Black and white, academic points for being hardworking and smart. The application fees had been waived. I got accepted to four schools, but Preston was the only one that offered a full scholarship.

So here I was.

I pulled open the heavy auditorium door and a blast of cold air whipped my hair, tossing coppery-blond spirals all over. I shivered and drew my dark-green blazer tight.

"Let's sit in the back," Blair said. As we got comfortable, I scanned the rows, taking in my fellow students for the year. Most of the freshmen looked terrified, but some of the girls gaped at Blair in awe. I bit back a smile. I'd looked at her the exact same way my first day. Who wouldn't? With her cool ivory skin and sleek mahogany locks, Blair Montgomery was a glamorous and preppy Snow White come to life.

My own first day was still clear in my head. I'd been scared out of my mind, surrounded by all those pretty people with their designer bags, expensive shoes, and sparkling jewelry that winked and gleamed. A sea of creamy white faces and straight, shiny hair.

What would they think of my wild curls, light golden-brown skin, and silvery-gray eyes? Did my Fjällräven bag or Aldo shoes scream "scholarship student"? And would anyone think less of me because they did?

It wasn't so scary now that I was a senior and everyone

knew who I was: Devon Kearney, top student and aspiring astrophysicist. And if they'd figured out that I was a scholarship student? So what? I was proud of that, too.

The seniors spread throughout the auditorium, some of them acting too cool to be here, not even sparing their classmates a glance.

Auden Cooper was not one of them. She stared right at me, flipping her Pantene-shiny strawberry-blond hair and sending me her smug grin. Like she knew she was going to knock me from the top of the class and nab Preston's college scholarship, awarded to every valedictorian. Like she was going to take everything and rock it better than I ever could. My skin burned when she looked at me like that, and she *always* looked at me like that.

"Ignore her," Blair said.

"Can't. Remember that saying about keeping your enemies close?"

"But she's annoying, like a bug. Someone needs to squish her." Blair's eyes narrowed. "Maybe that someone is me."

I lifted my shoulder, then let it fall. "Eh, competition's good for the soul."

She sat back and crossed her legs. "You know what else is good for the soul?"

I sighed. I knew that tone, and I was not in the mood. "Not this again."

"Oh yes," she said with a devilish grin, "this again."

"Do we have to talk about this now?"

"If we're going to make this year the best ever, it's time for you to let go." She started singing. "Let it go, let it *goooooo . . .*"

"What makes you so sure I haven't?" I stopped her before she embarrassed us both. Or worse, before people started singing along.

"The fact that you're still single despite going on how many dates?"

I tapped my Preston Academy notebook. "Boys can wait."

She fixed her blue eyes on me, steady and determined. "Look, I get that you're super focused, but you were a ball of stress last year, and we both know it was because of that boy."

I squirmed. "I'll have you know that I hadn't thought about him all morning, until you brought it up."

Her eyebrows shot up in disbelief. "All I'm saying is that it's time you toss your hat back in the ring. My bubbe says the best way to get over a guy is by getting under another."

I gaped at her. "Your grandmother said that? To you."

She shrugged and nodded.

"That explains so much."

"Good morning!" Our headmistress began Assembly with a big smile. "Welcome, everyone. I'm glad you're all here. This morning marks the beginning of Preston Academy's two hundred thirty-fifth year!"

A cheer rose from the crowd and I flushed with pride. My school's legacy was unparalleled. Preston had a long waitlist, and every single day I was grateful to be here. Even while freezing during Assembly.

I pulled my blazer even tighter while Dr. Steelwood gave her speech about the upcoming school year. There was so much to look forward to, like competitions, activities, and the Harvest

Ball. She pretty much gave the same speech every year, but there was something about starting a new school year that made me so optimistic. A clean slate, shiny and new, just like my fresh school uniforms and supplies.

Blair was wrong. I didn't need a boyfriend. My life was full enough: school, family, Blair. And right now, that was all I wanted.

The creak of the door behind me barely registered; I was so focused on Dr. Steelwood's speech. Then there was a presence beside me, one that came with a slight tinkling sound. One that filled the last empty seat in the auditorium, and filled my nose with the most familiar, amazing scent.

Strange. Being late to Assembly = at least one demerit. A demerit went on your permanent record. I glanced over at this brave soul and

Oh.

My.

God.

My breath stopped. My mouth went dry. Dr. Steelwood's speech ceased to exist. The auditorium ceased to exist. Everything ceased to exist, except the boy sitting next to me, frowning up at the lectern.

Because now I knew why I recognized that scent, like waterfalls cascading over the side of a mountain. I knew that golden-brown hair with its slight curl—I'd buried my fingers in it more times than I could count. I knew the heart shape of those lips because I'd kissed them a million times. And when he turned to me, no doubt sensing my stunned stare, there was no denying that face. Because despite what I'd told Blair, this face had been on my mind all morning. And haunting my dreams every night.

It was right next to me and I couldn't breathe. I could not breathe.

Breathe, Devon.

His eyes widened. His cheeks tensed. His gaze seared into me, his deep-set brown eyes mirroring my shock.

He was here. He was here.

He was here.

Yes, I wish on stars. And my biggest and most secret wish was that this boy, who I'd loved one summer, would come back to me. But wishes on stars didn't really come true, so how could he be here? After disappearing that summer without a trace? After leaving without a good-bye? How could he be here, sitting right next to me?

How *dare* he be here? After all this time?

"Devon!" Blair's voice sounded as if it were in a space vacuum. "Assembly's over. Let's go." She paused. "Devon?"

I yanked my eyes away from his and turned to Blair. But she was looking past me, her forehead wrinkled in confusion and rank suspicion. Then her glance flicked to me. Whatever my face showed her must have freaked her out, because her eyes widened as she grabbed my arm. "Let's go. Now."

Chapter 2

In Campbell Hall, the student center, I fell onto a squashy sofa and stared ahead without seeing a thing. How had I even gotten here? I didn't remember leaving Bishop Hall or walking across the courtyard. All I knew was that Ashton Edwards, the one person I never expected to see again, was probably crossing that same courtyard this very minute.

A deep breath, and the scent of Murphy Oil Soap coaxed me out of my trance. I looked around to ground myself. Yes, this was familiar. Steady. Students milling around the cubbies, pulling out notes or candy bars. Gamers hanging out in the computer lab. Flyers, sign-up sheets, and posters already decorating wood-paneled walls. Vending machines offering fruit and bottled water, and people lining up to get their caffeine fix at the hot beverage bar.

Blair stared at her compact and touched up her makeup. She was the only person I knew who got away with wearing red lipstick *and* red nail polish. I'd look like a clown if I tried to pull that off.

She really didn't need to touch up anything. She was giving me time to gather myself.

"Ready to talk about it?" she asked once she'd shoved the compact into her bag.

"I think so."

"Are you okay?"

"I am the furthest thing from okay." There was a slight hysterical twinge in my voice. "I'm the exact opposite of okay." I buried my head in shaking hands.

"Devon." She squeezed my arm. "Was that the Rat Bastard?"

"That was the Rat Bastard."

Her mouth dropped. "How the hell did he end up here?"

"I don't know." My voice shook.

Inhale two... three... four.

Exhale two... three... four.

It was all I could do to keep breathing.

To keep from crying.

Blair stared in disbelief. "Holy shit."

She had that right. Crap. Definitely not how I expected to start off the best year ever.

Her expression softened. "Are you going to be okay?"

No. "I don't know."

She glanced over my shoulder, and her voice dropped. "He's here."

I closed my eyes and let out a deep breath. Shook out my trembling hands. "I can't deal with this."

"Too bad he's such a good-looking son of a bitch," she muttered.

I tried to resist looking at him, but I couldn't help it. My stomach flipped as I turned. He pulled open his locker, then ignored it as he frowned at his phone. "He's perfectly engineered to make girls lose their minds."

And losing their minds they were. Blair and I certainly weren't the only ones looking at Ashton. Almost every girl who walked past him did a double take, and some of them weren't even trying to act cool about it.

"He seems so familiar to me, but I can't place him," Blair said. "A guy like him should not be forgettable. Look at that face. A perfect mix of masculinity and vulnerability. He's exquisite."

I sighed. Even she was falling under his spell. *Exquisite.* Like she was describing a valuable work of art, or a fine jewel.

"I never should've let my guard down with him," I said, turning away. "A guy like that? He can't do anything but hurt you."

"I don't know if I believe that," Blair said, tilting her head. "Not all beautiful people are evil."

Heh. Spoken like a Beautiful Person herself.

She leaned in. "He's staring at you."

A jolt zinged down my spine. "He is?"

"He's not even trying to hide it, Devon."

I turned again. She was right. His gaze was fixed on me,

strong and unwavering. The searing look was gone, replaced with a softness that made my heart skip. Was he…*happy* to see me?

God. How could I even think about calming down when he looked at me like I was the only person in the world?

"He needs to come with a warning," Blair said.

I let out a slow breath. "No kidding."

Someone stepped into my line of sight, blocking my view. I gripped the arm of the sofa and tried to center myself. To breathe. Blair watched me, her head still tilted, the gears clicking away. I turned from the scrutiny, letting my eyes skip to the different flyers on the walls. Intramural volleyball. Tea Tasting Club. The Harvest Ball.

"Is that your poster?" I asked.

Blair grinned, her cheeks flushing pink. "All mine."

"It looks great." And it did, with its golden background, script lettering, and simple graphics arranged to mimic an old-fashioned poster from the 1940s.

"I worked on it all summer." Her voice lowered. "Do you really like it?"

"I love it. It's elegant without being stuffy."

"I know, right?" She grinned. "Wait till you see the invitations."

"I can't wait."

"You're coming, right?" she asked, her eyebrows raised.

"Of course," I said. "Gotta support my girl."

Almost against my will, I glanced over at Ashton. Would he go to the Harvest Ball?

Then I mentally slapped myself. Just because he'd appeared at *my freaking school* was no reason for me to lose focus.

The first bell rang.

I pulled out my schedule. "Oh good. Everything I wanted."

"Let me see." Blair snatched the slip of paper from my hand. "Although I can probably guess. Advanced Geometric Calculus, Scientific Trigonomic Physics for College-bound Seniors…"

"Shut up." But I was grinning. She loved to tease me about my science-heavy schedules.

"No, seriously. Multivariable Calculus. Advanced Physics." Then she paused. "*Astronomy Methods?* What in the world is that? And why would they even offer it?"

"It's interesting."

"It's weird."

I snatched my schedule back. "You know what I want to study. It makes sense."

She looked thoughtful. "You're going to be a scientist. That's really badass, to be honest."

I nibbled my bottom lip. "First I have to get into college."

"Stop it. You're a shoo-in."

Maybe, but I wanted McCafferty University. Their astrophysics program was world renowned and highly competitive. I needed top grades so I could get accepted. And get scholarship money—McCafferty was also expensive.

Blair wrinkled her nose at her schedule. "Meanwhile, I get to suffer in Home Management."

I screwed up my face. "Home Management?"

"I *know*."

The warning bell rang.

Despite myself, I glanced toward Ashton's locker again. The person who had been blocking my view had gone. Ashton was still there. Still looking at me. Then he gave me the slightest of nods. My breath caught in my throat, then I returned the acknowledgment.

Blair glanced over my shoulder. "You're going to be okay. You know that, right?"

I took a deep breath. "I know. I will survive this. I'm strong and smart and capable."

"Damn right."

It was cute how she believed me so readily. Preston was a small school, and ready or not, I was going to have to talk to Ashton sooner or later.

God help me.

Chapter 3

The first day of school = a chaotic mess. The morning classes were abbreviated because of Assembly, but the teachers still tried to cram forty minutes of material into classes that were half the length. And because I preferred writing my notes instead of typing or recording them, my wrists were on fire by the time the last bell rang.

But my schedule looked promising. Astronomy Methods, yay! Multicultural Literature. African American History. Advanced Physics. Advanced Conversational French, because I was definitely going for an internship at the Paris Observatory, one of the largest astronomical research centers in the world. How awesome would that be?

And then there was Calculus. I did really well at math, so

the subject didn't scare me. It was Auden Cooper's smug smile that made me groan.

"Hey there, Ninety-Nine!"

One test. She got a higher score than me one time, and refused to let me live it down.

"How was your summer?" she chirped. "What'd you do?"

I forced a smile and turned to her. "It was good. I spent most of it with Blair in the Hamptons, and then a week at astronomy camp." I swallowed the pang that came with remembering how I'd skipped my usual summer with Stephanie. The Hamptons had been great, but I'd missed my favorite beach.

"Astronomy camp?" She raised her eyebrow. "Seriously?"

Grr. I turned my smile up until my cheeks burned. "How about your summer?"

"The best. I went to Paris and Jamaica." She held out her arm. "Look at my tan! I'm darker than you! If I keep this up, I'll practically be Black."

And there it was. One of the many reasons she irritated me so much. Things like this slipped out of her mouth constantly. *Practically Black*. Ha! Not even close, girlfriend.

I turned my attention to the professor and his lecture.

But she wasn't done. After class, she eased up to me and murmured, "You're going down." Then she whipped around, her strawberry-scented hair hitting me in the face, and slipped into the hall.

Oh hell no. This bitch was not about to yank away my valedictorian spot, and I definitely wasn't letting her nab the

Preston senior scholarship. Ten thousand dollars per year toward the college of the winner's choice. Auden drove a freaking BMW. I needed that scholarship way more than she did.

★·●·✕

I made it through the day without seeing Ashton, which was a miracle, considering how small our senior class was, and without having a nervous breakdown, which was another miracle, considering how rattled I was. Too bad I'd skipped lunch. Terrible decision, but I hadn't wanted to risk running into him in the dining hall. Now I was borderline hangry on top of everything else.

Blair stood at my locker, scrolling through something on her phone. "I figured out why your guy looked so familiar."

I was in such a funk that I almost didn't care.

"Wait. Eat this." She handed me a granola bar and waited until I took a huge bite. "And next time, don't skip lunch to avoid him."

Busted.

"What did you find out?"

"It just so happens that I attended lower school with the honorable Ashton Edwards."

"Honorable?"

"Ashton Bishop Carter Preston Edwards."

I froze with the granola bar halfway to my mouth. "Should that mean something to me?"

"His father is Tristan Carter Preston Edwards."

I sighed. People here were obsessed with what everyone's

parents did. Who had what job, and who could affect the economy of entire cities or the livelihood of working-class families. Blair's father worked in the entertainment industry, and when I say worked, I mean he had the final say in what shows got aired on a certain cable network each season. How did people even get that powerful? Or that rich? Hard work? My dad worked seventy hours a week, and while we weren't poor, we certainly weren't rich. Definitely not powerful.

I was so tired of hearing about everyone's fathers and how freaking important they were.

"Should this mean something to me?" I asked again.

"It should mean everything to you. Tristan Carter *Preston* Edwards," she repeated when I stared at her blankly.

Then it dawned on me. "What?"

"They founded this school. They are faculty chairs. And they're the reason Preston's endowment is so big."

Oh.

Oh no.

"Great. I hooked up with the guy who's bankrolling my education."

"You really had no idea?" Blair asked, eyebrows sky-high.

"It says *Preston Endowment Fund* on my statements. Nothing about Edwards. Are you laughing at me?"

She let the laughter bubble out. "This would only happen to you."

Appetite gone, I groaned and leaned my forehead against the cool metal locker. "How did you even figure this out?"

"I googled. Learned his last name in Photography class."

Photography? This shouldn't have surprised me. That summer, Ashton was constantly pulling out his phone and snapping pictures. He also had a really nice camera—he'd taken a bunch of photos of me at one of the beaches.

The memory crashed through me. Driftwood scattered in the sand, all smooth logs and wiry branches. The tide pools swimming with tiny silver fish. The sun sliding its way to the horizon.

Magic hour.

Ashton had stared at me, his lips slightly parted. "God, Dev. You're breathtaking."

He hurriedly raised the camera and the shutter clicked away. Ashton's smile peeked from under the camera body. "My sunset girl," he murmured.

His girl. I'd felt such a thrill over that.

Wait. No. Focus. "Why are *you* taking Photography?"

"I'm broadening my horizons. Also, I can learn how to take better pictures of the dresses I design and make."

Which made sense. Besides her Mercedes, Blair's sewing machine was her favorite possession. The clothes she made were gorgeous. Still... something else nagged at me. "How did he live here all along and we never knew?"

"Except I did know. I just forgot. But it's weird that you guys never talked about your hometowns. Didn't he know what school you went to?"

"We didn't really talk about school."

"What the hell *did* you talk about?"

"Oh my God. Our feelings. Our dreams. Stuff we liked.

Politics. Religion. Can I just say I never expected a rich white male to be so liberal? He's a total bleeding heart."

"Just like you."

"Sometimes we sang show tunes."

"You *sang* to him?"

"He said I had a good voice."

"Wow. That's disgusting. Cute, but disgusting." She shook her hair back. "Anyway, if you'd told me his last name, this mystery could have been solved last year."

I yanked open my locker. "Blair, he destroyed me. I wasn't about to google-stalk him."

"First of all, you weren't *destroyed*, just definitely not okay. Second of all, I'm trying to figure out what was so special about him that you were such a mess when you came back. Therefore, I totally google-stalked him." With a flourish, she held out her phone. "Behold."

My Calculus book hit the floor. "He has a Wikipedia page?"

"Well, his ancestors started the very educational institution we're standing in right now. He's kind of a big deal," she pointed out.

Except when you attended a school like Preston where *everyone* was a big deal, it became the norm. Unless, apparently, you were descended from the founders.

I sighed again. "Okay."

"He used to go to boarding school overseas. Which is weird, seeing as his family pretty much invented *this* school."

"Really weird." I picked up my book and shoved it into

my bag. "Why pay all that money when he could go here for free?"

"It's a rich-people thing," Blair said. "Like my dad. He'll take out a calculator at a restaurant so he doesn't overtip, but he'll spend three thousand dollars for the perfect desk chair."

"Wait, what?"

"I mean, it *is* a nice chair. Pisses him off when I twirl around in it. Anyway. Back to Ashton. His family travels every summer, but so do you. Maybe it was serendipity that you both ended up on that beach."

"It was something."

She shoved her phone into her bag. "Your boy is mysterious. Like I said, I went to lower school with him, but after fifth grade, he disappeared."

"He's good at that."

"So it's not like you'd have seen him around town. I wasn't friends with him or anything, so I didn't give him much thought when he didn't show up for sixth grade. When you told me your boyfriend's name was Ashton, it didn't even register. He completely fell off my radar. Until now."

I slammed my locker. "So now what?"

"Well, that's up to you, isn't it?"

★ · ● · ✕

Sometimes when Blair drove me home, we talked until our throats went dry. Today, we were quiet for the half-hour ride. The sky was a brilliant blue and Blair had the top down on her convertible. Classical music ("The Sleeping Beauty,

Op. 66: Introduction") floated from the speakers while she smoked cigarette after cigarette and the wind blew our hair everywhere.

The golf course gave way to gated communities. Then the gated communities faded away. The houses grew smaller and closer together until we were in my subdivision: Villa Park. The houses were definitely not villas, but we did have a park.

"You want to come in?" I asked when she pulled up to my driveway. "My mom's ordering sushi for dinner."

She looked tempted. *Really* tempted. Blair constantly told me that she liked my family's cozy ranch house a lot more than her family's McMansion.

"I want to," she said, looking regretful. Then she rolled her eyes. "My esteemed mother insisted I be home tonight for a formal dinner. Apparently she and Daddy are having important guests, and it's vital that Theo and I are there."

"Isn't your brother away at school?"

"That's how important this dinner is. They called him home."

"Yikes." Her family's formal dinners were the opposite of fun. And her brother—yuck. A cocky, self-important jerk who always looked at me with his lip curled.

"Whatever. I'll survive. I always do." She kissed my cheek. "See you in the morning."

I grabbed the mail and went inside. A stack of college brochures for me. Some boring trade magazines for my father, not that he had time to read them. Nothing for Mom, who was sitting on the couch, pecking away at her laptop. Her smooth brown skin glowed in the sun's rays that streamed through the window, and a mop of springy curls twirled all over her head. She worked in real estate, so her hours were flexible. She was almost always home after school.

I kissed the top of her head and inhaled her coconut scent. "Hi, Mom."

She took off her glasses and focused on me. "Hey, Bun. How was it?"

"Don't ask," I muttered.

She raised an eyebrow. But Mom knew when to back off. "Dad's gonna be late," she said. "New client's being a pain in the you-know-what."

I hung my blazer on the coatrack. "And that's different from when, exactly?"

She chuckled. Dad worked as an art director at an advertising agency and constantly got into it with one client or another. He thrived on fighting, at least while negotiating contracts.

"I'll order the sushi in about an hour," Mom said. "You want your usual?"

My stomach grumbled at the thought of salmon nigiri and a dragon roll. "Yeah, that sounds good."

"Give me a hug, baby doll," she said. I wrapped my arms around her and squeezed. When I went to pull away, she stopped me and looked closely at my face. "You okay?"

A brisk nod. "I'm fine."

"I don't believe you, but I hope you'll talk to me when you're ready."

"I'm going to start on my homework."

"Homework already? On the first day?"

"That's how you make valedictorian."

She was already back to her computer. I went into my room and closed the door. Lit an incense stick, hoping the sandalwood scent would calm my racing heart. Changed into yoga shorts and a tank top. Then I flipped open my laptop. While I waited for the Wi-Fi to connect, I dug deep into my documents folder, clicking through layers and layers until I got to a folder labeled *X*. I let the pointer hover, then double-clicked.

There we were, the stars of photo after photo. Huddled together in the sand, me in my bikini, him in swim trunks. Kissing on his parents' yacht on July Fourth while fireworks bloomed above us. Holding sparklers on Stephanie's birthday, laughing as if we'd had no cares in the world.

And then my favorite picture. *Used* to be my favorite picture. Ashton and me on the beach, the sky a tapestry of pinks and purples behind us. We'd been kissing when Stephanie called our names and pointed her phone at us. The way he and I were turned toward each other, the way his arm draped over my shoulders...it was obvious we were a couple. I'd felt so close to him. I'd felt like we'd had all the time in the world. Except that hadn't been the case at all. I closed my eyes as the sadness washed over me.

No! I wasn't about to start feeling sorry for myself.

Not again. Never again.

I slammed my laptop shut and grabbed my running shoes.

Time to refocus.

Chapter 4

I WAS GREETED THE NEXT MORNING BY A POUNDING HEAD and heart. I'd been having a delicious dream, and I wanted at least another hour of sleep. But my internal alarm clock went off at five forty-five every morning. And once I'm up, I'm up.

Wait.

That dream.

Ashton.

Oh my God.

I needed my subconscious to explain itself. Immediately. Because I certainly did not go to sleep wishing for freaky-deaky XXX dreams about me and my ex-boyfriend.

I rubbed my eyes and stared at my phone—5:46. Hours until I had to leave for school. Time for a vigorous, sweaty yoga flow to clear my head and set me straight. I hopped out of bed, twisted my hair into a bun, and stepped onto my mat. Then I took a deep breath, closed my eyes, and began. Inhale, arms reaching up. Exhale, folding forward, head to knee. Connect. Center. Balance. *Om.*

It didn't work. The images refused to leave my brain. I pushed until my heart was racing and sweat was dripping onto my mat, and Ashton *was still there.* Every stretch reminded me of being wrapped around him, getting lost with him. Every breath reminded me of the passionate nights when we'd kiss for hours. Touching each other everywhere, pushing each other to the brink.

I collapsed an hour later, more frustrated and confused than ever.

The frustration and confusion didn't end in the car ride to school while Blair babbled on and on about Louboutin shoes and Vuitton bags. Girlfriend was obsessed with all things fashion. Meanwhile, my mind played *what the fuck* on a constant loop. Because seriously, who has a sex dream about the boy who abandoned them?

The frustration and confusion expanded triple-fold when I got to my locker and spotted Ashton at his. Unfair. Why did he have to be here, and why did he have to be so yummy? The freaking school uniform made him look like he'd walked straight out of a Ralph Lauren ad.

Rat Bastard.

He deliberately picked through his books, slowly placing them into his bag. I was mesmerized by the way he chewed his bottom lip while he concentrated. By the way he blinked. The way he took a deep breath before closing his locker.

Longing and

anger and

desire and—

He turned, totally catching me.

My face grew hot, hot, hot. I tried to look away. I tried so hard. No luck. I was stuck. In. Place.

And now he was coming over. I promptly dropped my Astronomy book because apparently my hands forgot how to work properly.

He picked up the book and handed it to me. His fingers brushed mine, sending sparks all through me. "I don't think you want to lose this."

"Thanks," I managed to get out.

Ashton was at my locker.

Breathe.

"Devon," he said, that soft look on his face again. "I can't believe it's you. You look beautiful."

His voice had deepened slightly since that summer. I hated that it still gave me chills.

"Thanks," I said again.

"So, we should—" He froze then, his eyes focused on my neck. "You're still wearing it."

I touched the key-shaped pendant. "Yeah. I guess I am."

"Dev..." His voice shook.

The bell rang, making us both jump. "I–I have to go," I

stammered. And without another word, I turned and all but ran to my Astronomy class.

My lunch tray hit the table with a loud *smack*.

Blair, the unshakable bombshell, kept scrolling through her phone. "Rough morning?"

I sank into a chair and rubbed at the headache forming behind my eyes. "You could say that."

She leaned back in her chair and crossed her legs. "Does it have anything to do with your blast from the past over there?"

"Everything to do with it."

She raised her eyebrows, waiting not-so-patiently for me to elaborate.

"I talked to him this morning."

She dropped her phone. "Holy crap, Devon. Are you okay?"

"I'm fine."

"You're lying. You're so not okay."

I bit my thumbnail. "So?"

She tilted her head in his direction. "He's sitting by himself, like yesterday. He stared at his phone all period."

"Did he?" I kept my voice flat and disinterested.

But Blair didn't fall for it. "He's not very social, is he?"

"He likes to keep to himself."

"You guys are alike in that way." She picked up her phone, swiped at some things on the screen, then put it back down. "So, listen. I did some more research."

"Why?"

She picked up her fork. "Because I'm worried about you. I see how you look at him."

I squeezed mustard onto my sandwich. I didn't want to think about how I looked at him. It probably involved a blank stare and drooling.

"He's switched schools a ton of times. Switzerland. Germany. The UK. That's not normal unless you have military parents. Which he doesn't." She frowned and shook her head. "There's something there, but I can't figure it out. Did he get expelled? Did he leave on his own? It's like you said. He's good at disappearing. But... why? What's he running from?"

"How do you even find this stuff?"

She held up her hand. "If I told you, I'd have to kill you."

I had a feeling she wasn't joking.

Chapter 5

One of the best things about being a senior at Preston was that we got a free period right after lunch, two days a week. They called it Enrichment, the implication being that the time was to be used wisely, maybe for studying or an extracurricular. Blair joined an art club, one that focused on sketching.

After years of working on the staff, I'd been appointed coeditor of the Yearbook Club.

Along with Auden Cooper.

Professor Wilcox, the adviser, had said we were both too good, that she couldn't just choose one.

Fun.

Auden handed me a printout of a spreadsheet. "We don't have a lot of people on our staff. So I divided the duties like this."

Business manager, in addition to Clubs & Organizations Editor. "Auden, we should have decided on this together."

"I know, but I got all antsy and couldn't wait!"

"It wasn't even one day."

Whenever Auden got in her "take charge" mode, she pulled her massive amounts of hair into a ball on top of her head. She stuck a pencil in that ball now. "Do you want to handle the money or not? I mean, you know what you're doing with budgets and all that. I figured you'd be perfect."

How dare she appeal to my ego? "I'll do it. But next time, don't make any big decisions without me."

Tyrell Jenkins and Colton Myers, two boys who couldn't have been more different but were somehow the best of friends, strutted into the room like they owned the place.

Tyrell, tall with beautiful brown skin, deep dimples, and locs that hung down his back. Lover of jazz, anime, and painting. Blair's object of obsessive desire. Too bad he was loud and proud about his dating preferences, which did not include white girls.

Colton, also tall, with beige skin, blond hair, steely blue eyes. Football bro, whose dating preferences pretty much included anyone who was breathing.

"Tech Director! Photo Editor!" Tyrell pumped his fist. "Yes!"

"Auden, you lovely creature you." Colton wrapped his arms around her. "Assigning me to Sports & People."

"I had a feeling you'd be okay with that," she said, then glanced sideways at me. "I considered everyone's interests and strengths when sorting all this out."

Just then, Professor Wilcox swept into the room. "Sorry I'm late!"

"It's okay, professor," Auden said sweetly. "I've got it all under control."

Suck-up.

Wilcox handed a stack of papers to Auden for her to pass to the rest of us. "Agenda. We've got a lot to cover today. Main thing being: What will be our theme for this year?"

Auden and I looked at each other. The official motto of Preston was *Unity, Respect, Growth*. But that would not do for the yearbook.

"If you haven't been brainstorming yet, it's time to think about getting on that." Wilcox turned on the projector, and an image of her laptop screen appeared on the whiteboard. "But first you need to go over how to use the software."

Colton's voice piped up from beside me. "But—"

"I know what you're going to say, Mr. Myers: You know the software already. But it's been an entire season since you last worked on the yearbook. This is a refresher. It's actually pretty straightforward, but I'm a lousy teacher. I've cued up a couple YouTube videos for you to watch while I go get a cup of coffee." She hit PLAY. "I'll be back."

With a swish of brown hair, she was out the door.

"Hold up," Tyrell said. "How is she a teacher if she can't teach?"

While the video played, I jotted down ideas for this year's theme. It had to be a good one.

Chapter 6

"Devon! My favorite budding astrophysicist." Professor Trask beamed, his denim-blue eyes twinkling. With his round belly and rosy cheeks, my astronomy teacher/adviser could have been related to Santa Claus. As usual, Professor Trask had accessorized to the nines with Mickey Mouse. His tie. His watch. His suspenders. I'd never known anyone so obsessed with a Disney character. "Have a seat. I have your transcripts right here."

I plopped into a chair and watched as Professor Trask picked up my file. "How was your summer?" I asked him.

"Really good. I worked a part-time gig at Disney World, selling pins."

I chuckled. "Of course you did."

"You laugh now, but wait until you get to go."

"I've been! My parents took me when I was five."

He nodded appreciatively. "Then you should understand the magic. I'd love to talk your ear off about how you should go back as soon as possible, but we only have thirty minutes to discuss your college plans."

"Okay."

"You're already here on the second day of school. Very impressive." He flipped through the papers and then pulled one out. "McCafferty, huh?"

"It's what I've been working toward."

"I can see that. Your transcripts look wonderful. Straight As, top of the class three years running. Well-rounded extracurricular activities, great recommendations." He peered at me over his glasses. "On paper, you're a shoo-in."

I grinned. It was good to know that my hard work might actually pay off.

"But."

The grin slid off my face. "But what?"

"But so are a lot of other students, many of them right here at Preston."

I knew this. Of course I knew this. I couldn't eat/sleep/breathe this dream without this knowledge constantly pounding around in my head. Competition to get into McCafferty was fierce, and my classmates were some of my biggest competitors.

"One of the largest obstacles for you, Devon, is that you are not a legacy. The other is that you indicated you will need financial aid to attend. The legacy part can be overcome with your academic history," Professor Trask said, stroking his beard. "But the finances might be tricky."

I clutched my pen. Tight. "Would they deny me admission because I'm not rich? Can they do that?"

"Unfortunately, some universities factor finances into their selection process."

I took several deep breaths and tried to fight the dejection clawing up my spine. I hated how this process made me feel. As if I weren't good enough because I wasn't wealthy. So many of my classmates could write a check and attend school anywhere in the world. Money was no object at all for them, and I had to admit I was super envious of that.

I tried to ignore my sweaty hands. "Should I even bother applying?"

He took off his glasses and looked me in the eye. "Definitely. Don't give up hope. McCafferty has been known to generously reward those who show a tremendous amount of potential, and I believe you do. In fact, I'm going to suggest you apply early action. That way, if you get an acceptance in December, you can start making concrete plans for financing your tuition. But I want you to consider some other less expensive, yet still high-quality, options."

I *had* to go to McCafferty. Even the undergraduate students got to travel to the biggest telescopes in the world for research. Getting an assistantship during graduate school guaranteed placement at one of the top air and space associations in the country. There really was no other option for me. I'd apply to the safety schools, but I couldn't see myself at any of them.

Professor Trask gave me a bunch of scholarship applications.

"But I'm not Swedish," I said, reading over the top one.

"Look closer. It says preference given to students of Swedish descent, but what if no Swedish students apply? That money could go to you," he said. "What have you got to lose?"

I nodded. "Fair enough. And maybe they have scholarships for Black students. Or Irish ones. Or biracial ones. I could qualify for all of them."

"You never know. One thing I do know, though, is that if you don't apply, the answer is already no. That's why we're doing this." He nodded briskly. "Listen, deadlines will be here in a flash. I want you to have your Common App account completely set up, and at least three other college choices ready to go, by the end of the month. I'll look them over, and we'll move forward from there."

I gave him a nod back. "You got it."

Chapter 7

Grades, scholarships, McCafferty. Grades, scholarships, McCafferty. Grades, scholarships, McCaff—

"Hi," Ashton said, slamming my mantra to a halt. "I was wondering if we could talk." He sounded confident, but the slight pink in his cheeks betrayed his nerves.

"Okay." I didn't sound confident at all. I cleared my throat and slammed my locker door.

Ashton stared at me with those damn eyes that were full of galaxies, hypnotizing me, making my knees shake. "Hi," he said again.

My mouth opened slightly, then I closed it and shook my head. "I don't even know what to say to you."

He nodded, glanced at the floor, then looked at me again. "I don't blame you."

All I could feel was my longing to stroke his face. Even despite my anger, my embarrassment, my confusion.

He caught his lip between his teeth. "I need to apologize to you. Big-time. What I did . . . it was messed up. Inexcusable."

I was instantly transported back to that awful day. Sitting on the porch, my heart shattering. Humiliation suffocating me so I couldn't even breathe. The great horned owl hooting on the bird clock. Because it was midnight, and Ashton never came.

"Devon?"

Except now it was over a year later and he was here.

"Devon?" he said again.

I gripped my bag to keep from shoving him into a locker. "I thought you were dead."

He had a way of looking at me that haunted me all day and night. It was the way his face softened, the way his eyelids lowered slightly. As if he were trying to bare his very soul to me without saying a word. He stared at me with that look now, making my anger dissipate, but only a little bit.

"It was a shitty thing for me to do, and you never, ever deserved it," Ashton said, stroking the strap of his bag with trembling fingers. "And I'm sorry, Devon. I'm so, so sorry. I don't expect you to believe me, but I never meant for our summer to end that way."

Damn. The look in his eyes punched me right in the gut. Contrite. Nervous. Vulnerable.

I swallowed. Hard. "So why did it?"

He stood there, mouth opening and closing, face flushed. How sad was it that a tiny part of me felt sorry for him?

"I have so much to tell you," he finally said.

"There you are." Blair popped up beside me. "It's mani-pedi time. Are you ready?"

I blinked while the world came back into focus. "Huh?"

She threw Ashton a hard glance, then turned back to me. "We need to go."

"Oh, right."

She looked Ashton up and down like he was vermin.

"I'm Ashton Edwards," he said, his expression now neutral. He reached his hand out to her. "You're in my Photography class."

She reluctantly shook his hand. "That's right. Blair Montgomery."

"Nice to officially meet you."

"We used to go to the lower school together," she said.

He raised his eyebrows. "Sorry. I feel terrible that I don't remember."

"I don't expect you to. It was a long time ago." She turned back to me. "We have fifteen minutes to make our appointment."

"Dev?" Ashton's voice shook slightly. "Can we talk soon? Please?"

I stiffened, then nodded slightly.

To give Blair credit, she kept her mouth shut until we got to her car. But once the doors slammed, all bets were off. "Are you effing kidding me?"

"What are you talking about?"

"You should see your face. You're all... pink and glowy," she said, her own face flushed. "This is bad, Devon."

"I'm not glowy. I'm mad."

"Good. You should be." Blair's voice softened. "Remember how screwed up you were last year?"

Last year. It took everything in me to hold back a snort. There was no past tense about this. My feelings were happening *now* and I didn't even know what the hell my feelings *were* and seriously *screw him* for coming back here and—

Blair huffed. "I swear, I'm going to throat punch him. Twice. Once for hurting you. Once for getting you all flustered. Once for being so damned gorgeous."

"That's three times."

Her eyes flashed. "You're missing my point, Devvy. There was obviously something way deeper than a fling between you two."

"He was my best friend that summer." I looked down at my shaking hands. "He was amazing."

"Not that amazing, if he just up and left you. What did he want, anyway?"

"To apologize."

"Good," she said again. "You should make him grovel. Beg, even. I want him on his fucking knees."

"Blair. This morning. He freaked out about my necklace."

She froze mid-cussword. "Necklace?"

I pulled out my key pendant. "This."

She yanked the pendant closer to her. "Why would he freak out over your necklace?"

"He gave it to me."

She stared at me. "He gave you a Tiffany necklace after dating you for what? Two months? Are you serious right now?"

"One. He gave it to me on the anniversary of our first date. Monthversary. Whatever. And how did you know it was Tiffany?"

She stared harder. "Devon. Did you forget who I am? I know jewelry. He spent at least two hundred dollars on that thing. After being with you for a month. No guy does that. It's not normal. It's almost kind of creepy."

"It wasn't creepy. It was sweet."

"Except for the part where he abandoned you." She frowned. "I thought your parents gave you that necklace."

"Nope."

"You need to get an explanation out of him, and it better be good or he's going to be sorry he even showed his face here."

Blair started the car. Eerie violins and haunting brass filled my ears and made me squirm. Beethoven: Symphony no. 7 in A Major, Op. 92: II. Allegretto. This composition always felt like a chastisement.

"This is bad news," she said. "I don't know how I feel about him weaseling his way back into your life. I saw how you were looking at him. Like you wanted to slap him and then throw him down and have your way with him. Devvy, you need to be careful."

But *would* I be careful? That was the million-dollar question.

At the red light, she studied me closely. "Do you think he still wants you?"

I stared at the light, willing it to turn green. I knew what I wanted the answer to be.

"Devon? Do you want him to still want you?"

I didn't hesitate. "Yes."

"You're kind of a train wreck."

"You think?"

She tilted her head in that thoughtful way. "Here's the thing. You're going to do what you want. But I sure as hell don't trust him."

I nibbled my nails, which I only did in supreme hot-mess mode.

This was not good.

Ashton was distracting me way too much. Look how quickly he'd managed to make me forget about scholarships and McCafferty and school. Look how I was *sitting here right now* trying to analyze him when I needed to just stop. But I couldn't stop. Memories from that summer rushed back like comets. Him and me, walking along the boardwalk, holding hands and sharing our hopes and dreams and fears. Sitting in the surf together, laughing while the waves knocked us around. Kissing deeply under the stars. I'd known his every heartbeat, his every breath, and I'd wanted it all. I'd wanted all of *him*... and I'd wanted him forever.

"I know," I said. "But—"

"The heart wants what it wants."

"Exactly."

"And judging by the way you were looking at him, other body parts, too," she muttered.

And now we were back to that dream.

That dream.

It wasn't even based in reality. Ashton and I came close, but we never "sealed the deal." I'd flip-flopped between being glad about it and regretting that I didn't take the chance, but now I knew it was for the best we hadn't. Because it was a summer fling, right? But silly me had thought this was different. I'd thought *we* were different. But nope. And ever since, I'd been stuck with an emptiness in my heart that I hadn't been able to fill.

Sleeping with him now would not fix it.

Telling myself that was one thing. Believing it was quite another.

"Devon?"

"Yeah?"

"Promise me you'll be careful. Okay?"

How could I promise that to her when I couldn't even promise it to myself?

Chapter 8

"Hours for your community service projects need to be turned in by October 2," Professor Trask reminded us in Advisory. "That's three weeks. Some of you," he said, glancing around the classroom, "have your work cut out."

Cue the moaning and groaning. Most of my classmates would rather write a check than set foot in a disadvantaged neighborhood or spend time with sick kids or old people. But that didn't matter. If you wanted to graduate from Preston Academy, you had to clock forty hours of actual community service.

"Sign-up sheets are on my desk," Professor Trask continued, "but you need to hurry. Top choices are going fast."

I'd already done most of my hours, so my mind was a

million miles away, at Ashton's locker, which had stayed shut all morning. It was only the third day of school, during a short week, and he was already skipping?

Blair's tormented groan ripped me out of my reverie. Alarmed, I whipped around and stared at her. How had I missed how pinched her forehead was? "What's wrong?"

"I really don't have time for this," she groaned. "The Harvest Ball is in three weeks. *Three.* I need to be focusing on that, not community service. Devon, if this dance isn't the best that Preston's ever had, I'll die." She buried her head in her hands and whimpered. Then her head snapped up. "I need copious amounts of caffeine, and I need uppers."

My mouth dropped. "Uppers? What the hell, Blair?"

"I'm kidding, Devon."

But the thing is, I wasn't sure she actually *was* kidding.

She flipped open her bullet journal. The page was completely black, a million to-dos checked off and a million more that weren't. "This sucks big hairy banana balls. What are you doing tonight? I need to buy an espresso machine. Wanna come with me?"

"I've got a field trip to the planetarium with my Astronomy class. We're going to study Cassiopeia."

She stared at me. "Who?"

"It's an asterism."

"A *what*?"

"So, okay. I know you've heard of constellations?"

She shrugged. "Sure. Big Dipper, Orion's belt. All that jazz."

"Except not. Most people think the stars are what make up the constellation, but a constellation is a specific area of the celestial sphere. An asterism is a shape of stars that make up the patterns you're used to seeing. So the Big Dipper asterism is part of the constellation Ursa Major, which means Big Bear."

"You're making my eyes glaze over, Devvy," she said with affection. Then she stared at her planner again, her face crumpling.

I grabbed her hands. "Blair. You got this. I promise."

"If you two are done with your lovefest," Professor Trask's voice floated over to us, "the bell rang two minutes ago. You should get a move on."

I gave Blair's hand one more squeeze before heading to Multicultural Literature.

★ · ● · ✕

Happy Paws was the only no-kill animal shelter in town. Since it was funded entirely by grants and donations, volunteers were essential. I was excited to finish my community service requirement here.

I stepped into the bright, airy lobby with its picture windows, dark bookcases filled with white binders, and large reception desk. A couple sat on a sleek black couch and filled out paperwork on a square coffee table. The animals were separated by glass doors, Doggie Town to my left and Kitty City to my right.

"Good morning!" A petite, goth-looking girl bounced up to me. "Are you one of our Preston helpers?"

"Yes. I'm Devon."

"Angelica, volunteer coordinator. I'm so glad you're here." She pumped my hand aggressively. Holy cow. Way too perky for a Saturday morning.

She gestured to the reception desk. "You can sign in over there. I was thinking I'd put you in with the dogs."

"Whatever you need." I printed my name, then scribbled my signature on the sheet.

Angelica checked her clipboard. "Looks like there's only one more student volunteer coming in today. He's been here before, so we won't wait for him." She led me into a small office and thrust a stack of papers at me. "Go ahead and fill these out, then I'll show you around."

"Thanks." I looked over the forms. Official Preston letterheads. A medical release. A sheet for filling out my hours. An evaluation form. By far the most intense onboarding of any volunteer hours I'd done.

"Hey, Angelica."

I dropped my pen. Oh God, no. Not him.

"Good morning, Ashton! I'm glad you're here! There's one other volunteer, and I was thinking I'd pair you up. You might already know her."

I wasn't ready for this. An entire day with him?

Deep breaths. I had this. By the time Angelica brought Ashton into the room, I'd managed to compose myself. Calm, cool, and collected! That was me!

"Dev!" His face lit up. "I didn't know you were volunteering here."

"Service requirement," I reminded him.

"This is a great place to do it," he said. "I'm going to keep volunteering when my forty hours are done." He hung up his jacket. "Be right back. I need to wash my hands."

I stared at him as he left the room. He looked gorgeous in his dark jeans and light-blue T-shirt.

Damned gorgeous.

My heart fluttered like hummingbird wings. A billion beats per minute.

Inhale... two... three... four.

Exhale... two... three... four.

Get a grip, Devon.

Now.

Angelica tossed me a peach-colored apron and walked me to Doggie Town. Seven dogs charged, barking and jumping, until Angelica whistled, making them stop in their tracks. I shrieked when a tiny brown Chihuahua skidded into my leg. He sat there, stunned, then sniffed my shoes and ran off again.

Ashton was already in the room, nuzzling a medium-size black-and-white mutt. "You're such a good boy," he cooed, stroking the dog's broad head. Then he looked up at me. "This is Buddy. Isn't he incredible?"

Cautiously, I knelt down beside the dog. "He's what they call special needs," Ashton continued. "See how he doesn't have a right eye?"

I touched Buddy's nose and a pink tongue came out to lick my fingertips.

"No one knows what happened to him. They say he's been here forever." Ashton scratched Buddy's ears. "He's awesome."

Why is he talking to me like everything is good between us?

The tips of Ashton's ears were bright red. They only did that whenever he was nervous and uneasy. Maybe I'm a terrible person, but seeing him a bit aflutter made me feel a lot better.

And Buddy really was awesome.

Ashton was nuzzling Buddy again, and Buddy seemed as if he were in heaven, his tail thumping against the floor.

Lucky, lucky Buddy.

Yeah . . . this wasn't going to work. I jumped up and started gathering squeaky toys and slobbery plush animals.

"Time for breakfast!" Angelica called. "Ashton, can you handle? I've got to submit this paperwork now or the director will have my head."

"I got this. Come on, Dev. Let me show you how to feed these rascals."

Dev. He kept calling me by that nickname. I could even hear the affection in his voice, the same lilt from that summer. It made me want to melt.

Or smack him. I wasn't sure yet.

Once the pooches were happily munching, Ashton and I finished picking up dog toys and cleaning. There was a lot of work to do, but that was a good thing. I could focus on tasks instead of my emotional turmoil.

After lunch we had cleaning duty again. Washing toys and shaking out bedding. Sweeping up kibble and mopping up pee. Keeping myself busy so I could avoid Ashton and those deep brown eyes.

He did the exact opposite. He'd look right at me, almost as if he were daring me to keep staying away from him. Then he'd look off into the distance, his face troubled. He'd freeze in place, only moving when one of the dogs jumped onto his lap, snapping him out of his reverie. Then he'd brighten, burying his face in fluffy canine fur.

His mood swings were super confusing.

Every bone in my body ached by the time the dogs went for their afternoon walk. I wanted tea, I needed a nap, and instead I got Ashton poking his head around the corner and grinning at me.

"You look like you could use a break," he announced. "Come with me."

I took one step, then hesitated. "Where?"

"Trust me."

"Why?"

He blinked those eyes, turning on the charm full blast. "Please?"

Dammit.

"Lie down and close your eyes," he said once we came to a bright room in the far corner of Doggie Town.

"Excuse me?"

"Trust me," he said again.

I actually lay down on the floor. But because I was very tired, of course.

As long as I kept telling myself that, it would eventually come true.

"The key is to give in." Ashton's voice came from above me. "Surrender to what's about to happen."

What the hell had I gotten myself into? "Which is what, exactly?"

"Shh." And suddenly I was buried in a whirlwind of little paws and wet noses and puppy breath. I shrieked and opened my eyes, and there was Ashton on the floor beside me, a look of utter happiness on his face as the puppies jumped from me to him, their tiny barks echoing all over Doggie Town.

"Oh my God," I said, not even trying to hold back my laughter. "Where'd they come from?"

"Their foster just dropped them off. This is the intake room."

I scratched the tiny black puppy nipping at my nose. "Best energy boost ever."

Ashton gave me a heart-melting grin. My hands trembled with the effort of trying to resist it. To resist *him*. But damn, if this boy wasn't an abyss.

I turned away and focused on the puppy, who had settled onto my stomach with a plop and a sigh.

But I was still so aware of Ashton lying there. What was he thinking? Feeling?

I turned to face him, and he was looking at me, a gentle smile playing around his lips. One that mirrored the pure joy in his eyes. Was he so happy because being buried in puppies was the best thing ever, or was it because he was here with me? Did it even matter?

God, this was so hard.

"These little cuties are all cleared for adoption." Angelica's perky voice broke the spell. "I need you to bring them to Puppy Palace. Everything's all set for them, but I want you two to get them settled in their new home."

"How do we do that?" I asked.

She grinned. "Easy. Play with them!"

Ashton saluted her, hopped up, and started gathering the squirming, yapping puppies. "Best day ever."

Angelica shook her head and left the room.

"Duty calls," Ashton said to me.

And it kept calling for the next three hours. Puppy Palace was huge, with floor-to-ceiling windows that let in streaming sunlight. There were fluffy doggie beds and rubbery balls and bowls of food and water. And toys. So many toys for them to absolutely destroy.

I couldn't keep ahead of them. I'd pick up all the toys, and the puppies would immediately have them all over the place. Rubber strips and ripped-up stuffed animals and random squeakers covered the floor. On top of that, not all the puppies were potty trained, so the mopping was never-ending. There was no way I could take control, and I was *this close* to full-on give-me-*all*-the-junk-food meltdown mode.

But then the biggest puppy, a golden cutie named Darby, totally obliterated a stuffed mouse and left the carnage in a puddle of pee.

"I'm gonna cry," I whimpered, letting the mop clatter to the floor.

Ashton glanced over, saw what I was gaping at, stared at me in disbelief, then collapsed to the floor in laughter. He laughed so hard his cheeks turned red and he snorted. He actually snorted. That set me off, and we both started howling. Which made some of the dogs howl. Which made us laugh even more. Every time Ashton and I caught each other's eyes, the snorts bubbled up again and again.

"I'm sorry I suck," I said between gasps.

And there was that tender look of his. "You don't suck. This place falls apart every single day. Believe me, it's not you."

"It's you?"

A devilish smirk. "You caught me."

Dammit, Ashton, stop with all the nice stuff. I'm furious at you, and I'm determined to stay that way. I crossed my arms. "Now what?"

"We wait for the dogs to settle down. Then we clean again."

That wasn't what I'd meant. At all.

Another deep stare, and no Angelica to interrupt this time. Just a cold, wet nose burrowing into my ear. I squealed and jumped up. Happy for an excuse to get away from Ashton. To center myself. To breathe. This up-and-down was taking its toll and I needed to sort myself out. Now. "Hand me some more paper towels."

By four o'clock, I was exhausted and covered in fur, but happy. Because honestly, it was impossible to stay sad after playing with dogs all day. And now I could go home, take a bubble bath, and be Ashton-free until Monday. Tuesday if I was really lucky.

I've never been really lucky.

"Did you have a good day?" His voice came from behind me as I was washing my hands.

Why couldn't he be a straight-up asshole? Then it would be easier to hate him. But no, he had to be nice. He'd always been nice. Maybe that was part of the problem.

Sometimes "nice" wasn't enough.

I stood up straighter. "It was okay."

He nodded and moved in to wash his own hands. The silence stretched out the awkwardness. I shook droplets off my hands and stopped dead when my stomach decided to break the tension with a loud growl. Ashton's mouth dropped open, then his face relaxed into a slow grin.

Embarrassed, I concentrated on drying my hands. But I could feel his eyes on me. Imploring me. Pulling me in. Almost against my will, I glanced at him. He watched me with a thoughtful expression, then: "You wanna...grab a bite?"

I did. "I should get home."

He nodded. "Okay."

My stomach betrayed me with another loud growl. He raised his eyebrow, but didn't let any other emotion cross his face.

"We can't just..." I shook my head.

"I know." He tugged the zipper on his jacket. "But I'd like to start by getting you dinner."

"You don't have to do that."

"I want to."

I counted to five in my head. Told myself I was making a huge mistake. But then I said, "Okay."

Chapter 9

In the parking lot, there was a definite bite in the air, a crispness that showed the time for apple picking and hay-rides wasn't too far off. The scent of burning leaves tickled my nose, reminding me of jack-o'-lanterns and hot cider and cozy nights in front of the fireplace.

"This is your ride?" We'd stopped at a black Porsche Panamera.

He gave me a bewildered look. "You've never seen my car?"

"We only walked or rode bikes at the beach. Remember?"

He opened the door for me, and a blast of heat nearly seared my eyebrows off. Someone had apparently parked in the sun all day. "You're right. We took a million walks that summer."

That summer.

Normally I would have been geeking out over this luxury car with its leather seats and wooden panels and clean car smell. But I was too nervous, nibbling my nails and not really seeing our small downtown blurring past. I took deep breaths, trying to calm my racing heart and cool my flushing skin.

"Is fast food okay?" Ashton asked. "I'm craving fries."

Quick and easy. Great. "Sounds good to me."

We pulled up to a burger joint. "I don't even care that I smell like dog hair," he said. "I want to eat inside. That okay?"

"That's fine. I hate the drive-through."

We ordered burgers, fries, and apple pies. My stomach grumbled again, earning me a teasing grin. "Your stomach means business," he said, eyes twinkling.

"It doesn't like missing meals. Or snacks. Or candy."

"Too bad I didn't know that. I'd have given you some of my M&M's earlier."

"You should have given me M&M's anyway, selfish."

"Sorry. They're my favorite."

Of course. His massive sweet tooth. How could I have forgotten? It was one of the main things he and I had in common. We'd spent so many nights on the beach scarfing down ice cream or funnel cakes or cotton candy, then making out in a whirl of sugary bliss.

Focus.

"I'll grab ketchup and napkins," I murmured.

By the time I'd filled my drink and gathered the condiments, Ashton had made his way over to me with a tray of steaming food. We had our pick of tables, and I slid into a booth across from him.

We focused on unwrapping our burgers. Salting our fries. Checking for rogue onions.

Maybe that last part was just me.

"Dev, it was fun working with you today."

I'd had fun with him, too. But he didn't need to know that. He didn't need to know my heart and my brain were engaging in a whirlwind of confusing, conflicting feelings. Anger. Desire. Fury. Lust. I gripped my fruit punch and tried not to squeeze.

"Same," I finally said.

He gave me a small smile. "You're so formal sometimes."

My grip on the drink relaxed. "I'm not sure how to act around you."

"Is that why you've been avoiding me?"

"Yeah." I fiddled with my straw. "You're bad for my sanity."

The smile faded.

"I'm kidding," I said.

But not really.

We were quiet for a while.

"Is this weird?" he asked.

"Definitely weird."

We got quiet again.

These silences were killing me. So I blurted out the first thing that popped into my head. “You weren’t at school yesterday.”

Great. Why did I have to say that? Now he probably thought I was a stalker.

He looked down at his food. “I have a lot on my mind.”

I should have let it go. Instead, I dragged a fry through my ketchup and took a deep breath. “Want to talk about it?”

He hesitated before meeting my eyes. “I don’t want to dump on you.”

“Is everything okay?”

“I don’t know.” Then he was quiet for a long time. Sliding his fingers back and forth across the table. His expression telling me his mind was light-years away, and that it wasn’t nice, wherever that was.

My heart ached, desperate to comfort him. To bring back that annoying heart-melting grin from earlier.

My skin ached, desperate to feel him warm and smooth against me.

My brain ached, because God, what was I doing here?

“Ashton,” I said quietly. “Where are you?”

The raw vulnerability in his eyes almost knocked me over. “Do you ever get overwhelmed? By everything?”

I thought about the emotional roller coaster I currently had unlimited tickets for. “Constantly.”

“So you get it, then.” His fingers stilled as he gave me another small smile. “You always have. More than anyone.”

You are angry at him, Devon. Furious. Stay strong! This boy had flaked on me big-time, so why was I trying to make him open up to me? It made no logical sense. But something would not let me be that flippant to another person.

Sometimes I hated that about myself.

"Tell me," I said.

He buried his head in his hands, then mumbled something under his breath.

I leaned across the table. "I didn't hear you."

He shook his head. "It's so messed up."

I could've sworn he'd said *I'm so messed up.*

He crumpled his burger wrapper and squeezed it in his fist. "My father says he's at his 'wit's end' with me. That I need to toughen up. Apparently, I have one more chance to mess up before I get shipped to military school."

"Military school?"

"I'm not down on military school or anything. But I know myself. It would kill me." His expression turned from pained to thoughtful. "Maybe I *should* go there."

"To get killed?"

He shrugged. "Probably easier than doing it myself."

I dropped what was left of my burger. "What?"

He shook his head. "Nothing. I'm being stupid. Don't pay me any attention."

Yeah, okay. Fat chance of that happening now.

"Ashton, do I need to be worried about you?"

"No. Like I said, I was being stupid."

I frowned. Here was the thing: Memories of that summer were still constantly flowing into my brain. Times when he'd say things that seemed a bit off. Like one time when he'd gotten into it with his dad and said, "He'd probably be happier if I wasn't around." And the time he'd said, "I need to just be done with everything." I'd taken it as Ashton needing to get away from his family for a while. That he'd be fine once he cooled off. But now that he was still talking like this...maybe it had been more.

I wanted to pry it all out of him, but it wasn't my place to push. *Was it?*

"I wish you wouldn't say those things about yourself," I said softly.

"I wish I didn't think these things about myself, but there you go." He made a fist and pressed it into the table. "We should talk about something else. How's your food?"

The abrupt subject change threw me off. "Um, what?"

"Your food. Is it good?"

I picked up my burger again. "What do you want me to say? It's fast food."

His hand relaxed. "We had fast food in France, but it wasn't as delightfully crappy as it is here."

"You lived in France?"

He broke his apple pie in half and nodded. "Went to school there this past year. It was nice because I could see my grandma during my breaks instead of coming home. She lives in Monaco."

I smirked. "You probably got into all kinds of trouble."

A real smile this time. "Surprisingly little. When I was really young, I hated going there. Which didn't make any sense, because she spoiled me rotten. But I guess it felt too much like my parents sent me there because they didn't want me around, and that's a shitty feeling. But then I realized how awesome Grandma is. I love hanging with her. I talk to her about everything."

Then the smile turned into a frown. "How are we talking about me again? God, I'm the biggest asshole."

"You're kind of fascinating," I admitted.

He let out a snort. "I'm really not. Not even a little bit. You're the fascinating one. Are you still studying your stars?"

"Absolutely."

"Awesome. I love how you see pictures *and* stories in the sky. Like that night you told me about that one star. Arc—?"

"Arcturus."

His face relaxed into a wistful smile. "I remember it."

I remembered, too. It had been such a magical night. A banana moon. The scent of saltwater filling the air. The cool ocean waves crashing over our toes as the tide rolled in. He'd asked me a million questions about the moon and the tide, and he'd asked me to point out my favorite stars to him. I'd taken his hand and pointed to Arcturus—but he wasn't looking at the sky.

He was looking at me.

He was looking at me as if he would rather look at nothing else. As if I were the only thing that existed and he still couldn't get enough. Then he'd gently tugged me so that

I tumbled against him. I could feel his heart pounding. His warm breath against my lips. Then his lips against my lips.

Our first kiss.

"That was a good night," Ashton said quietly.

Blinking slowly, I reluctantly came back to the restaurant. To right now. "Yeah. It was."

He was gazing at my mouth with the kind of stare that could unsettle the most stoic of stoics. The kind of look that sent fire to my stomach and made my fingers tremble.

He shook his head slightly, as if he were coming out of a trance, and said, "I love that you know this stuff. About the stars. It's one of my favorite things about you."

And when he said stuff like this…it was hard to stay so infuriated with him.

"But don't quiz me or anything. I'm not going to remember. It's been a long time," he said. And all the hurt came crashing back.

"That's not my fault," I said quietly.

"I know." He looked down at the table. "Our summer shouldn't have ended that way."

"But it did."

"And I hate myself for it," he said, his expression so miserable.

Coming here had definitely been a mistake. I didn't even know what I'd been trying to accomplish, but feeling bad for him? Concerned? Not even. He should be feeling bad for *me*. I'm the one who floundered for a year, wondering where the hell he'd been all this time when I'd been here. *Right here.*

"Why did you leave me?" My eyes and throat burned, but I needed to know.

"I didn't want to."

"That's not what I asked."

He looked at the crumpled wrappers. "This isn't a conversation I want to have here."

"Then let's go somewhere and have it."

He nodded and picked up the tray. "Let's go."

Chapter 10

"Thanks for dinner," I said in the Porsche.

"Of course." He started the car. "I like spending time with you."

"Me too."

Our gazes locked. And despite every warning going off in my brain, I didn't look away. I let myself study the contours of his face. The deepness in his eyes. The light flush in his cheeks.

I wanted to kiss him so, so much.

I gripped my key pendant. "We've got to talk."

"I know," he said, his expression serious. "Let's go to my house. We'll have privacy there."

I should have made him take me home right then. Actually, it would probably be better to text my mom for a ride so I could get the hell away from him. He'd changed. I was sure deep down was my incredible boyfriend who'd surprised me with picnics on the beach and won me stuffed animals at silly boardwalk games. But now his happy-go-lucky nature was tempered by darkness. Now he was a hurricane, with pain behind his eyes and scary words escaping his lips.

Like about military school. All the talk about him losing it.

I didn't know what to think.

The tension made the fifteen-minute ride seem way longer. After what felt like ages, we pulled up to a gated property that stood alone rather than as part of a community of McMansions.

The Founder's Mansion. A landmark in our quaint, scenic town. The brick Georgian-style house was mammoth and intimidating, with shuttered dormer windows and a neatly manicured lawn. Perfectly round juniper bushes stood on each side of the portico while pink chrysanthemums bloomed in uniform flower beds. A circular drive wound around a white three-tiered fountain. Ashton bypassed that and drove straight back, behind the house.

The Founder's Mansion. Because of course I had to have fallen for one of the most important people in town.

Ashton parked in a garage filled with a bunch of luxury cars and then we made our way into the kitchen, which looked like a set from a Food Network show. Gleaming stainless steel appliances. Loads of counter space. A bowl of fresh fruit on the island. I didn't like to cook, but if I had a kitchen like this, I'd be willing to start.

"My humble abode," he said as I tried not to gape.

"Humble," I repeated. "Did I see a Maserati out there?"

"You sure did. And I know this place is ridiculous. There's only the three of us living here, too." He looked at me, a thoughtful expression on his face. "You're into cars, aren't you?"

"I like foreign ones that are pretty and go fast."

He nodded. "So does my father. You should see our other garage."

Other garage. Holy Christ.

He opened the Sub-Zero fridge and peered inside. "Can I get you something to drink?"

"Water, please," I said. My mouth was suddenly so dry.

"Coming right up." He pulled out two Smartwaters and handed one to me.

"Thanks. Where are your parents?"

He screwed up his face. "My father's traveling for business, and my mother is at some D-O-R function."

"D-O-R?"

"It might be D-*A*-R. Daughters of the Revolution or something like that."

I screwed up *my* face.

He gave a slight smile. "Yep, that about sums it up. Let's go sit in the garden."

"No tour?"

He threw his jacket on the counter. "I can take you on one if you really want, but I'm a lousy guide."

"I was kidding." Although I kind of wasn't. I really did want to check out the rest of this house.

I immediately loved Ashton's garden. It was like one of

those conservatories by the zoo, complete with statues and benches and birdbaths and butterflies. Fat bumblebees hovered around daisies, and the scent of roses hung in the air. My throat was already itching, but I was too enamored by their beauty to care.

Then I remembered why I was here. My nerves turned up to one hundred, and suddenly I wasn't so sure I wanted answers about that summer at all.

"Ashton. Are those swans?"

He grimaced. "My mother's idea. Don't go near them. They're mean as hell."

I gave him a sideways glance. "Sounds like you're speaking from experience."

"They don't like it when people try to pet them. They really hate it if you try to pick them up."

I couldn't help smirking. "You tried to pick up a swan?"

"Oh sure, laugh at my pain." He clutched at his heart.

"I'm sorry, but the thought of you wrestling with one of those things is too much."

"It was messed up. That's what it was."

I looked at the pond again. The swans—all-white, except for their black bills—floated peacefully. Trumpeter swans. How rich did you have to be to own trumpeter swans? "What are their names?"

"Freddie and Flossie."

"After the Bobbsey Twins?"

He nodded. "Yep."

"Did you name the swans?"

"I did. Maybe that's why they hate me so much," he said thoughtfully. "I should've named them Edgar and Agnes."

"Why those names?"

"'Cause they sound cranky, like the swans."

I shook my head. "I can't believe this is your house. What does your family even do with all this space?"

"Fill it up with useless crap." He shrugged. "My mother loves antiques. The house has been in my family for generations."

If Preston Academy was founded 235 years ago, then Ashton's family had to have been here well before then. Wow. Talk about a legacy.

"My ancestors felt that they should have an impressive and imposing place," he added.

"It's both of those, all right."

"It's a lot to live up to," he said quietly, all smiles gone. "Come sit down."

We settled on a gray stone bench that was halfway hidden behind a giant sugar maple. Far enough from the roses so my allergies didn't flare up too badly, but close enough that I could appreciate their beauty.

Not that I was paying much attention to the flowers. My mind reeled. The familiarity. The way we finally started falling back into our easy pattern of that summer. It lulled me into a false sense of security.

And now every cell in my body wanted to be as close to Ashton as possible. God, this was so frustrating. This up and down and back and forth. No wonder I was so wound up, as if any touch could set me off. I took a sip of water to calm the heat building inside me. This was the perfect setting to pick up where we'd left off that steamy summer.

But I needed to be stronger than that.

I took another drink of water.

Ashton nudged my foot with his. Dark-brown Top-Sider boots bumping into my black Converse hikers. "Hey."

I sat up straight. Waited.

His eyes softened. "I still can't believe it. After all this time, you're sitting in my *garden*. I never thought I'd see you again."

"Yeah. About that."

"About that," he repeated, then rubbed the back of his neck. Then he stared at his shoes for what felt like ages.

"Ashton. Just tell me."

"It's complicated."

"I think I can keep up."

He nodded. Then he let out a world-weary sigh. "So, my family. There's this history. We've got these bloodlines.... My mother goes on and on about how we need to stay within our circles"—his voice lowered to nearly inaudible, and he cringed—"and with our kind."

Silence. Then, "Your parents didn't like me?"

"Mother did like you." The color in his cheeks deepened as he ran his fingers through his hair. "My parents. They're old-fashioned and conservative. Said you were nice enough, but not suitable for our family."

My jaw clenched. "I wasn't white enough, you mean?"

He sucked in a breath, his face on fire. "My mother thought I was experimenting. Said she expected me to. But I brought you to the beach house. Multiple times. That's when it sank in that you weren't a fling. That's when the bullshit started."

My breath thinned. "Experimenting? What does that even mean?"

He gave me a pained look. "Do you really want me to say it? Because I don't want to say it. I don't want to think it."

And then I got it. *Experimenting.* Tasting the naughty, forbidden fruit before settling with the socially acceptable WASP princess for a lifetime of snobby, white-bread bliss.

I wish I could say I was surprised, but I knew better. You don't attend an exclusive private school with an endowment without learning about the politics of old money. Generations of wealth. Legacies that had built entire towns and industries. And schools.

My legacy wasn't power and money and control. It was camping trips where we snuggled together in a tiny tent, Dad telling ghost stories that weren't scary at all. Eating pasta until we had to crawl from the kitchen table. A mom who could sell a million-dollar mansion but would never own one. Whose quiet pride and strength enveloped my entire family. A dad who was addicted to Nestlé Crunch bars and watched *Riverdance* and tried to imitate the steps when he thought no one was looking. Who worked his butt off so I could focus on my studies instead of working an after-school job. Parents who would never make me choose politics over someone I loved.

Stuff like that didn't matter in Ashton's world. Seemed like all they cared about were appearances. Having pure blood. Well, I seriously doubted I had any blue blood in my veins. My father: 100 percent Irish. My mother: 100 percent Black. Me? Apparently not good enough for Ashton's family.

I wasn't surprised, but it still stung like hell.

"I'm not proud of it," Ashton said. "Any of it. And I made it worse. Instead of standing up to them, I ran."

"Why?"

"My father is the ultimate authority. When he talks, you listen, you do what he says, and you get the fuck out of his way." Ashton's expression grew stony. "He terrifies me, Devon, so that's what I did. Instead of standing up for you, instead of *being up-front* with you, I ran."

"Yeah. You did."

He didn't turn away. If anything, he became more focused. More intense. "There are no words for how sorry I am, not that you want to hear them anyway."

"I mean, I kinda do want to hear them," I admitted.

A small smile, then he grew serious. "You made that summer so *good* for me, and I repaid you in the shittiest way possible."

"I waited for you," I said quietly. "I sat there for hours."

"Oh." Another deep breath. "I suck. *God*, I suck. Devon, I don't even know how to begin making this up to you."

"You can start by letting me kick your ass."

He raised an eyebrow. "You want to kick my ass?"

"I want to hurt you like you hurt me."

He winced. "I deserve that."

I was hurting all over again. Not so much because of the race stuff. Eighteen years of microaggressions coming at me every day had made me good and numb to that. But his mother's lying. Her phoniness. Smiling in my face while thinking God knows what about me, my family, my heritage. *That* was bullshit. And I didn't know if I could forgive her for that.

I couldn't even make sense of the emotions rushing through me now. It was too much. And also not enough.

"Why did you bring me here?" I asked. "Was it to show me what I'm not good enough for?"

"No! Devon!"

"I'm sitting here in this gorgeous garden and looking at your beautiful house, and all I know is that people live there who think I'm not good enough because I wasn't born the right color and I don't have the right size bank account. Do you know how shitty that feels?"

"My parents suck," he spat out. "I'm ashamed to share their so-called bloodline."

"They're your family."

His cheeks darkened again. "I'm not like them."

"Sorry not sorry I don't exactly believe you right now."

He groaned and rubbed his face. "I don't blame you." Then he was looking at me again, full-on. Completely open. "I missed you every single day. I dreamed about you every single night."

I raised my eyebrow.

"Well, sometimes I had dreams about zombie Easter Bunnies or giant beanstalks, but that's beside the point."

I stared at him. Was he joking? Now? But, no. There was no crinkle around his eyes.

"I'd wake up thinking you were there," he continued. "I wanted to touch you so much. Make sure you were real. But you never were."

"I'm here now," I said, my voice shaky.

"Wearing the necklace I gave you." He reached toward my pendant, then pulled his hand back slightly. "I still want to touch you."

There was no mistaking the longing in his eyes. It was the same look he'd given me before he kissed me for the first time. Like he thought I'd hung the very stars I loved so much. The same look that could slowly melt all my anger and tamp down my frustration and make me forget everything except right here and right now.

"What's stopping you?" I asked.

A long pause. Then, a new look on his face. It was heartbreaking, but not as much as what came out of his mouth. "I have a girlfriend."

Hell. No. My hands shot out to shove him, but he caught my wrists, restraining me.

"Let me go."

"Devon."

My fists clenched. Focusing on that kept my eyes from stinging. "Let. Me. *Go!*"

Because *of course* he had a girlfriend. Of course he did. I wanted to throw something. I wanted to throw *him*.

"I left," he said. "And even if I'd found you again, why would you want me after that?"

I yanked my wrists away. "You didn't even try to find me!"

He froze. "That's not true."

"Again, sorry not sorry for not believing you."

"You're the one who's not on social media."

This boy had one more time to try me before I went *off.* "Don't you dare try to blame this on me. You had my phone number. You had my email."

"Devon, my parents took my phone and my computer. They made me delete my email account. I eventually got new ones, but I couldn't get any of the old info back."

I stared at him so hard he started to squirm. "Were you with her when we were together?"

And now he had the nerve to look offended. "You really think I'd do that to you?"

"I don't know what to think. I feel like I never knew you!"

His face crumpled. "You were the *only* person who knew me."

"You have a girlfriend."

"And you don't have a boyfriend?"

Inhale...two...three...four.

Exhale...two...three...four.

Don't punch him in the face.

"Number one: not your business. Number two: What does it matter now?"

He jumped up and began to pace. "When I saw you the first day of school, I was shocked. Knocked clear on my ass.

But I figured I'd apologize and we'd go our separate ways. Then I saw the necklace. The key to my heart." He stopped in front of me. "You still wear it."

I stroked the chain. "So?"

He stared at me, the expression on his face tortured. Then his meaning crystallized.

I drew in a gasp. "Oh."

His eyes locked on mine. Then, the slightest of nods. "I never stopped, Dev."

For a second I was wildly happy. Then my heart sank with a pang. "But what about her?"

He collapsed onto the bench again and buried his face in his hands. "Rochelle."

Rochelle. She had a name. That made her real. And I'd bet anything she was beautiful and rich and the perfect shade of ivory. His parents probably didn't have any problem with *Rochelle*.

My lips wouldn't stop trembling.

Fuck. No. I wasn't going to cry. I refused.

Ashton rubbed his forehead. "Hooking up with her... it made sense at the time. I've known her forever, since we were kids."

And that was that. How could I ever compete? They had history. All I had was a summer.

We sat in silence. Bees moved from the daisies to the roses. A light breeze lifted my hair and tickled my nose. But I was still too aware of him beside me.

I took several deep breaths. This was so unfair. Why did

it have to be this way? Why couldn't I have him? Or at least *hate* him? I closed my eyes and tried to fight all the love washing over me. I tried to grab my anger and hold it close, bury it in my heart so I wouldn't do something irrational. My head pounded with the effort. My emotions were spinning out of orbit, and I was terrified of crashing.

"You are a bastard," I said, my voice shaking. "I can't be around you." My voice had steel in it now. No way was I going to show him I was falling apart.

His eyes pierced mine. "I'm going to make things right. I promise."

"How? By telling Rochelle that your old flame from two summers ago waltzed back into your life?"

"That's exactly what I'm going to do."

I couldn't listen to this. "Take me home. Please."

We didn't talk except when I murmured directions to my house. It was dusk by the time we got there, the brightest stars already popping out. Those damned stars. Since when did any wish on them come true? Why did they have to bring him back? And why hadn't I been more specific? *Next time, bring back the boy without the crappy parents and the girlfriend, thanks.* The girlfriend. Did he twirl her hair in his fingers when he kissed her? Did she know he had a mole at the top of his right thigh? Did she kiss him there like I used to?

When we pulled into the driveway, the front curtain parted slightly and the outline of my mom's Afro appeared in the light. Then the porch lamp snapped on.

I unlocked the door. Then I paused. "Are you sleeping with her?"

He stared at the steering wheel, chewing his bottom lip.

"Okay." I got out of the car and slammed the door.

It was not okay.

I was not okay.

Chapter 11

Even though I'd been staring at the night sky for years, I still found something new every time. That was the thing about the universe. I'd never be able to explore it all. Most of the time, I was okay with that, because no matter what, I could always find my center here. This was my heart and my soul and my world.

Every time I stargazed, I focused on something new. Let it consume me. Like now, lying on a sleeping bag in my back-yard, looking for the Orion Nebula.

Really trying to distract my mind from Ashton, and from tonight. Trying to stop the heartache and concentrate on my future. The stars. But the memories were relentless, sneaking in every time my mind went blank.

So I let my eyes slide out of focus, blurring the sky like a van Gogh painting, and gave in....

"Hey." Poke. "Hey." Poke poke.

I grabbed his finger. "What are you doing?"

He pointed up to the sky. "What star is that?"

I squinted at him. "Is this how you get your kicks? By giving me astronomy quizzes?"

"As opposed to . . . "

"Kissing me?"

He grinned. "I mean, I should at least pretend I'm not just hanging out with you 'cause you're hot."

I shoved him so hard he fell over into the sand. Laughing, he pulled me so I tumbled down next to him.

"You didn't answer my question," he said.

"It's Deneb. The brightest star in the Cygnus constellation. Part of the Summer Triangle."

"Does this mean you can't see it in the winter?"

"Yes."

He frowned. "That sucks. Can you believe summer is over?"

"I know. Feels like I just got here."

"Best two and a half months ever. Not looking forward to going back to my regular life."

"I kind of am," I said. "Astronomy isn't going to learn itself, you know."

"Okay, first of all, that makes no sense. Second of all, you are weird. But I'm not even surprised. How else are you going to get that doctorate?" He smiled. "Devon Kearney, PhD. I will always love the way that sounds."

I swallowed. "Do you think we'll still know each other then?"

He went quiet, staring out at the sea. "I hope so. Already seems like I've known you forever."

"I feel the same. Is that weird?"

He kissed my forehead. "Maybe. But I don't care. That first time I saw you, I knew you were going to be important to me. And you are."

I glanced over at him. "Do you believe in soul mates or twin flames?"

"I don't even know what a twin flame is."

"Ashton." I poked his shoulder. "What do you know?"

He grabbed my finger and kissed the tip. "I know that you come here every year. You love sushi and sub sandwiches, but you hate the sound of people chewing. You got the money for your first telescope by doing odd jobs for your neighbors. I know you love the stars and would take them home if you could."

"But that's a bunch of stuff I told you. What do you know*?" I put my hand on his chest. "In here."*

And then he looked at me as if he'd rather do nothing else in the world but *look at me. "I know the thought of not seeing you every day just feels wrong, because when I'm around you, everything actually makes sense. I know you make me excited about the future. This summer has been so perfect. It scares me how perfect. And it scares me how much... how much I love you."*

Heart pounding. Breath shallow. "What?"

"I'm falling in love with you."

Oh wow. I hadn't expected this. Why, I didn't know. Because I felt it. Every time I looked at him, my stomach fluttered like someone with her first crush. Every time he touched me, my body tingled so much it was a miracle the vibrations didn't shock him. I could spend hours with him and still get thrilled when he called or texted not even ten minutes after saying good night. When we were together, we were the only two people in the world. No one else needed. No one else allowed.

My breath caught as I stroked his face with trembling fingers. Traced his lips with my thumb. Then said, "I'm falling for you, too."

"Yeah?" He grinned. "I love you. I love you. I'll never get tired of saying that." He grew solemn. "I love you, Devon."

"I love you, too."

And then we were kissing as if the whole world had disappeared. All that existed was his skin against mine. His soft breathing. His intoxicating sweet, salty taste.

"I don't want this to end," he murmured, "just because the summer does."

Summer romances were supposed to be fun, intense flings that got filed away into warm, glowing memories. I didn't know anyone who tried to make it more than that. But with Ashton... I wanted it to be more.

I drew a heart on his chest. "Tomorrow's our last day together."

"I think we should try to make it work," he said.

"Is that realistic?"

"I want to try. I know after tomorrow we have to separate, but I'm going to make sure it's only for a little while."

"Tomorrow's going to suck."

"No. We're going to make our last day together awesome. The whole day, the whole night, just me and you. And then, it's going to be me and you forever."

I gripped his shoulders. "Don't say it if you don't mean it."

He fixed steady eyes on mine. "I want you forever, Devon. And I absolutely mean it."

But he hadn't, had he?

Because now he had a girlfriend.

He had a girlfriend.

I ripped up a clump of grass.

Whatever. I'd been doing fine all this time. I would certainly be fine again. I didn't need him. I didn't need him. I did not need him.

I stared at the Orion Nebula, observing what looked peaceful but was really a swirling, evolving phenomenon, a stellar nursery churning out new stars by the hundreds. It reminded me of myself. A tower of control on the outside, a wild, unpredictable spiral on the inside.

I needed to resolve the things causing my heart to race and my breath to catch...and I needed to resolve them now. Nothing could stand between me and my dream. No boys. No heartbreak. No pain. From now on, it was going to be hard work, dedication, and focus.

I had this.

Chapter 12

THREE AND A HALF WEEKS INTO THE SCHOOL YEAR, THE Yearbook Club was still fighting over the theme. "It's got to be impactful, but comforting. Universal, but unique. And truly representative of our class."

My head hurt from Auden's posturing. Why couldn't anything ever be simple with her?

"You're thinking about this *way* too hard," Colton said.

"Someone has to!"

"Okay, yeah, because in a year, people will care. Get a grip, Auden." Tyrell tossed his pencil and caught it. "It's not that serious."

"It is to me. What about you, Devon?"

I mean, it was, but... "Don't bring me into this."

Professor Wilcox yawned. "You folks need to come up with

something *today*. Even if we have to come back after school and stay here all night."

Oh hell no.

"How about *A Splash of Class*?" Auden asked.

"Absolutely not," Tyrell said. "Way too cute."

"I *like* cute."

"That's because you *are* cute," Colton said with a wink.

Auden flushed with pleasure, but crossed her theme off the list. "Fine. What do you have in mind?"

"A Year to Remember."

"That's basic as hell," Tyrell protested.

"I don't see you coming up with anything, Jenkins."

"That's because brilliance takes time."

Colton put Tyrell in a headlock, which Auden and I ignored. Because this happened at every single meeting.

I didn't talk much at the meetings, which was silly, considering I was supposed to be one of the people in charge. It's just that Colton and Tyrell had such big personalities, and Auden was so freaking bossy, it was easier to sit back and let things unfold. I spent most of the time calculating sales and billing advertisers anyway.

Everyone in school eventually bought a yearbook; it was just a matter of how soon we could make the sales. The sooner we got funds, the more cool stuff we could add to the book. This year, Colton's charm had the things flying off figurative shelves.

"You need to get serious," Wilcox said. "I can't even think of working out a color palette until the theme is locked."

"How about *These Are Our Moments*?" I asked.

Silence. And then: "Let the crowd say amen!" Tyrell pumped his fist, his voice ringing out like a gospel preacher's. "She hast spoketh, and brilliance hast poureth forth."

Wilcox beamed. "That's it, Miss Kearney. That's the theme. Anyone have any objection to Devon's idea?"

We all looked at one another, then at Wilcox, whose smile grew. "Great. Now on to the next. Who's covering the Harvest Ball this weekend?"

"I'm on it," Auden said. "I've got my fancy camera ready to go."

"Perfect," Wilcox said. "Let's do this thing."

Chapter 13

I knew the Harvest Ball wasn't going to be an ordinary dance, but this was beyond anything I could have imagined.

The President's Club, located down the street from Preston Academy, was another staple in the ritziest neighborhood in town. The stone building glowed under golden spotlights as limo after limo dropped off beautifully dressed students.

The ballroom took my breath away. Gauzy material and twinkling white lights stretched across the walls, giving the room a dreamlike ambience. Crystal chandeliers threw rainbows against gleaming platinum pillars. Huge orange lilies decorated every table. A DJ spun lush remixes of the popular songs that everyone claimed to hate but still danced to.

"This is... wow."

Blair looked around, her eyes shining. "I'm so happy with it. With everything."

"You should be. You poured your heart and soul into this thing."

"I did, didn't I?" She grinned. "Let's party!"

I'd never seen so many pretty dresses outside of red-carpet specials on TV. My classmates looked like movie stars, but no one came close to outshining Blair in her long, slinky red dress.

My dress was a golden A-line with a sweetheart neckline. Tonight, I felt like a movie star, too.

"Smile!" Auden held the official school camera up. "Wait, where are your dates?"

"Devon's my date," Blair said, throwing her arm around me and kissing my cheek.

Auden's eyes gleamed. "I knew it!"

"Knew what?"

"You guys are totally lesbians! Oh my God, this is so cool." And then she snapped about one hundred pictures.

After dinner, the dancing really started. The floor filled with sweaty bodies and teachers trying to keep the dry humping to a minimum.

Guys pulled Blair onto the dance floor left and right. I danced with my share of guys as well, but I was most surprised when Auden took my hand, twirled me around, and then spun away.

I seriously did not understand her sometimes.

"What's up, Devon!" Tyrell bounced up to me, looking like a snack. Good enough to eat. I just wished he would consider asking Blair out. But there was that whole anti-dating-outside-his-race thing, which sucked for my best friend.

"Are you seriously wearing sunglasses?" I asked, laughing.

"Am I pulling it off?"

"You kinda are."

"Nice." He looked around appreciatively. "This party is off the hook. Blair organized all this?"

"She did."

"Yeah . . . this is her style."

Hmm. Curious. I tilted my head and raised my eyebrow. "And how would you know her *style*?"

He gave me a look like I was the densest person alive.

I looked at him like he'd lost his ever-loving mind. Tyrell was never one to be nervous about a girl. Dude was as cocky as they came. Then realization dawned. "Oh my God. Wait. You like her?"

"She's all right."

"Tyrell."

"I know. But I'm trying this new thing called 'keeping an open mind.'"

I smirked. "That's because you like her."

Tyrell's jaw twitched. "She scares me."

"And I don't?"

"You scare me on a different level, Devon. But not like Blair does."

My smirk turned into a grin. "You should ask her to dance."

He glanced over at her and smiled. I knew that expression—the dopey look guys got when they saw the girl of their dreams doing something they thought was absolutely adorable. Blair had her eyes closed, her hands waving in the air, while spinning in a circle. She looked ridiculous and totally blissed out, and therefore, breathtakingly beautiful.

I nudged him. "It's one dance."

He nodded, a thoughtful expression on his face. "You're right. I will."

After the song ended, I made my way over to the refreshments table. I watched Tyrell tap Blair on her shoulder. She spun around, and the look on her face lit up the entire room. They started swaying, looking absolutely stunning together. Seeing all the couples twirling around the floor made me achingly sad, but I found enough room in my lonely heart to be thrilled for Blair. She looked so happy, and I loved to see my friend glowing like that.

"I need another dance with my best friend forever." Grinning, Blair pulled me back out to the dance floor.

"Let's do this!" We threw our hands in the air and yelled *woo* and shook our hair and shimmied and it was awesome.

Blair shone like a star, brilliant and radiant. Her party was a major success, and people kept coming up to her to compliment her handiwork. I'd bet good money this was the best Harvest Ball ever.

Laughing, Blair and I held hands and whirled around and around. When the song ended, we collapsed against each other, still laughing, my head spinning with exhilaration.

And then I spotted Ashton.

He glanced around, taking in the scene, his expression one of deep appreciation.

I couldn't look away.

He was like the sun, blinding and painful. His dark suit did nothing to dim the glow emanating from his entire being.

"Oh," I sighed.

"What?" Blair shouted over the music.

I turned away from him and focused on her. "Nothing."

She glanced over and her eyes shone with mischief. "You gonna ask him to dance?"

"No."

"He's looking over here."

"I don't care."

"Bullshit," she sang. "You totally care."

"I really don't."

"He's coming over," Blair said.

Breathe, breathe, breathe.

I turned toward the guy nearest to me. Tall, curly dark-brown hair, ivory-colored skin, shining green eyes. Jeremy something or other. Played basketball. Happy to dance with me.

I could see Ashton, though. Frozen in place, the expression on his face dark as he watched Jeremy and me dance to hip-hop that spat out rapid-fire rhymes.

Ashton would not stop staring.

Even when the song changed and I grabbed Colton Myers. And good Lord—the boy danced like a stripper. Downright obscene. His blue eyes sparkled while he gyrated to the DJ's dubstep remix of the latest and greatest by everyone's favorite pop diva.

Ashton was still there. On the sidelines. Unwavering.

Then there were four of us: Blair, Jeremy, Colton, and me. R & B. Hip-hop. Fast, sweaty, exhilarating. I tried to get lost in the dancing, but I could feel Ashton's eyes burning into me, calling to me, tempting me. But I refused to turn around. I refused to give in.

"Last dance," the DJ murmured into the mic as the beats faded away and the slow song filled the air.

I glanced at Blair, but she was back in Tyrell's arms. Jeremy and Colton had disappeared. I swallowed and turned to go grab a soda...and came face-to-face with Ashton.

He traced a light fingertip down my arm. *Oh God.* Breathing, thinking, reasoning became a distant memory as my skin flooded with sensation. I stood there, shaking. Trying to resist...and giving up as he pulled me close. I melted right into him. Gave in to the passionate look in his eyes and his hands on my body. The way the music moved us. The shrinking distance between us.

I tried not to inhale too deeply, lest I become intoxicated by the scent of his skin. I tried not to tremble as he trailed his fingers down my back. I tried not to lose myself in the feel of his arms around me, his warm breath against my neck, his heartbeat next to mine.

I completely and utterly failed.

We were so close right now. My fingers tickling the back of his neck. Our lips brushing. My mouth aching to be pressed against his. I could almost taste the mint on his breath.

I wanted to taste it. *Him.* I wanted to taste him.

Then the song ended. The lights rose and the voices around us grew louder. The world slowly came back into focus but I couldn't—wouldn't—look away from him.

"What are we doing?" I whispered.

"Longing," he answered in a low voice, his eyes still locked on mine.

"What now?" I asked.

But I knew exactly what he wanted. It made me shiver to see him smoldering with such blatant desire.

"Give in," he said thickly.

I wanted to. So much. But what did that say about him? About me?

"Come home with me," he said, his gaze intense.

My fingers curled, crushing his shirt. "Why?"

"You know why," he said. "You know exactly what I want to do with you. All night. Every night."

Yeah, I knew. And I wanted him to do everything he wanted. Again and again and again.

"Dev..." His voice trembled.

And that did it. Unbearable heat shot through me and I was desperate to do something about it. Was this the best course of action? Hell no. But I'd long left the Land of Rational Thought and was straight-up cruising toward Yes Please Even if Only for Tonight Town.

"Are you still with Rochelle?" I managed to get out.

Abruptly, he let go.

That answered my question.

Chills ran down my body like a bucket of water dumped over my head. Then exhaustion. I was tired of his intense desire. I was tired of being frustrated and lonely. I was tired of the back and forth and the up and down and all of it. I was just done.

The solution was obvious. But I couldn't be the one to point it out to him, and I wasn't about to be one of those girls who thought she could run someone else's life. I could take control of mine, though.

"Stay away from me."

Chapter 14

I didn't go inside after the limo dropped me off. Instead, I slumped on the stoop and searched the skies for Aquila, the Flying Eagle. In Greek mythology, Aquila belonged to Zeus and carried his thunderbolts across the sky. He also kidnapped the son of the king of Troy—Aquarius, another of my favorite constellations. I liked that they were up there, playing out their story night after night. But right now, clouds ran across their stage, obscuring my sight. I wouldn't find comfort in the stars tonight.

I heard the door open and shuffling behind me. "Pumpkin?"

"Hey, Dad."

"When did you get home?"

"About an hour ago."

"Feel like company?" he asked as he sat beside me, so I guess I was getting company no matter how I felt. "I never see you anymore."

"You work too hard."

He bumped my knee with his. "So does my daughter."

I looked up. "I have big dreams."

"I know you do. It's *why* I work so hard." He paused. "So. Mom and I have been talking. About your college."

I studied his face. Dad had bags under his eyes and lines on his forehead that hadn't been there before the summer. His chestnut hair was a hot mess, tousled every which way and even sticking straight up in some places. "Oh?"

"I know you have your heart set on McCafferty. I don't know anyone who deserves to go there more than you do."

I straightened. "But?"

"McCafferty is very expensive."

I sighed. "I know, Daddy."

"You know I'd give you the whole world if I could. I just don't know how much Mom and I can give you for McCafferty."

I shook my head. "No, I get it." We were in this weird no-man's-land where my parents made too much for me to qualify for aid, but not enough to pay for school outright. "I filled out a billion scholarship applications. I'll take out loans. I'll do whatever it takes. I never expected you and Mom to foot the bill for my education."

"Well, maybe it won't be quite so bad," Dad said. "We *do* have a college fund set aside for you. There's no way it's going to completely cover your tuition, but it will help make a dent. And the Preston endowment will open up some scholarship doors."

"I'm counting on that."

"Have you considered living at home for your first two years, then getting an apartment for the last two?" Dad asked. "I know you want the dorm experience, but that's going to tack on an extra twenty grand a year."

I hadn't considered that at all. In my mind, college meant living in a too-small room with a roommate, sleeping on a bunk bed, and eating cereal, popcorn, and ramen noodles every day. Mom had showed me this music video from the nineties that had three Black girls living in a college dorm. The feeling of *belonging* I got while watching it—it stuck with me. If dorm life was anywhere near that cool for real, I wanted to be a part of it.

"Think about it," he said. "As I told you, we have a chunk put aside, but we don't have the three hundred grand to cover everything."

I shook my head again. "I'll figure out a way to make it work."

"*We'll* figure out a way to make it work," he corrected.

I wrapped my arms around him and breathed in his dad smell. Mint and Irish Spring soap and chocolate. "You've been snacking again, haven't you?"

He smiled and ruffled my hair. "Don't tell Mom."

"Your secret is safe with me." I held out my hand. "For a price."

He fished a mini Nestlé Crunch bar out of his pocket and dropped it into my cupped palm. "How was the dance?"

I groaned. I'd almost forgotten about the dance. And Ashton. "It was great. Up until the end."

"What happened?"

My face warmed. "Forget it. It's nothing."

"*That* I refuse to believe, when you're squirming like a spider crawled up your leg."

"Daddy, I would not be sitting here if that happened. I'd be running all over the yard screaming like I was on fire."

Dad started laughing. "Do you remember—?"

The screech of car tires startled me so much, I dropped my candy.

Dad shot up. "Who in the hot green hell?"

Holy crap, holy crap, holy crap. I knew that car, and I knew the person driving it. I was standing, Dad's hand heavy on my shoulder, when Ashton popped out and ran up to me.

"I'm going to break up with Rochelle," he blurted out.

Stunned, I couldn't do anything but stare at him. Then Dad cleared his throat.

"Dad, can we have a minute?"

"Everything okay?"

I waved him away. "It's fine."

"What I did at the dance was uncool," Ashton continued once the porch door closed. "I never should have been so close to you tonight."

"You're right," I said. Then I sighed. "But it's not like you were dancing by yourself."

"Doesn't matter. I'm the one with a girlfriend." He shook his head. "I was being extremely unfair to both of you. I've been unfair for a long time. Too long."

I wasn't about to argue with that.

"Rochelle's in France. For school." He held out his phone. "I just bought a plane ticket."

I stared at the boarding pass. "Ashton…"

"I have to do the right thing, in person." He also stared at his phone. "I don't want to be the jerk who left a girl hanging again."

"Okay."

He lifted his eyes to meet mine. "I'll be back soon."

"Okay."

"Dev." He pulled me close and I relaxed into him, reveling in the feel of his arms around me. His fingers in my hair. His heart beating against me.

I wanted to hold on forever.

"I have to go," he whispered. "I can't miss this flight."

SHINE

Chapter 15

"You're awfully quiet," Blair said at my locker Monday morning. She'd slicked back her hair with a plaid headband, so her eyes looked enormous. And all the more penetrating. "Anything you need to tell me?"

Two could play at that game. "I could say the same about you. I tried calling yesterday. Where were you?"

Her cheeks turned pink. "Ty and I went to the zoo."

My mouth dropped. "And you didn't text me?"

"I forgot to charge my phone."

This was suspect. Blair was never without a fully charged phone and a battery pack to keep it that way.

I studied her face. "Are you keeping secrets from me?"

"Of course not." Her eyes shifted from side to side. "I'm telling you now, aren't I?"

All kinds of shady.

"So, what's going on?" I asked.

"He bought me blue cotton candy and a stuffed giraffe. I named her April."

"Cute." Then it dawned on me. *"Ty?"*

She huffed out a breath. "It's not a big deal."

"Not a big deal? That's a nickname. Nicknames are special." My suspicions grew. "What else happened?"

Her cheeks turned crimson.

I gasped. "Did he kiss you?"

She nodded, her cheeks flaming.

I grinned and rubbed my hands together. "What else?"

"That's all. Pervert."

"Whatever. You're totally a freak."

She smirked. "I'm saving my freak side for our second date, I'll have you know."

I raised my eyebrows. "*Second* date? Hey now!"

"We're going to the aquarium. Should be a nerdtastic time."

"Blair, that's awesome. I'm so happy for you."

"Don't book the temple yet. Speaking of, I hope you went to church or something yesterday, because that dance Saturday night was downright sinful!" She fanned herself. "Have you recovered?"

"Well, get this..." I told her about Ashton's plans.

"I'll be damned. It almost justifies you giving him another chance."

I looked down.

With a gentle smile, she shook her head. "You're totally giving him another chance."

"Is that bad?" I asked in a small voice.

"Well, to give him credit, it's romantic as hell that he's doing this because he wants you that much. I just don't want you to get hurt again."

"That summer was like a dream. I have to see if it was real."

"Before Saturday night," she said, "I would have been a real hard-ass on you. But since this thing with Tyrell? I get it. I don't understand it, but I get it." She shrugged. "Love just kinda happens."

I regarded her flushed cheeks. Her sparkling eyes. The smile that she tried to tamp down. "You said *love*."

She rolled her eyes. "You know what I mean."

Yeah, I knew. But that didn't stop me from thinking she might be actually falling for this guy.

Chapter 16

THURSDAY EVENING, I SETTLED IN TO STUDY THE WONDERS of the electromagnetic spectrum. The doorbell rang, but I ignored it. It was probably a solicitor anyway. Which would make Dad happy. He loved arguing with them.

Then Mom sent me a text:

Sum1's @ the door 4 u.

Why couldn't she text like a normal person? She and Dad were the only people I knew who used shorthand like that.

I texted back:

Mom:

A q.t. pie

A jolt zinged through me. Because no effing way. There had been no trace of Ashton since Saturday after the dance. Why was he here now?

Mom:

Want me 2 send him away?

Me:

Be right there

I pulled on my zip-front hoodie and brushed my face with powder, then headed to the living room.

The jolt turned to a rush of adrenaline when I saw Ashton *standing in my house*, looking rumpled and travel-worn in a pullover hoodie and jeans. His hair stood up all over his head, like he'd been running his fingers through it over and over.

I wanted to run to him. I wanted to freeze in place. I wanted to throw myself into his arms, and I wanted to hide away.

"Can we go somewhere and talk?" he asked. "Please?"

I was rigid with tension. Then I took a deep breath and nodded. "Okay."

Dad, who had probably been gearing up for a fight with a salesman or whatever, cleared his throat. "Don't be too late."

"We'll be back before ten."

"Where are we going?" I asked Ashton once we were in his car.

"It's a surprise," he said. Then he switched on the radio. Heart pounding, I settled back and listened to the DJ wax poetic about "no money down, six months same as cash" furniture.

"How was your trip?"

"Let's put it this way," he said. "I'm glad it's over."

"That bad?"

"Truth? All I wanted was to be back here with you."

He knew the right things to say, that's for sure. My guard slowly slipped away. "Did you come straight from the airport?"

He nodded. "I'm exhausted."

"You didn't sleep on the plane?"

"Couldn't."

We drove for an hour, the sun setting in a swirl of fiery cotton clouds as we raced along the highway. "My second favorite time of day," I said.

"I know," he said. "Sunset girl."

I let the nostalgia wash over me. "You used to call me that."

"I know," he said again.

I didn't say anything else the rest of the ride. Just watched the sky put on one of its spectacular autumn shows before the night took center stage.

"You probably figured out where we were going by the signs," he said as we pulled into a parking lot.

"The planetarium? Yeah, I did. Why are we here?"

"I had a feeling you'd love it here."

"I do," I said quietly.

So now my palms were sweating...as he made his way around the car and opened my door. As he reached out his hand and helped me out, giving me the most heartbreakingly beautiful smile.

"What's going on?" I asked in a shaky voice.

"Do you trust me?"

"To be honest? Not really."

His face softened as he looked into my eyes. "Can you trust me for the next five minutes?"

I wanted to. "I'll give it a shot."

"Ah, Mr. Edwards! Welcome!" A tall, wavy-haired, pale-skinned guy bounced from behind his desk to shake Ashton's hand. "Everything's ready! Right this way."

"Ben. Dude." Ashton shook his head as we walked. "Too much."

"I'm being professional," Ben said, then he winked at me.

Ashton turned to me. "This dork is my best friend, Ben."

I raised my eyebrow. "Your best friend works at the planetarium?"

"Indeed, he does," Ben said, his dimple deepening as he grinned. "He's also a lifeguard and a barista."

"And he talks about himself in third person way too much," Ashton said.

"You work three jobs?"

"Acting lessons don't pay for themselves," Ben said. "You must be Devon. I've heard a lot about you."

"Oh no."

"Good things. I promise. Anyway," he said, making a gesturing motion, "the Star Theater. It's all yours for the next hour."

Ashton tried to slip Ben some cash, but Ben pushed it away. "You know where I am if you need anything."

"Thanks, man." Ashton took my hand and led me into the dark theater.

I'd been here many times. Of course I had. But tonight was different. No parents. No strangers. No classmates and no astronomy professor. Only the domed ceiling, the reclining seats...and us. Ashton and me.

The lights turned down and the stars turned up.

"What is this?" I asked, my voice trembling.

"It's the sky from the night we met," Ashton said.

I whipped my head around to stare at him. "What?"

"That night, Devon. I'd never met anyone like you, and I don't think I ever will. My life changed. Did yours?"

I swallowed. "It did."

"All I can think about is what we had, how perfect it was, and how I messed it up." He looked up. "I watched the stars every night because they reminded me of you."

"The whole time we were apart?"

"The entire time."

We stood quietly, staring at the ceiling, my mind reeling.

"France was a shitshow," he said. "I mean, it absolutely sucked. But it was also the easiest thing I've ever done, because I knew you were here."

"Even though we're not a sure thing."

He nodded. "I had to do the right thing. It was never fair to Rochelle, because I couldn't let you go. I never let you go."

"So now what?" I asked softly.

With shaking hands, Ashton took mine in his. "I want to be with you. I can't think of anything I want more than that."

My first emotion: numbness. Or maybe denial. I'd been waiting for this for so long that I didn't even know how or what to feel right now. Could I trust him? Was I willing to try?

Second emotion: fear. Because letting him in right now meant the chance of more heartbreak. I wanted to believe I was strong. But I had a feeling he was going to test that strength, and I wasn't sure if I was ready.

Third emotion: relief. It was done. No turning back from that. It was done and he was here and he was right now. And I loved him. No turning back from that, either.

"I'm so scared you're going to hurt me," I admitted.

He nodded, catching his lower lip between his teeth. "I did a lot of things wrong. I know this. You have every right not to trust me, and I wouldn't blame you one bit. But I know this, too: I don't want to be away from you anymore."

He wasn't lying, not with the desperate hope I saw in his eyes.

"I want you to be happy," he said. "I think I can make you happy. If you'd just give me another chance."

It would be so easy right now to let go of the past and let him in again, 100 percent, no-holds-barred, full-on relationship. And I wanted to.

But something told me to guard my heart a little longer. "I'll think about it."

The expression on his face... This look of trying to be strong but barely holding on. It almost broke me.

He nodded quickly. "That's more than fair." Then he brushed a curl behind my ear. "Is it okay if I hold you?"

I took a step toward him. "Yes."

He slid his arms around my waist and pulled me close. We stood there, the two of us clinging to each other, bathed in a sea of stars. Heartbeats in sync. Breathing in sync.

Our eyes locked. Long, torturous seconds passed while we stared at each other. He reached up to caress my cheek, looking at me like he couldn't look long enough. Like he could never look long enough. Then my hands were clutching his hoodie, pulling him closer, closer, closer. My eyes fluttering shut.

Our lips came together in a collision of breath and salt and skin. Stars and galaxies and entire universes. And I was falling into him. His passion and his hunger and his heat, consuming me and mirroring my own. We were a supernova, expelling all our layers, clinging to the core of us.

"Devon." Again and again, he said my name. A mantra between breaths. "Devon."

I ran my fingers over his flushed cheeks, over his trembling mouth. He closed his eyes and planted small kisses in the hollow of my neck. A moan escaped my lips, and his arms tightened around me. *Closer, closer, closer.* Breathless, he leaned his forehead against mine and we stood together, gasping. Shaking. Wanting.

"Ashton," I whispered. My own prayer.

He let out a shuddering breath and buried his fingers in my hair. "God, I missed this. I missed you."

"Then don't leave again."

"I'm not going anywhere," he whispered against my lips. "Promise."

I put my hand on his chest. "I still don't trust you."

"I know."

"And I still don't forgive you."

He twirled one of my curls around his finger. "I wish more than anything I didn't mess up that summer, but I'm excited to spend time with you again." His voice lowered. "Kiss you again."

Just don't hurt me again.

Chapter 17

ASHTON WAS WAITING AT MY LOCKER THE NEXT MORNING. "Happy Friday! I got you tea. Or should I say 'syrup'?" He grinned. "Three sugars, three drops of honey?"

A goofy smile spread across my face, then I took a sip. "It's perfect. Thank you. I can't believe you remember how I like my tea."

"I remember everything about you."

"Oh no." Blair's groan came from behind me. "Don't tell me you're going to be one of those super-sickening mushy couples."

Now Ashton's eyebrows were raised. Then he smiled and turned to Blair. "I would love it if Devon and I became one of those ooey-gooey whatever-you-said couples."

We stopped outside homeroom. "This is me," I said.

Blair stepped close to Ashton. "Listen up. The second you turn my best friend's smile upside down, I will knock your ass back to the beach where she met you."

Ashton stared blankly at her. "Okay."

"I mean it. You hurt her again, you answer to me. And you won't like what I have to say."

"Oh my God. Come on." I yanked her into the classroom. "See you later," I said to Ashton.

He kissed his fingertips and pointed them toward me, then headed down the hall.

"I can't believe you threatened him," I said to Blair after we'd gotten settled.

"Do you even know who I am? Of course I threatened him. It's because I love you."

I squeezed her hand. "And I appreciate it. But you might have scared the crap out of him."

"If that scares him then he's not worth the floor you walk on, Devvy."

"I know."

She pulled out her compact. "You're happy now. I like that. For all our sakes, I hope you stay that way."

"Blair is a piece of work," Ashton said in his kitchen that afternoon.

"She's my best friend."

"No one's ever talked to me that way before."

I watched him closely. "Does it bother you?"

He shook his head, his expression thoughtful. "It did at first. But it's not like I don't deserve it."

"Well, I'm not going to argue with you there."

He grabbed an orange from the fruit bowl and rolled it back and forth across the counter. "Thanks for coming over."

"Thanks for inviting me." I looked around. "I still feel weird here. Your parents—"

He tossed me the orange. "It's my home, too, and you're my guest. Okay?"

"Okay."

"So." He ran his fingers through his hair. "We probably have a lot to talk about."

I raised my eyebrow. "Probably?"

"Definitely."

"Good afternoon." Ashton's mother entered the kitchen, her navy suit perfectly pressed, her ivory skin silk smooth, her blue eyes like glass. "I didn't realize we were having company."

"Mother." Ashton stood up straight, and his hand clasped mine. "You remember Devon."

Her lips curved into a polished, political smile, but the way she clutched her pearls betrayed her. "Of course I do. How are you, dear?"

"I'm well, thank you."

Ashton didn't seem to mind the buckets of sweat pouring from my palm, so I let out a breath and tried to relax.

"That's wonderful to hear." She turned to Ashton. "I need to speak with you. In private."

He stood like a wall. Immovable. "You can't say what you need to right here?"

"It's quite sensitive." She turned that political smile on me. "I'm sure we wouldn't want to bore Devon with it."

With an apologetic look, Ashton squeezed my hand and then joined his mother outside the kitchen. I could hear a few whispered snatches—it did not sound like a fun conversation. Nor was I having fun, standing there feeling all awkward and gawky.

I returned the orange to the fruit bowl. My appetite was gone, anyway.

By the time they came back, I'd managed to compose my face into (I hoped) its own political smile.

"Make yourself at home," Mrs. Edwards said to me. To Ashton, she threw a look that clearly said, *This isn't over.*

Ashton stiffened, then grabbed my hand again. "Let's go upstairs."

"Is everything okay?"

"Is it ever?"

Ashton's room was more like a suite. There were two sections—a sitting area with a squishy love seat, a leather recliner, and a huge TV, and a sleeping area with a cozy-looking bed.

A sleek silver laptop sat closed on his desk, next to a mug full of pens and a bowl filled with M&M's. His room was so tidy, almost sterile. No knickknacks. No toppling mountain of laundry, no shoes scattered all over. But there were photos everywhere. Beaches and landscapes and sunsets. Pictures of his horse and those mean swans from his garden. The only thing missing from the photos was people.

I picked up a photo of a towering mountain. "You took this?"

"I took all of them."

I looked around again. "They're stunning."

He shrugged. "They're okay."

"No, this is more than okay." I turned to look at him. "I knew you took photos. But, Ashton, you're super talented."

"I have fun."

"This kind of fun could make you rich." I paused. "Oh wait."

"Ha ha," he said with a smirk, which then slid away. "I can't really pursue it, anyway."

"Why not?"

He pointed to himself. "Family business. It's all on me someday."

Oh right. Of course. A lot of people at school had to deal with that. No matter what they wanted, their futures were already mapped out and tied up with family expectations and reputations. At least I had the freedom to make my own choices, as long as I was willing to work for them.

Ashton dropped his book bag and sank into the recliner. Then he looked up at me. "What?"

"Are you going to get in trouble?"

He shrugged. "It doesn't matter."

"Except it kind of does. Should I be here?"

"Of course you should be here. You're my guest. You're my *girlfriend*."

I held up my hand. "Whoa."

"Eventually," he corrected. "I hope."

"But I don't want to be ripping your family apart."

"You won't. Once they see how important you are to me, they'll come around."

"Do you really believe that?"

A long pause. "I'd *like* to."

I studied another photo. "What did you do when we were apart? Besides the girlfriend thing?"

"Mostly scrambled around trying to get my shit together, failing, and then giving up. Over and over and over."

I looked over at him. "Elaborate."

"Not much to tell, really. Spent a lot of time playing catch-up at school. I'm not that keen on going to class."

So I'd noticed.

He shrugged out of his blazer and tossed it onto his desk. "I struggle a lot with my grades. It's one of the many reasons my father wants to send me to military school. Preston is the last resort. If I embarrass him there, I'm done."

Here's what I couldn't understand: If Preston was his last resort, why did he keep skipping school? Why didn't he seem to take it seriously?

Ashton picked up one of the photos. "The one good thing about boarding school was that we took a lot of trips. Something about broadening our horizons or something. I saw some seriously impressive things. I met cool people, ate awesome desserts. Took a lot of pictures." He handed me the photo. "This was my favorite."

A distinct temple. Tall trees. A stunning sunrise. "Your school took you to Angkor Wat?"

"Oh my God, Dev. I've never seen anything like it. It was incredible."

"It looks like it." I set down the picture. "You know what's even more incredible? How much I need your bathroom right now."

"Right through the closet."

"Thank you."

Ashton's closet was twice the size of my bedroom and perfectly organized. Preston blazers, all in a row. Suits arranged by color. Shoes arranged by style and season. And then the bathroom. Double sinks. Huge soaking tub. One of those rain showers with the big flat heads. And there was his cologne. Ashton's scent, right there in a bottle. I picked it up and inhaled. Fresh, like rushing river rapids. Like grass waving in the wind.

Like him.

It was while I was drying my hands that I noticed the medicine cabinet was ajar. I shouldn't have been snooping, but I couldn't help glancing inside before I closed it.

So. Many. Pills.

One. Two. Three. Four bottles. I nudged the cabinet open farther and studied the labels. They were all his. I didn't recognize the names of the drugs, but they all had multiple refills. What could he need so much medicine for? Was he okay? Then I stepped back, ashamed. I shouldn't be prying. He'd tell me in his own time. *If* he told me at all.

"Hey, Dev, did you fall in?" Ashton called.

I jumped and barely stopped myself from slamming the cabinet shut. Then I burst out of the bathroom.

"I hope you sprayed some air freshener," he said, smirking.

My cheeks grew hot. "I did not go number two!"

Laughing, he grabbed my hand and tugged me so I tumbled into his lap. When our lips met, my body came alive with tingles that made my heart pound.

Pills completely forgotten.

I slid my hand under his shirt and rested it on his warm, smooth skin. He planted gentle kisses in the hollow of my neck, making me shiver. I moaned as our lips met again. And again. And I was lost. Lost in the thrill of this deep, passionate kiss. Lost in the way his fingers slid under my blouse, stroking my waist and tracing my belly button. Lost in the way he expertly explored underneath my bra.

Amazing that a kiss could erase all doubts and trepidation from my mind, at least for a moment. Amazing that my body responded completely opposite to what my brain would suggest...if it were working.

Amazing how a kiss could completely stop my brain from working.

For at least an hour we made out, touching each other, breathing each other. Thrilling each other. I didn't want it to end. I wanted to stay forever in this recliner, in his arms, in this universe we'd created. So much could happen, and I kind of wanted it to.

No.

Not yet.

"Wait." I pulled away and put my hands on his chest. "It's too fast."

He wrapped his fingers around mine. "Sorry."

Breathless, I leaned my forehead against his. "We really should take our time. But sometimes—"

"I know. I just want everything to be okay with us. I'll do anything to make it okay."

"You can start by being completely open with me."

"Okay."

"And I'll be honest with you." I nibbled my thumbnail. "I looked in your medicine cabinet."

He flushed. "So you saw my pills."

"I'm sorry. The door was open and I—"

"It's fine. Maybe it's better you saw them."

"Will you tell me about them?"

He hesitated, looking down, then met my eyes. "Remember when I told you I was dealing with stuff?"

I nodded.

"The medicine helps me deal."

"Elaborate," I said for the second time.

He sighed and trailed his fingers lightly down my back. "I don't want to scare you away."

"You won't. Unless you're a serial killer or a rapist or a pedophile. Are you any of those things?"

"What the fuck, Devon? Of course not."

"Okay then. Tell me."

He did one of his slight nods—as if he'd made a choice. His final answer. "Sometimes I get depressed."

"Like, really sad?"

"It's more than that." His eyebrows furrowed. "It's like having this big black weight constantly pushing down on every part of you. Everything is dull and dark and scary. And you feel helpless because you can't stop it. Outside, you're pretending you're okay, but inside you're screaming." He sat for a while, that faraway look on his face again. "No one hears because you're too ashamed to say it out loud. Because saying it out loud makes it real." He stared at me then, his expression solemn. "And you don't want that to be real."

I'd been hurt. I'd been sad. But I couldn't fathom the depth of feeling pain like that. And I hated that it happened to him. "I'm so sorry."

"I hate it, which is why I take the medicine, even though I hate that, too."

"How long have you been taking it?"

"It feels like forever. I don't like needing it."

"But why? If it helps you, that's a good thing, right?"

"Not everyone thinks so. They think people like me are unstable. Irrevocably fucked up."

I tried to catch his eye. But his eyes darted back and forth, looking everywhere but at me.

"I'll never think that," I said. "What about you?"

He was quiet for a long time. Then: "I hope you don't run away, now that I've dumped all that on you." His tone was light, but there was a strain around his mouth that hinted he wasn't joking at all.

"You didn't dump. I asked. And even if you weren't okay, *I'm* not going anywhere. Are you?"

"What do you mean?"

"Are you going to let this come between us? Because if so, then I should know now. I'm not waiting around to be dumped again."

"I told you, Dev. I'm not leaving. Not again."

"Okay."

He stared at me. "You don't believe me."

"No. I won't for a while. But I'm here. Does that count?"

He nodded. "It does. And that's all I want right now."

After dinner, I sat at my desk.

Depression.

I typed the term into Google, and the results came up instantly. The first four sites were ads. I clicked on the fifth: National Institute of Mental Health. The site listed five different types. I scrolled down to the SIGNS AND SYMPTOMS for clinical depression.

> **Fatigue**
>
> **Feelings of worthlessness or guilt**
>
> **Diminished interest or pleasure for almost all activities**
>
> **Suicidal thoughts**

I tapped my desk, thinking. A few things came to mind.

Especially the first time Ashton and I had gone to his family's beach house. His parents weren't supposed to be there...but they were. Which meant awkward introductions and trying to cover up that Ashton and I had been looking for a place to be alone so we could make out...and maybe more.

Eleanor Edwards was tall and had a presence that demanded respect. Tristan Edwards was broad and imposing, with tan skin that suggested loads of business deals done on golf outings. They were handsome, in a severe, old-money kind of way.

They scared the crap out of me.

But what was worse was how much Ashton changed around them.

My playful, passionate boyfriend turned into an uncomfortable, formal young man with ramrod straight posture and a mouth that couldn't smile. His father seemed to go out of his way to put Ashton on the spot—warning him about straying away from his set path, almost threatening him if he even *thought* otherwise. His mother studied both of us, her eyes narrowed over the rim of her wineglass. Still, her voice was pleasant enough when she asked me about the things I was interested in. She seemed charmed by how Ashton and I met. She seemed to even like me a little.

But Ashton seemed a shell of himself. He answered questions mechanically—until he talked about me. He lit up in a way that made his mother's eyes narrow even more.

I thought he'd go back to normal when we were alone again, but instead he stayed pensive. "Can you believe it's always like that?" he'd asked.

And then he said something that should have scared me at the time, but I'd been too caught up in our romance to notice:

"I can't imagine living the rest of my life like this."

God. How did I not see it?

I didn't know much about depression. I didn't know if it came on suddenly or if it was a gradual thing. Was it different for everyone? How come some people seemed to function okay with it, but it brought others to the brink of death? Or beyond? And where was Ashton on that scale?

I didn't know what to think. Was I getting in over my head? What did this mean for me and our relationship? Did it mean anything? Did it matter? Because God knows I was falling for him again.

I sat on the floor and took deep, calming breaths. Things were different this time. They were new and wonderful. Everything would be fine.

Chapter 18

"Horseback riding," Ashton announced after I climbed into his car Saturday morning. "I can tell you've been stressed. I think this will relax you. Plus, I want to show you what I do when we're not together."

What I saw at Bishop Stables made me feel out of my element, with my minimal riding skills.

Expert riders sitting astride marching, shining horses, some hunched over and racing around a track. Other riders straight and proud, jumping with their horses over what looked like hurdles or fences. One body, one motion. Spellbinding.

"Equestrian." Ashton pointed out the jumpers. "And dressage over there."

I blinked. "Those horses are dancing. Why would someone teach a horse to dance?"

"It's how horses were trained for the military a long time ago."

"Have you ever done dressage?"

He laughed. "Not really my thing. Give me a trail and nice weather and I'm good."

I looked down at my jeans, white blouse, and black Converse. "Should I have worn boots?"

"I'll grab you some before we start riding." We stopped at a stall inside the whitewashed stable. "First, I want to introduce you to Leander."

A chocolate-colored horse with a white muzzle regarded me with big brown eyes before gently nudging Ashton's hand. Ashton opened his palm, revealing a large sugar cube that vanished between Leander's enormous jaws.

"He's gorgeous," I said. "Can I pet him?"

"He'll love it."

I stroked Leander's silky face. "He's got a sweet tooth, like you."

Leander blinked and bumped me with his nose.

"He's a gentle guy, but you have to let him know you're the boss," Ashton said quietly. "Don't let him push you around."

"Okay." I planted my feet and refused to sway when Leander bumped me again.

"Good," Ashton said, his voice full of affection. "I really want you to like each other. He's my best friend in the world."

"Should I be jealous that I'm number two in your life?"

"Number three. You forgot about Ben," he said with a wink.

"Smart-ass."

He flicked my hair. "I arranged to have Maisie saddled up for you. She's smaller and extremely gentle. Great for beginners."

I'd taken the mandatory class at Preston when I was a freshman, but that had been so long ago. I didn't mind having the mare at all.

"That's her right there."

I gasped at the sun-dappled horse grazing in the pasture. "She's all white! Ashton, she's stunning!"

"Let me get you a helmet and some boots," he said, smiling. "I'll be right back. Then we'll go on the trails."

It was a stunning fall day, a last hurrah before the cold set in. The leaves burst off the trees in fiery reds and oranges. The bright-blue sky stretched on for days, the breeze a warm caress. I inhaled deeply, taking in the friendly scent of fresh air and horse.

Maisie chewed some hay and looked bored, but Leander watched me with big brown eyes. I kept petting his nose, then I leaned my head against his, letting out a sigh. I could see why Ashton loved this horse so much. Leander's very presence was relaxing.

Ashton handed me a hot-pink helmet. "You two are getting along really well."

"I like him. But Maisie won't have anything to do with me."

"She's just shy. Come here, baby girl," he said to her, clucking his tongue. She walked right over to him and gently nudged him. "Would you like to meet Devon? She's the girl I've been telling you about. She's going to take you on the trail today."

This time Maisie nudged *me*.

"See?" he asked. "Told you she likes you."

"I like her, too," I said, smiling. "And I like *you*."

He kissed me then, his lips as gentle as that warm breeze. Sweet and lingering...and interrupted by an impatient head bump from Leander.

"I guess it's time to hit the trail," Ashton said, laughing. "Ready?"

I pulled on the tall black boots. "Ready."

"Then let's ride." He put his hand on my back. "I'll help you up."

Yikes. I'd forgotten how high I'd be sitting. The ground seemed miles away, and my head spun. I had to take a few deep breaths when I settled into the saddle.

"You okay?" he asked me once he was on Leander.

I held tight to the reins. "I will be."

Once we were on the trail, I relaxed. Golden leaves floated from skinny trees as we wound our way through the woods, Maisie and Leander clip-clopping slowly on the paved roads. The scent of nature put me at ease and the gentle rocking of the horse calmed my racing heart.

"This is nice," I said. "I can see why you spend so much time with him."

"It's peaceful," he agreed. "I come here to get away from my parents. They've been fighting."

"Oh no."

He sighed. "Basically, the only way they communicate is by fighting, unless they're both pissed at me. Then they get along great. But it's been worse lately."

"Do you know why?"

"My father wants to stop paying for counseling. He thinks I just want attention. I mean, yeah, I'd like my fucking father to talk to me without ordering me around all the time, but I don't fake being depressed for him to do it. My mother thinks he should just pay the bills and get off my case."

"And what do you think?"

"I think if they stop my counseling, it'll get really bad for me. And I get scared my father is going to win that fight. He can be really loud and persuasive."

"When you say really bad, what do you mean?"

He grew quiet. Then: "My therapy helps keep me from falling apart."

A monarch butterfly landed on Maisie's mane, flapped its wings once, then flew off again. "Do you feel like you're falling apart, Ashton?"

He looked down and waved his hand, like he was throwing the subject away. "What scares you?"

"I get scared you're going to hurt yourself," I admitted.

"Dev. I'm fine. Really." He tugged at his collar. "Tell me something about you."

I stared down at Maisie's mane. White as snow, glowing

brilliantly against the gold that surrounded us. "I'm afraid of failing. I have all these goals, and I worry that all my hard work is for nothing... because what if I don't make it?"

"It blows my mind that you, of all people, worry about this stuff," he said.

"What do you mean, 'of all people'?"

"You're smart, and you work so hard. Not like me. I get to go to McCafferty because that's how it's been done in my family for generations. And then you come along, working your ass off to get what you want, while it's all been handed to me. It's not right."

Jealousy burned bitter in my throat. "You've been accepted? To McCafferty?"

He fidgeted, and his voice lowered. "As good as. Legacy, you know?"

"Is that how it is?" Dismay descended over me like a shadow. "All the spots get taken up by people like you?"

"Not all. Enough, though."

I slumped. "Is there any point in me trying?"

"Every point. They need you."

"I hope you're right," I said. "The hundred and twenty dollar application fee would scare me off if I didn't want it so bad."

He stared at me in disbelief. "A hundred and twenty dollars? To apply?"

"I guess they want to make sure they only get serious applicants." Or wealthy people who'd have no issues paying their tuition. McCafferty was the only school on my list that didn't accept fee waivers.

"Well, that's definitely you," Ashton said. "I can't think of anyone who deserves it more. And for what it's worth, I'm one hundred percent sure I'll see you on campus next year."

"We'll see, I guess. Maybe we can take some classes together."

He grinned. "That would be awesome."

We rode for another half hour, then stopped to let the horses drink from the stream and to have a snack of our own. By now the sun burned overhead, making the golden leaves glow all around us. As if we were in the middle of the sun itself.

"This is so relaxing," I said. "You come here a lot?"

"Almost every day."

"It's your sanctuary."

He spread peanut butter and Nutella on an apple slice and handed it to me. "It really is."

"Thank you for sharing it with me."

He slid his arm around me and squeezed. "You're my sanctuary, too."

"Yeah?"

"I love being around you. Makes me happy."

"Ashton, that's so sweet."

"It's the truth." He gazed at me with that tender look. "Even the first time I saw you. Remember how we met at that party? I saw you that morning, when Todd and I first arrived. You were wearing this shiny blue bikini and trying to get up the courage to get in the water. It took you forever."

I smiled. "The water is always freezing there."

He looked off into the distance. "First, you kept dipping your toes in and jumping back and squealing. Then you went for it, letting out this adorable scream when you finally got in. You were laughing so hard. Your laugh. It's like music, Dev. I swear I fell in love with you right then."

"And then you met me that night."

"I almost lost my shit when you walked up to us." He nibbled his lip. "I told my cousin I was going to marry you someday."

I handed him a Nutella-covered strawberry. "Marry me, huh? What did he say?"

"He told me to quit being a pussy."

I snorted. "Figures."

He paused, then looked at me. "I still think that, you know."

"That you were being a pussy?"

"No. Dork." He grew serious, his cheeks slightly pink. "I still think about marrying you someday."

It took a moment for the words to truly sink in. "But... Ash. I'm still figuring out what we even are right now."

He didn't even try to hide the hurt. "You're still not sure?"

"Sometimes I'm okay. Really okay. But then I remember. You said you loved me, but you left. And we're only eighteen."

"I know we're too young. But I think about it a lot. Don't you?"

I dipped another strawberry into the Nutella. "Here's the thing. I can't imagine my life without you. But marriage is so far off my radar."

"I get it."

"Did you and Rochelle ever talk about getting married?"

"No way." He shook his head. "My parents talked about it, though. It was all planned."

"You're kidding."

He grabbed the knife and started slicing another apple. "They want to get the family lineage thing squared away as soon as possible. Mother wasn't happy when I told her I broke up with Rochelle. Said I was ruining all their plans."

"Plans? Like an arranged marriage?"

"Not quite. But, yeah, in a way."

"Could they make things worse for you if you don't go back to her?"

With rapid slashes, he finished slicing the apple. "Every move my parents make has nothing to do with my happiness and everything to do with their image and growing our empire."

"But isn't growing the empire going to help you down the road?"

He handed me another peanut butter–covered apple slice. "You're determined to give them the benefit of the doubt."

"I don't want you to hate me for breaking up your family."

He rolled his eyes. "They say things like, 'What do you have to be depressed about? You're a descendent of the most powerful family in the county. You will never want for anything if you do what's expected of you.' Which means fall in line and marry *her*, and everything will be peachy keen. Except it won't."

He grabbed another apple and started slicing. "Sometimes I wish I were one of those ruthless motherfuckers who did whatever he wanted, no matter the consequences. But I'm not, so I guess that makes me a failure."

I frowned. "Do you really wish you were that kind of person?"

"It should be enough that I'm taking over the business. They shouldn't get to choose who I marry."

I absolutely agreed with that. "Why do they want you with her so much, anyway?"

"Her family is powerful. My family is powerful. A merger like that?" He let out a long, low whistle. "We'd be unstoppable."

"What *is* your empire, anyway?"

He screwed up his face, thinking. "The newspaper, the museum, the library, some of the housing developments, Preston Academy, of course, and the bank."

"All of that's coming to you?"

"Not all. I have cousins."

"Do you want *any* of it?"

He shrugged. "Here's the thing. I still want my parents to be proud of me. Even if I don't agree with ninety-nine percent of the shit they preach. Isn't that pathetic?"

"No. Of course it's not. I mean, despite everything, you love them, right?"

He went still. "I don't know."

Oh.

Wow.

Had he ever admitted this out loud? I didn't think so. Not with the hauntingly sad look washing over his face. *Good going, Devon.*

"I'm sorry. I shouldn't—"

"No. It's fine." He shook his head. "Things are complicated with my parents. I'm an only child, so all this pressure is on me. But I'm not great at school, I'm not dating the girl they want. I'm doing everything all wrong, and they don't know how to relate to me because I'm not acting how they think I should act. I can't be who they want me to be. And sometimes? I hate it. I hate *me*."

"But of course they don't hate you?"

He shrugged again. "Mother is protective of me, but I don't know if it's because of the family name, or if it's because I'm her kid, you know?"

I didn't know, either. So I didn't say anything. I squeezed his hand instead.

"And my father," he said. "His father was hard on him. I think it's the only way he knows how to be."

"Even with your grandmother?"

"I think she didn't start speaking up more in the family until my grandfather was gone. I don't remember him much. He died when I was a baby."

"God, Ashton. I'm so sorry."

He swatted at a fly. "It is what it is."

"But they're your parents."

"It is what it is," he said again. Case closed.

Since I was already tossing out the heavy hitters, I swallowed and forced out the next question. "Would you have married Rochelle?"

The sun cowered behind a thick bank of clouds. "Maybe."

His answer punched me in the gut and made my skin burn. "Did you love her?"

He fixed troubled eyes on me. "Does it matter, Devon?"

"It shouldn't. But it does."

"She and I have a lot of history. But I don't love her like I love you. I'll never love anyone like I love you."

I looked down. "That's not an answer."

"Dev, Rochelle's my oldest friend. I love her in that way. *Only* that way."

"I feel like if anyone could take you away from me, it's her."

"No. You've got me. All of me." He sat quietly for a moment, then asked, "Do I have you?"

I caressed his cheek. With a sigh, he closed his eyes and kissed my palm. And that's when I knew my answer. I'd known for a long time.

I touched my trembling lips to his. Let myself fill up on his taste, his scent, his sweet, salty essence. Whereas our kiss in the planetarium had been explosive and dramatic, this one was tender, slow, and soft. Binding and emotional and true. I felt it through every part of me, through my soul and beyond.

"Dev?"

"Yes," I whispered.

"Yes?"

"You have me. I'm yours."

He put his hands on my cheeks. “I won’t let you down again.”

“No. Don’t do that. Don’t make a bunch of promises. Not today. Just be with me.”

He opened his arms so I could lean into him. “I can do that.”

Chapter 19

I COULD NOT SLEEP.

Saturday night. Halloween. Most of my classmates were probably out, or just getting home. Blair was at her grandmother's for the weekend. Ashton was probably in bed. He was like me, one of those people who turned in impossibly early, even on the weekends, and woke up bright-eyed before the sun rose. Except tonight. It was almost midnight, but I was wired. I lay in bed and stared at my ceiling. The glow-in-the-dark stars had faded hours ago. My eyes were gritty, and I couldn't stop yawning, but my mind would not turn off.

I threw off the covers and grabbed my laptop. The bright monitor temporarily blinded me, but my eyes adjusted quickly. My fingers flew across the keyboard as I typed in the McCafferty web address. Then I logged in and stared at my profile.

There was another reason I lay here wide awake. It wasn't just any Saturday night. Tomorrow was November 1: The deadline to turn in my early action application.

My application, my essay, and my scholarship paperwork sat neatly in my account. My letters of recommendation, transcripts, and test scores had already been forwarded to the admissions office. Everything was ready. Everything except me.

I hadn't been able to bring myself to click the SUBMIT button. Even though everything had been vetted by Professor Trask. He'd said it was "go for launch." Yet, I was still so nervous. What if everything wasn't perfect? It *had* to be perfect.

My essay needed to be written from the heart, but not show weakness or begging. Did I outline my accomplishments without bragging? I'd agonized over every single word. I had to strike the right balance. They had to think they needed me, not the other way around.

I gave up on sleeping, grabbed my phone, and shot a text to Ashton. Unlikely he'd be up, but I needed to blow off some steam. I'd feel better, and he'd get the message in the morning.

I lay back and stared at my ceiling. Again.

The phone buzzed and I jumped, knocking my stuffed bunny to the floor. I clutched my chest as I answered. "You're up."

"I'll be there in fifteen."

"You don't have to—"

"I want to. Besides, I have something to show you."

I was so glad to hear from him. "See you soon."

I pulled on yoga pants and a hoodie, and when my phone

beeped, I padded into the living room. My parents were snuggling on the couch.

"We're watching a documentary," Dad announced. "Conspiracy theories. Project Monarch and all that."

"Why?"

"It's fascinating," Mom said. "Want to join us?"

"No, thanks. I'm going out for a bit."

Mom sat up. "So late?"

I slipped on my tennis shoes. "It's not a school night."

She studied me carefully, eyebrows raised, then nodded. "Be safe."

"I think you're in more danger than I am, watching that weird stuff."

"Don't be out too long," Dad called.

I pulled on my sneakers and headed outside, where Ashton sat in his car, his fingers dancing across his phone in that playing-a-game sort of way.

A grin spread across his face when I opened the door. "Hey, you." He shoved his phone into his pocket, then leaned over to give me a quick kiss. "I'm so glad you texted."

"I'm surprised you were up."

"Couldn't sleep."

I paused. "Everything okay?"

The grin evaporated as he rolled his eyes. "Is it ever? But this isn't about me. It's about you."

"Ashton, if you need to talk about anything—"

"I don't." He put the car in gear. "I want to show you something. It's a surprise."

I stared at him, but his face was impassive, his profile brightening and darkening as we passed the lights on the street.

"Ashton—"

He reached over and took my hand. "No. It's really okay." His shoulders relaxed. "I'm sorry for snapping."

I looked out the car window and tried to decipher where we were heading. We passed the old-fashioned soda fountain and ice-cream shop. The flower shop run by cranky Mrs. Armstrong, who thought teenagers were "hoodlums," except when it came time to buy all her corsages. The locally owned coffee shop that had a line out the door, and the Starbucks that didn't.

"We're here," he said after about thirty minutes.

A park. One outside of town. I sometimes ran here, but tonight, it was deserted. Peaceful. We walked until we got to the playground. He stopped me with a gentle touch on my shoulder. "Look up."

And wow. Above me was the Milky Way, swirling in its majestic glory, all purples and blues and hazy white clouds. Vast and sweeping, broad and infinite. Stunningly gorgeous. I drew in a breath and let the awe wash over me. This would never, ever get old.

Ashton stepped behind me and slid his arms around my waist. "I discovered this a few weeks ago when I needed to get the hell out of my head. Came here to think, and then I looked up. I knew right away I had to see this with you."

"I'm glad you brought me. I haven't seen it like this since I was a kid." Observatories, yes. Google images, definitely. But not with my boyfriend, who I was falling harder for every day. Not when his waterfall scent, mixed with the night air, helped empty my mind. Filled it instead with magic.

The sky was so clear. Only a half hour away from my house, but the park didn't have orange streetlights and trees blocking this glorious view. How did I not know about this?

He rested his chin on my shoulder. "Tell me about your first time."

I smiled. "Yellowstone. My parents took me camping. I stayed up so late staring at the sky, watching the stars move. When I got home a few nights later, I googled 'why do the stars move.' I fell down a rabbit hole and learned it was actually us moving. That's when I figured out I wanted to study astrophysics."

"Do you keep falling down these rabbit holes?"

"All the time. Did you know there are hundreds of billions of planets in the Milky Way?"

"I had no idea," he said, looking at me in wonder.

"And maybe even a trillion stars. All kinds. Lots of supernovae." I shook my head. "God, it's so beautiful."

"Do you think there are others out there? I mean, we can't be the only ones, right?"

I nodded. "And I want to find them."

"Dev, you're going to get into McCafferty. They need someone who loves this like you do."

I stiffened, then turned to face him. "If I send the application."

His forehead furrowed with wrinkles of confusion. "What do you mean *if*?"

"This is my one shot, and I'm terrified I'm going to blow it."

"Dev. You are young, scrappy, and hungry. You're not throwin' away your shot." Then he sang the last two words. "Rise up!"

I let out a small laugh. "Are you singing *Hamilton*?"

"I'm singing a variation of 'My Shot' from *Hamilton*." Serious again, he put his hands on the sides of my face and stared into my eyes. "Devon. Promise me you'll send that application."

I nibbled my thumbnail. "I'm scared."

"Why?"

"What if they don't let me in?"

"Devon, if you don't send it, the answer is already no."

"That's what Professor Trask said."

"Professor Trask is a very wise man." Ashton gently pulled my thumb away from my mouth. "Devon, do you promise?"

I let out a trembling breath, steamy in the cool air. Then I nodded. "I promise."

"Good." He brought my thumb to his lips and kissed it gently. Then he leaned close and pressed his mouth to mine, making me forget everything except him and me and the twirling stars above us.

Chapter 20

"Let's go to my house," he whispered later.

"Why?"

"I wanna make out."

"What about your parents?"

"Out of town."

I smiled and let him take my hand.

"I feel so naughty, sneaking around like this," I said once we got to his room. It was mostly dark, the only light coming from a small lamp on his bedside table.

He edged me closer to the bed. "You *are* naughty."

Our clothing rumpled. Our hair grew wild. But the kissing

was nonstop. Warm, slightly salty, all him. Deeper than a sugar rush, sweeter than candy. The best kind of intoxicating drug.

Since getting back together, we'd only made out with our clothes on, wandering fingers exploring heated skin under our shirts. Tonight, something reckless came over me, and I pulled off my hoodie and T-shirt. Then we kissed again.

"I want to see you," I said against his lips. "It's been so long since I've seen you."

Ashton sat up, his chest rising and falling with his breath. Then, with his dark eyes locked on mine, he slowly pulled off his T-shirt. I let my gaze skim over his golden body. He was thin but toned, with slight definition in his arms and abs. I ran my hand over his warm, smooth skin, then smiled.

"What?"

"You're so skinny."

He raised an eyebrow. "So?"

"You've changed. Since that summer." I traced a heart onto his arm. "I like that you're not a beefcake."

He burst out laughing. "Beefcake? Who talks like that? And you've changed, too. Your boobs are bigger."

I stared down at my chest. Leave it to him to point it out.

He drew in a breath as his eyes swept over me. "God, Devon. You're flawless."

My face grew warmer. "No way."

"Every way."

We were kissing again, his hands moving along my back, unhooking the clasp on my bra. Then his fingertips slid down my bare shoulders, taking the dainty straps with them. His lips followed, planting delicate kisses along my collarbone and shoulders, sending electricity everywhere they lingered. Then his eyes met mine again, silently asking if it'd be okay if he slid the straps all the way off.

It was okay.

We lay back down together, our kisses growing in passion and urgency. Flesh against flesh, heartbeat against heartbeat. My body aching as those kisses traveled all over my face, my neck, then back to my lips again.

"I want to touch you," he murmured. "Everywhere."

"I want you to," I admitted, then trembled.

Another deep kiss, then his fingers were dipping below my waist. He hadn't forgotten what I liked. His fingers brushing just the right spot, making my heart beat faster. Intense sensations that made my toes curl. He still remembered how to make the feelings spiral out until I was lost in a state of breathless bliss. God, *he still remembered.*

"Good?" he asked.

"Mmm."

"Like before?"

"Better."

"Good," he said again, his eyelids lowered, his smile lazy and content.

I kissed him again, then trailed light fingertips down his abs. "Now it's your turn."

★ · ● · ✕

"I'm finally getting sleepy," I said with a yawn later, then reached for my hoodie. "I should probably get home."

"I want you to do something first," he said. Then he led me to his desk and flipped open his computer. "Send it, Dev."

And just like that, my palms were sweating and my knees were trembling. The warm contentment from earlier was gone, replaced with stark fear.

"I get that you're nervous." He stroked my wrist. "But you'll regret it big-time if you never send it."

Why was this so hard? All I had to do was type in *McCaffertyUniversity.edu*.

Enter my username and password.

Hit SUBMIT.

But instead I froze, staring at the screen.

"I'm right here," Ashton whispered, his breath warm and comforting on my neck.

"Maybe you can do it for me," I joked, but not really.

"This is your dream," he said gently. "It has to be you."

The screen burned in front of me. "No pressure or anything."

"You shouldn't do it if you're not truly ready." Now he was stroking my arm. "But I think you are."

"Then why can't I do it?"

"Because it's a big deal, Devon. And once you hit that button, it's out of your hands. That's scary as hell."

I ran my fingertips over the slick black keys. "Event horizon."

"What's that?"

"Like you're at the edge of a black hole, and once the gravity catches you, that's it. No turning back. Have you ever felt like that?"

He nodded. "When I got on that plane to France. I knew I was going to piss off my family, and Rochelle would not be happy. But once I was in the air, it felt right. And so will this."

"Do you regret it?"

"Not one bit, Dev. I can't think of anywhere else I'd rather be right now."

I wrapped my arms around myself. Why the hell was I shaking? It was a college application. Not a big deal. Seriously.

Not. A. Big. Deal.

So why couldn't I hit SUBMIT?

"Dev, you've wanted McCafferty forever. If you don't do this, you're already doomed. Then what?"

"I'll beat myself up."

"And neither of us wants that."

He was right. I needed to get a grip. This was my dream. Time to get my head on straight and do this thing. Now.

I pulled out the leather chair and sat. Then I clicked through the uploaded documents one last time. Application. Essay. Scholarship applications. Everything was still there. I typed in Dad's Visa information—memorized by this point. Closed my eyes and said a tiny prayer. Took three long, deep breaths, and finally hit that SUBMIT button.

A white screen, a twirling gray circle, then:

Thank you for applying to McCafferty University!

And I felt . . . nothing. No relief. Not a drop of impending fear. Just ordinary. As if this was how it was supposed to be all along. My palms stopped sweating. My knees stopped shaking. And everything was okay.

I was okay.

Ashton squeezed my shoulder. "Now I can take you home."

Chapter 21

I HATED WHEN IT SNOWED BEFORE THANKSGIVING. THREE weeks ago, we'd been horseback riding. Now Ashton's car was slipping and sliding as he pulled up to my house after school.

I let go of the bar above the window. "I think you should stay for dinner."

Ashton swallowed. "Tonight?"

I nodded. "Mom just texted. They want you to."

His hands trembled on the steering wheel. "What if they don't like me?"

"They already love you." I brought his hand to my lips and kissed his wrist. That's when I noticed the scar. Silvery white, almost faded. Easy to miss if you didn't look too closely. I traced it lightly, then turned to him, asking the question with my eyes.

He was looking at the scar, too, his nostrils flaring with his breath. Then he shook his head. *Not now*, his expression said. His voice said, "Okay. I'll have dinner with your parents. But if I don't make it out alive, I'm blaming you."

"Come on."

Ashton looked, well…*ashen* as we stepped onto the porch.

I touched his cheek. "It'll be okay. I promise."

His expression indicated he believed the exact opposite of that.

"Take that, you rat soup–eatin' lowlife son of a bitch!"

Ashton froze, his hand gripping mine. "Was that your *mom*?" he asked in an urgent whisper.

"And if you attack her again, I will annihilate you and your cow!" Dad this time.

I rolled my eyes. "They're playing video games."

A look of comprehension dawned. "Makes perfect sense."

I dragged him into the living room.

Mom and Dad threw their headsets aside and smiled big ole Kool-Aid smiles. No one would ever guess they'd probably been making twelve-year-olds cry thirty seconds ago.

Mom sat there in all her hippie glory, wearing a tube top and a long flowing skirt. Dad had on a Hawaiian shirt (a Hawaiian shirt!) and cargo shorts. Because somehow, neither of them had gotten the memo that it was snowing outside.

"Well. Look who we have here," Mom said, a mischievous glint in her eyes. "The person who's been making my daughter glow like a glowing thing that glows!"

"Thank you for inviting me in, Mr. and Ms. Kearney."

Then he gave me a look like *Am I doing okay?* Of course he was. His political self was on, the epitome of perfect manners and charm.

"So." My dad cleared his throat and rubbed his hands together. "What are your intentions with my daughter?"

Mom closed her eyes and shook her head. My mouth dropped. "Dad."

But Ashton didn't seem shocked at all. "I like hanging out with Devon and getting to know her." Then he gazed at me with his soft look. "I hope we stay close for a long time."

"You're staying for dinner, right?" Mom asked. "We're having spaghetti. Unless you have a food allergy? Or restrictions? Because if you do, I can rustle up something else. Or we could order out. We're especially fond of sushi."

Ashton's mouth formed an O. "You have no idea how perfect that sounds, Ms. Kearney. I haven't had spaghetti in forever."

"Lori," she said. "I insist. And welcome to our home. We're glad you're here."

With that, Ashton's shoulders relaxed. "Thank you."

"Let me give you the grand tour." I squeezed his hand.

I tried to see my home through Ashton's eyes. It wasn't a grand, stately mansion with a million rooms. It didn't reek of old wealth, and it wasn't full of museum pieces. But it was warm and comfortable. Rich with history, like my growth marks on the bathroom wall. Like dried spaghetti noodles on the kitchen ceiling from Mom's al dente tests. And like the glitter in the carpet from last spring's BananaCon costume.

Mom's bohemian signature echoed throughout every room. Fairy lights strung along the walls, the scent of Nag Champa incense permeating the hall. Beaded curtains adorning the windows, wild green plants reaching for the ceiling, and books tumbling onto scuffed wooden floors.

Ashton's face took on a faraway, serious look as we poked our heads into the family room, the kitchen, the formal living room that we never used except for holidays or family parties.

I bumped my shoulder with his. "You okay?"

"There's so much love here. It's palpable. Like, yeah, *this* is a home."

I slid my arm around his waist. "And now you're part of it."

He fixed those mesmerizing eyes on mine. "Do you mean it?"

"Yes," I whispered, and kissed him. His lips were trembling.

I touched his cheek with my thumb.

He slowed down to study my "hall of fame": school pictures from every year since preschool. "You were a very cute kid."

"Thank you. I wonder what happened?"

"You grew up to be a knockout, that's what happened." He picked up a beaded frame from a side table. "Are you wearing a Cinderella dress?"

"I was at Disney World! Of course it's a Cinderella dress."

He gave a slight smile. "Damn, that's adorable." Then his expression became solemn again. "I've never been there. To Disney World."

I squeezed him. "I'll take you someday."

He set down the frame and nodded slowly. Then he wrapped his arms around me and rested his chin on my shoulder. "I'm kinda jealous of your childhood. And by 'kinda jealous,' I mean really jealous." He pulled away slightly and picked up the picture again. "Look how your dad is looking at you. He still looks at you like that, Devon. You are literally his little princess. My parents—they never look at me like that." His mouth turned down. "They never look at me at all."

"Ashton—"

"No." And as quickly as it had appeared, his somber mood was gone. He was bright again, like a fire that burned too hot. He broke our embrace and glanced down the hall. "Show me your room."

I pushed open the door and led him inside. Then I watched as he ran shaking fingers across my desk, over and over and over. "Ashton? You sure you're okay?"

He jerked his head. "I'm fine."

He wasn't fine. The way he wouldn't look me in the eye, the way his mouth turned down at the edges, made that clear. But he was sure putting a lot of effort into trying to convince me, and probably himself.

"Wow," he said, looking around my room, his smile forced. As if the gleam of his white teeth could scare off whatever was trying to take him over. "Exactly how I pictured it. Yoga mat on the floor. Desk with a huge stack of books. Telescope. What kind of bed is that? It looks like it really wants to be a couch. I like the canopy, though."

"It's a daybed. Couch by day, bed by night. Ashton—"

"And who's this?" He picked up my stuffed bunny and nuzzled her nonexistent nose. "She looks very loved."

I sighed. "That's Honey. I've had her since I was a baby."

"She's sweet. Like you are." And then he set her down oh so carefully and gave her a gentle pat on her head.

"I wish you'd tell me if something's wrong."

"I told you. I'm fine." He pulled me close again. "Why's it smell so good in here?"

With reluctance, I let it go. He changed the subject every time, and it was starting to frustrate me. But no point in forcing him to talk when he didn't want to.

"I burn incense constantly," I said. "In fact, I'm going to light some now."

He tossed his blazer onto my bed, then walked over to the window. "Is this the telescope you saved up to buy?"

"I can't believe you remember that. I told you that forever ago."

"One of these days you're going to believe me when I tell you I remember everything you said that summer." He bent and peered through the eyepiece. "Do you use your telescope to stargaze or to spy on your neighbors?"

I laughed. "Have you seen my neighbors? Trust me, no one wants to spy on that."

"I wonder if any of them are spying on *you*." He looked up and waggled his eyebrows. "I know I would be."

"Ew."

"I'm kidding."

"I really use it to stargaze, for your information. It's a basic refractor, so I can see some cool stuff. But I really want a reflector. Or a catadioptric."

He stretched, making his shirt pop out of his pants. "What's the difference between this one and that... whatever you said?"

I pointed. "Well, with this one, I can see planets and stars, but with a reflector or a catadioptric, I could see deep space. Galaxies and nebulas and things."

"I don't even know what a nebula is, but it sounds cool." He slid his arms around my waist. "You're going to be the best scientist."

"I hope so."

"I know so. No one as passionate as you could be bad at it." Ashton was completely relaxed now, his agitation from earlier vanished. Or maybe well hidden. He moved forward, pressing me against the wall. "Now if you don't mind, I'd really like to kiss you right now."

"Only if you promise to never spy on me."

"I promise to never spy on you, stalk you, or do any other creepy things to you," he said solemnly. "My hot scientist girlfriend."

His soft lips worked their magic as the kiss grew deeper and more urgent. Wandering fingers eased under my shirt to stroke my skin and shoot bolts clear to my toes. I could taste his hunger and his passion, and it made me think reckless things.

Sexy things.

"Ahem!" Mom cleared her throat.

Ashton and I jumped apart so fast he knocked two books off my desk.

Mom threw me a knowing look. "I was coming to see if Ashton wanted something to drink, but—"

The tips of his ears flamed. "I'm fine, Ms., er . . . Lori."

She smirked at him. "I'm sure you are. Maybe you two should join us out here."

Faces burning, Ashton and I followed Mom to the family room.

"Sorry," he muttered.

Dad stalked in behind us and thrust a video game at Ashton. "You play?"

Ashton stared at the game, his mouth wide open. "This is *Tidal Destruction III*. But it's not even out for another month. How—?"

"That, I'm afraid, is classified."

"No, that's cool . . . but . . . wow." Ashton was all but drooling. I'd never seen him look so undignified. It was both adorable and unnerving.

"Wanna play?" my dad asked.

Ashton didn't hesitate. "Yes. Yes, I do."

"We'll leave you boys to it," Mom said, then she and I went into the kitchen. "So, your boyfriend." She gave me an appreciative look. "Dang, girl."

My face warmed. Okay, it was one thing for girls my age to fall all over Ashton. It was quite another for my *mom* to do it.

"I ain't mad at *you-ooo*," she sang, filling a pot with water.

Now I was hot all over. I could barely focus on chopping the lettuce, I was so embarrassed. "Can you not?"

"Hey, I might be off the market, but that doesn't mean I can't enjoy the selection."

"MOM!"

She was laughing. "You have got to stop embarrassing so easily. Your boyfriend is very handsome. Enjoy it."

"Believe me, I do," I said without thinking. And now I was officially on fire.

She stared at me in wonder. "You're in love with him."

I relaxed and smiled. "Madly."

She raised her eyebrows. "Do we need to talk birth control?"

"I think so. We haven't needed it yet, but..."

She finished breaking the spaghetti, and put her arm around me. "But it's getting close?"

I was having a hard time keeping my clothes on whenever Ashton and I were alone these days. To be honest, it's not like I tried that hard. Or at all. There was something about opening up emotionally with him that made me want to open up physically. The more we shared, the closer I wanted to be to him. I was addicted to the sensation of his flesh against mine, and I wanted to feel all of him. *Getting* close? We were practically there.

A slow nod. "Yeah."

"I figured," she said. "I can tell by the way you two look at each other. And the way you two were all over each other when I walked in on you."

Now I was burning up again. “Sorry about that.”

She squeezed me, then went to stir the noodles. “Hey, like I said. Enjoy it. Enjoy him.”

“You don’t think we’re moving too fast?” I asked in a small voice.

“I’m your mother. You can be married with three kids and I’ll think you’re moving too fast. Do *you* think it’s too soon?”

I started tossing the salad. “Not at all.” *Not soon enough* is what I wanted to say.

“Well, if you feel ready, and you’re responsible enough to handle it, I say ‘your body, your rules.’ ”

“Does this mean I can get his name tattooed across my chest?”

She turned and stared at me, the look on her face worth every embarrassing moment I’d just suffered in this kitchen.

“Mom, you know I’m kidding, right?”

“God.” She fanned herself. “You almost gave me a heart attack. Please never get anyone’s name tattooed on you.”

“But you said my body, my rules.”

She sighed. “I’d *prefer* it if you wouldn’t get someone’s name tattooed on you.”

“I know Mom. I love you.”

Later that night, I sat at the same desk Ashton had run his fingers over.

Depression.

I'd been typing the term into Google every day since Ashton told me his diagnosis. The results were always the same:

Fatigue

Feelings of worthlessness or guilt

Diminished interest or pleasure for almost all activities

Suicidal thoughts

My hand froze. The scar on Ashton's wrist. The desperate look in his eyes when I'd noticed it. As if he wanted to disappear. As if he wanted the car to swallow him whole.

What if he'd tried the unthinkable?

I closed my eyes and took deep breaths. Then I did another search. Found a link to a site on supporting a loved one with depression. Bookmarked it.

Just in case.

Two knocks, then Mom walked in holding a little paper bag. I closed my laptop and leaned back in my chair, crossing my legs lotus-style. "What's that?"

"What we talked about earlier," she said, closing the door.

Oh right.

Mom had given me "the talk" years ago, so I knew the mechanics of sexual intercourse. What I didn't know were the other things: How did it feel? Was it scary, being so close and so vulnerable with someone?

Would it hurt?

"Condoms," she said. "Brochures. A list of websites for the things you're too embarrassed to ask me about. And if you decide to go on the pill, here's the name of my gynecologist.

You can go by yourself if you want, but I'll be happy to take you, too."

"Did you have this stuff waiting for me?"

"As soon as you started spending all that time in the driveway with him. Don't think I didn't notice those foggy car windows."

"Um..."

"And, Bun? Talk to him. If you can't sit down and have a frank discussion about sex, you shouldn't be having sex with him."

"What do we talk about?"

"What *don't* you talk about?" she countered. "Talk about everything. Birth control, your history, testing for STDs. And don't forget the logistics, like when and where, what you both like and don't like, and how much you're willing to explore together. Talk about it *all*."

That made perfect sense. "I will."

She pointed to the bag. "Look through that, and if you have questions, come to me. Okay?"

"Okay." I sifted through the bag, then I looked up at her. "It's all very serious, isn't it?"

"Damn right it's serious. I've tried to be sex-positive and open-minded with you, but I have to give it to you straight. It's a big deal when you let someone get so close to you for the first time. If you take that step, he's going to make you feel things you've never felt before. That can do a number on your head and your emotions. There are a lot of risks, and I'm not only talking about getting pregnant or STDs."

I nodded. "I know, Mom. I'm not taking this lightly. I love him. Deeply."

"I know. But it wasn't that long ago you were crying over him. I like him, but I don't quite trust him yet." She kissed my forehead. "However, I do trust you. And I hope he's worth it. You only get one first time. I want yours to be special."

Chapter 22

"My teachers have lost every ounce of sense," Blair groaned the Wednesday after Thanksgiving. She didn't look panicked this time. Just annoyed. "I have to come up with a budget for Home Management—like I know anything about budgeting? That's what we have accountants for. And it's not like I can slack off. The Fashion & Design Institute will be checking my grades until I graduate, so I have to do *everything*." She faded out, muttering under her breath and cursing various Preston instructors. When she got like that, it was time to step back and let the steam work itself out of her ears.

My planner didn't look so great, either. The homework would not stop coming. I spent a lot of time in the library, digging around the stacks, trying to find that certain thing that would give my projects an edge. My laptop went everywhere with me, and I was constantly making charts and spreadsheets, typing papers, even editing videos. Then there were the exams themselves. In addition to statewide testing, there were Preston's own stringent exams to pass. No, not just pass. *Ace.*

When I wasn't working on school projects, there was Yearbook. Hours sorting pictures, coming up with clever captions, laying out pages. Keeping track of orders and balancing the ledgers. It was slowly beginning to resemble an actual yearbook instead of endless blank ladders—diagrams outlining what was going in the yearbook—that looked insurmountable.

This was my legacy. It had to be perfect.

Hard.

Core.

Pressure.

And then there was Ashton. I had so much work, but let's be real. It was hard to concentrate when all I wanted to do was rip his clothes off.

I craved him. Constantly. Closing my eyes and losing myself in the scent of him, the feel of him. His deep, deep kisses. That delicious thrill when he unbuttoned my shirt, then trailed tiny kisses all over my chest and down my belly. His skin against mine after I slid off his shirt and tossed it to the floor. The questioning look in his eyes as his fingers stroked beneath my skirt, wordlessly asking if it was okay for him to explore more. And, finally, I craved the shiver that came after I told him yes.

"Earth to Devon." Blair waved her hand in front of me.

"Did you want to come over after school today? Model some dresses for my portfolio?"

"Oh man. I'd love to, but I already have plans with Ashton."

"Sexy plans?"

My face got hot. "Maybe."

She shook her head. "You have it bad."

She had no idea.

After school, Ashton and I rushed up to his bedroom, as we often did. Lay in his bed and kissed until our lips were swollen. Let our fingers start to wander to those secret places. But this time, I stopped him before we got carried away. "We should talk," I said breathlessly.

Talking was the last thing I wanted to do.

"This sounds ominous," he said against my mouth, his eyes half-closed. "Is everything okay?"

"Actually." I touched his bottom lip. "I don't know."

His eyebrows drew together. "What's going on?"

I flipped his hand so the silvery line on his wrist showed. "I need to know. Did you...?" The words caught in my throat.

He didn't say anything for a long time. And then... a slight nod.

I squeezed his hand. Hard.

"It happened that summer," he said quietly. "Our summer. I used a razor blade. My mother found me."

Our summer...

"My parents took me away. Stuck me in a hospital." He stared at his lap and lowered his voice. "That's the real reason I didn't get to tell you good-bye."

I swallowed, then brought his wrist to my lips. Tried to stop from shaking. I loved being right as much as the next person, but I hadn't wanted to be right about this. Never this.

"Why did you do it?"

"I don't even know how to explain it, Dev."

"I just... I want to know. I want to know *you*."

He rubbed his face while he found the words. "I call it the Dark. It's always there, sleeping right under my skin. Most of the time I can live with it. I don't like it, but I deal. But then something happens to wake it up. And when it's awake, I want to rip my skin off." He gripped a handful of his hair and yanked. "That night? I was already upset the summer was ending and I wouldn't get to see you all the time. Then my parents forbade me to see you at all. Like, ever. So by now, the Dark was roaring. Asking me why I couldn't ever do anything right. Telling me I was the worst person ever, since my parents were always pissed at me."

"Oh my God, Ashton." I put my hand on his cheek.

"It just keeps going, telling me how I'm a loser. Making me wonder why the fuck I'm even wasting space here." He squirmed. "That night, I knew that no matter what choice I made, someone was going to be upset. I knew it would make you cry. I couldn't bear it. So..." He drew in a breath. "I decided I was a shitty person. And shitty people don't deserve to live."

"You're not shitty, Ashton. Not even a little bit."

He shook his head. "The Dark doesn't care about that stuff. And I was desperate. I slit my wrists to get it out so it would finally leave me alone. Even if it meant I had to die."

He'd talked about the darkness inside him before. And I'd seen hints of it. Him going inside himself. His mouth a straight line as the thoughts took over. But then he'd turn to me and smile brightly enough to convince me everything was okay.

But his darkness was bigger than I'd imagined. He thought of it as an actual *entity*, something that could consume him. Completely.

"Do you still think about . . . doing that?" I couldn't bring myself to say the words. Saying it would make it real, and it felt real enough already. "Does the . . . is the Dark still trying to consume you?"

"Dev . . ." He buried his face in my neck.

"Is it?"

He nodded slowly. "Yeah."

"Ashton." I wrapped my arms around him. Closed my eyes and tried to swallow the fear.

"My counselor calls it 'suicidal ideation,'" he said. "I think so much about death, and how much better off everyone would be if I were gone, that it feels like a part of me. It's like a reflex. I don't even know I'm doing it half the time."

I squeezed him tighter. "How serious are these thoughts? I mean, I know they're serious, but . . ."

"I don't have plans to go through with it. Not anymore."

Not anymore.

"Do you promise?" I bit my lip to stop it from trembling. "I don't want to lose you."

"I promise."

I studied his face for hints that he was lying. But he looked normal. Whatever *normal* meant.

I wasn't so sure anymore.

"I messed up on so many levels that summer," he said, his fingers drumming the bed. Moving so quickly they blurred. "But leaving you like that? I'll never forgive myself."

"Ashton. We've worked through that already."

"I should've tried harder to find you."

I grabbed his hand. Intertwined his fingers with mine until they stopped jerking. "You were in the hospital."

"There was no excuse. I went with what was easy instead of what was right, and that whole time, I never stopped loving you. I never stopped thinking about you, missing you, wanting you. Not even once." He sat for a bit, clenching and unclenching his free fist. Then his expression turned thoughtful. "I need to show you something."

He hopped up and went to his desk. Dug through a drawer, then handed me a book.

A photo album. "Wow, this is so old-school," I said lightly. But then my throat caught. The album had fallen open to that photo of us I loved so much. Sitting in the sand, his arm lightly around my waist. My hand on his chest. Our curved lips close, as if we shared a secret. Our secret. And then page after page of photos from that summer. Pictures of me and him, our feelings obvious in the way we filled each other's space. Pictures from the day we went to that driftwood beach and he took a billion photos of me. There were photos of the sand, the sun, the moon, the water, but most of the album was about us.

I was so in love with him then. And I was so in love with him now.

"I don't expect you to believe me," he said, "but not a day went by that I didn't wonder where you were. What you were doing. If you still loved me." He stroked my cheek with trembling fingers.

"Even when you were with Rochelle?"

"She's not you, Dev."

I kissed him. Deeply, passionately. Desperately. We kissed like the world would end if we stopped. We kept kissing until we were breathless and our hearts were beating fast. And then we kissed some more.

We pulled away slightly to catch our breath, but we stayed close, our noses touching. Our eyes locked. There was turbulence in his. And now these afternoons of making out and touching weren't enough. I wanted to take things further. I wanted to share all of me with him.

"Dev . . ." He undid the top two buttons of my blouse, then planted kisses against my collarbone.

"I want you," I murmured.

His head popped up, his eyes wide. Then he swallowed. "Right—right now?"

"Soon."

"You look terrified."

"I kinda am. I've never done it. Had sex, I mean."

"That's okay. We'll figure it out together. Just warning you, though—it'll probably be messy and awkward." He gave me the most adorable sheepish look.

"Messy and awkward?"

He pulled me close so I could settle into his chest. "*Mmm-hmm.* Sex is a strange thing, Devon. You sure you want to do it with me?"

"Positive."

"Good. Because it can also be an amazing thing, and I really want to share that with you." He stroked my thumb. "I've wanted to for a long time."

"Same," I said softly. "But I don't want to make bad choices because we're so caught up in the moment."

"I'll make sure we do everything right."

"*We'll* make sure," I corrected.

"Even better."

Chapter 23

"I CAN'T BELIEVE I LET YOU TALK ME INTO THIS." BLAIR pursed her lips at the SATYA YOGA sign. "We should be heading to the nail salon for our Friday ritual, and instead you're making me do this. You know my delicate skin can't handle exercise."

"But your 'delicate skin' can handle anal bleaching?"

"That was one time," she grumbled.

I pulled open the door. A small reception desk covered in plants sat off to the left, a coatrack to the right. Photos of yogis in various poses graced the walls. Sunlight streamed through windows while girls with ponytails padded across shiny wooden floors. The scent of white sage permeated the air. I inhaled deeply. So did Blair.

"Smells like someone's smoking up in here," she muttered.

I poked her shoulder. "It does not."

"Says the girl who's never smoked up."

"Devon?"

Oh God. Not her. Not in my happy place. "Hi, Auden."

Auden came out from behind the desk, bringing with her the strawberry scent of her hair. "I didn't know you took yoga."

"And I didn't know you worked here."

"Sort of work here," she said. "It's part of my seva."

"What's seva?" Blair asked.

"Selfless service. A way of giving back to the yoga community." Her smug smile. "I'm doing it as part of my teacher training."

Blair stared at Auden, a skeptical expression on her face. "You're going to be a yoga teacher?"

Auden's grin turned up to toothpaste-commercial bright. "Alongside physical therapy. School for PT is intense, so I'm getting my teaching certification now. Are you guys taking the five o'clock class?"

"I'm considering it," Blair said, her suspicious expression intensifying.

Auden beamed. "Oh, you totally should! I'm apprenticing, so I can teach you a pose." She glanced inside the studio. "I need to go set up. See you in there!" And with a toss of her ponytail, she was gone.

"Auden Cooper. A yoga teacher. Who'd have thought it?" Blair mused.

"No kidding." As we made our way into the studio, I tried to squash down a flicker of resentment. Maybe this had nothing to do with me, but my heart wasn't about to listen to reason. Auden had her shit together. I wanted to have *my* shit together.

But yoga is about being present, so I needed to try to do that. I inhaled the sage scent. I enjoyed the warmth of the sun-warmed studio. I focused on the altar, with its green cloth covering and its candles, with its statues of Hindu gods such as Shiva, the god of creation and destruction, and Ganesh, the remover of obstacles. I certainly could think of a few things I'd like removed. Such as all the stress I was currently under.

I settled on my mat and rolled my shoulders. Yoga. Mani-pedis later, and sushi for dinner. All with my best friend. Today would be good for me. It had to be.

"This seva stuff sounds like a scam, but that's just me." Blair glanced around and frowned. "I'm having second thoughts."

"Why?"

"It's weird." She pointed to the altar. "What's up with all those statues and things? And what if they make us chant or something?"

"They won't make you chant."

"Wait, you're saying there *will* be chanting? Devon?"

"Hi, everyone. I'm Serena," the instructor said in a dreamy voice. "Welcome to yoga level one. I'm so glad you're here today. Make your way into a comfortable seated position, and we will begin our practice by bringing awareness to the breath."

This was good! This was fine! I could always get behind connecting with my breath.

"Inhale deeply, allowing your stomach to expand with the

breath. Exhale smoothly, allowing your stomach to become soft."

Inhale... two... three... four.

Exhale... two... three... four.

"Envision a white light at your heart center. As you inhale, imagine that light expanding, filling your entire chest. As you exhale, imagine that light spreading out, surrounding you, like an egg."

And that's when I checked out.

The worries of the past few weeks bum-rushed my brain like a runaway train.

I'd turned in my application to McCafferty over a month ago. Had they gotten to it yet?

I'd turned in all my scholarship applications, but no word from them, either.

Auden. Sitting on a bolster next to Serena, looking confident and secure in her future. Already doing something tangible to reach her goals, while all I had was a legacy of hard work and a head full of dreams. Would it even mean anything if I couldn't get the money to fund those dreams?

Ashton. His depression. How far he went to try getting away from it.

Our love. Making love.

I didn't want to be here. I wanted to be where he was. But I needed to focus and be present, like a good yogi. Except the worry kept rushing through me so intensely I could barely lie still on my mat.

"If you find your mind wandering, allow the thoughts to

come, but don't dwell on them. Simply watch them float by, like clouds in the sky."

Too late.

Later, in the nail spa, I sank into the soft leather chair and tried again to relax.

"You know," Blair said, "I always thought meditation was a bunch of woo-woo hippie bullshit, but it really helped me today. I feel a lot better about Tyrell."

Instantly my guard was up. "Do I need to smack a bitch?"

She laughed. "No. He's just struggling with his beliefs about interracial dating while dating me. He talks in circles a lot. Like, a *lot*. And I decided that I'm going to let him figure it out on his own instead of trying to 'fix' him or whatever."

"And you're okay with that?"

"I am now! Seriously, meditation is the best thing ever." She tilted her head. "In fact, I think it could help me stop smoking."

"That would be great. I'd love it if my best friend didn't die of lung cancer."

The salon was playing Mozart. Sonata no. 11 in A Major. Rapid, bouncy piano, which usually made me hyper and totally did not match with this conversation.

"Anyway. What's got you all agitated?" A look of realization dawned. "*Ohhhh.* Auden. Of course."

I watched the nail technician smooth citrus-scented scrub on my calves. "She's got all her shit together. Meanwhile, I'm supposed to hear from McCafferty this week, and I'm freaking out. What if...?" I shook my head. I couldn't even think it.

"I know what I think should happen, but the universe doesn't always have the decency to listen to me. I wish I could tell you everything is going to work out how you want. But I can't, Devvy."

"And then there's everything with Ashton."

Her shoulders tensed. "He's fucking up already? Because I might be happy from meditation, but I can still cuss out a Rat Bastard."

"No! It's not that." I spilled everything. It felt good to get it out of my head, but now I was darn near hyperventilating.

"Look. I'm going to ask you something, and you might not like it," she said. "You have so much going on, do you really need to add Ashton's stuff to the mix?"

"I love him. And you don't give up on someone you love."

"But at what cost?"

"There's no price."

The look she gave me—a mixture of sadness, pity, and understanding. "But this is heavy stuff. I'm scared you're going to lose yourself."

I swallowed as the technician colored my toenails a soft green. Maybe I was a bit scared, too.

Chapter 24

Deferred.

First, there was shock. Cold blood. Icy fingers. Then there was shame. All-encompassing, consuming, burning shame. It licked through my veins, taking away all the cold and filling me with fury. All I'd talked about was going to McCafferty. Everything I'd done was to ensure my admission to my dream school, and now I was reading an email that told me I didn't get to live my dream just because I'd dreamed it.

I stalked into the living room and thrust my computer at my parents, who were playing some game where they built forts and killed people. I don't know. They stared at me with furrowed foreheads, then at the laptop screen. Mom's face fell. Dad's did, too.

"Oh, Bun," Mom said in her soothing, rich voice. "I'm so sorry."

I didn't say anything. Just stood there, fighting to keep the pooling tears from falling.

She pulled me down to sit next to her. "It's not the end of the world. There's still a chance you'll get to go to McCafferty."

It hurt to force the words past my throat. "And if not?"

"Then, frankly, it's their loss," my father said. "I can't imagine what the hell they're thinking!"

"I know, right?" I took the computer back and stared at the email.

We are writing to inform you that your application is being deferred for further review.

I slammed my computer shut. Because fuck this. Seriously.

"Didn't you apply to five other schools?" Mom asked.

I gritted my teeth. "Yes."

"And they have excellent science programs, right?"

I shrugged. "I guess."

"So you won't be selling yourself short if you go to one of those schools instead."

"But I won't get the assistantship and the specialized astrophysics curriculum. I want McCafferty." I pouted.

"And you should have McCafferty," Dad said.

"James, you are not helping."

"I feel like such a trash human being right now." I was being overdramatic, but I did not care. My dreams had just been shattered to pieces. Surely I was entitled to one temper tantrum?

“Listen.” Mom held me at arm’s length, her eyes fixed on mine. “I’m going to say something, and you won’t like it.”

Why did everyone keep telling me things I wasn’t going to like?

“Sometimes what we think we want is not always what we need,” she said.

I fought to keep from rolling my eyes. “I love you, Mom, but I can*not* with the hippie stuff right now.”

“Devon.” Dad’s voice held a warning note. “I’m upset, too. But your mom is a fountain of wisdom. Maybe give her a listen.”

Unfazed, she continued. “Maybe you’re being pointed in a different direction. You’ve been so single-mindedly focused on this one school that you’re oblivious to what else is out there. Maybe there’s a better fit for you.”

I wasn’t trying to hear any of that. I’d applied to the safety schools because I had to have alternate plans. It just never occurred to me that I’d need to use them.

How arrogant of me.

The thought of rearranging the next several years made my heart ache. But the thought of going nowhere hurt even more. So now what?

I stared at Professor Trask’s desk as he searched through his file cabinet. His Mickey Mouse collection had grown since the last time I’d been in here. Even his office accessories were Disney-fied. “New mouse?”

He grinned. “You like?”

"It's shaped like Mickey's glove. What's not to like?"

"You have great taste. Have I ever told you that?"

Professor Trask sat and handed me a pamphlet that read *Deferrals and Waitlists: Now What?* The cover featured a girl staring at a piece of paper in disbelief. Probably with the same expression I'd had.

"So, Devon. I know you're disappointed, but the first thing you need to do is realize that you're still a strong candidate. They would have flat-out denied you if you weren't."

That's what all the websites had said, but so what? "All I can think is that if I was so strong, why didn't I already get accepted?"

"Could be a number of reasons, but what's done is done and it's not going to do you any good to dwell on it."

"You're right," I said quietly. Tough love. Professor Trask was an expert at doling it out.

"McCafferty likes for its deferred students to make a case, so now you need to follow up," he said. "Write a letter to the admissions counselor spelling out your commitment to McCafferty. Talk about the professors you've researched and desire to study with, and be sure to outline the opportunities they offer that aren't offered anywhere else. Be specific about what draws you to McCafferty."

"That'll be easy."

"You're in the regular admissions pool now, which could be advantageous for you, Devon. Follow all their directions, keep studying and working hard, and most important, don't give up hope."

I stuck out my lower lip. “That part’s not so easy.”

“Even if so, it’s time to focus on the future.”

I nodded. “Onward and upward and all that.”

He tapped his desk. “Get that letter written, and give it to me to look over. We’re going to do what we can to get you on that campus next year. But know this: Even if McCafferty doesn’t work out, you have some great options. You’ll be fine no matter what.”

Chapter 25

"LET'S GO STRAIGHT TO MY PLACE TODAY." ASHTON STARTED the car and pushed the button to turn on the heated seats. "The weather's supposed to get cray-cray."

I laughed. "Cray-cray?"

He grinned and switched on the *Hamilton* cast album he loved so much.

"Will your parents be around?"

"Nope. They're upstate at a fund-raiser or something, and I'm so glad they didn't drag me with them."

"Me too." Last weekend, Ashton's parents had carted him off to some boring political event downstate. He'd texted me the entire mind-numbing play-by-play of the speeches, fake conversations, and power plays.

"Would definitely rather spend my Saturdays with you," he said now, taking my hand.

"How was Happy Paws this morning?" I asked.

"Busy. Lots of people wanting to adopt." He screwed up his face. "I had to sneak time with Buddy. I really want to bring him home, but my parents would be furious."

"My parents never let me have a pet, either. Not even a goldfish."

"I don't get that. Well, I kinda do in my case. I was away at school." He frowned thoughtfully. "Just seems like all kids should have a dog or a cat or something."

"I wanted a bunny."

He looked over at me. "Bunnies are cute. Like you."

I squeezed his hand. "At least you have Leander. He's pretty awesome."

"I do love that horse. But it's not like having a dog in the house, you know? Someone who's always happy to see you no matter what. Buddy was so thrilled when I came in this morning. Especially when I gave him a new bone to chew on."

"I'm glad today was good for you. But Ash, you need a shower."

He grinned again. "What, you don't like Eau de Puppy?"

I wrinkled my nose. "Not really."

"Meh. You just don't appreciate my fine essence."

"Dude, have you smelled yourself? You are *ripe*. Did you even bother to shower before you went to the shelter today?"

He shrugged. "No."

At his house, he hung our coats in the coat closet and then we went to his room. I watched as he pulled off his clothes and tossed them into the hamper. I loved that stripping down in front of each other wasn't a big deal.

"Wanna take a whiff before I wash it all away?"

I wrinkled my nose. "No, thank you."

He made a motion as if he were going to smash my nose into his armpit. "You sure?"

"Get away from me!"

"I'll be out soon," he said, laughing.

I didn't really mind his natural scent. It was undeniably him, comforting and arousing. But no shower plus dog hair and slobber? Not so sexy.

While he showered, singing "The Story of Tonight" at the top of his lungs, I looked more closely at the photographs displayed around his room. There were new ones now. One of Buddy demolishing a ball. One of a golden full moon. And one of me from the day we went horseback riding, the sun's rays streaming through my hair and illuminating my skin. I looked ethereal, glowing. Is this how he saw me? No wonder he called me his sunset girl.

The weekend after Thanksgiving, Ashton and I had gone to the art museum. He'd pointed out a photo essay by some famous photographer whose name I didn't remember. "I want to take pictures like this," he said. "See how they tell stories?"

"I think your photos tell stories," I said, but he shook his head.

"No, mine are okay. Some of them might be good, I don't

know." He shrugged. "I want to move people, even if my picture is just a sunset or a mountain."

He was selling himself short. I could guess exactly what mood he was in when he snapped each shot. Even the ones from that summer. The early ones were bright and cheerful. Lots of sun and colors. But by the end, they were jagged glass and dark driftwood, all sharp points and edges. His newer photos were colorful again, but more muted. And that photo of me? I could hardly believe it *was* me. But it was obvious the photographer was deeply in love with his subject.

Photo tour done, I settled into the recliner with my astronomy book.

Ashton and astronomy. Both so large in my life right now. Both competing for the same spot in my brain. My body in perpetual adrenaline overload. *This isn't sustainable* constantly thrummed in the back of my mind. Maybe some spreadsheet calculating was in order. Just to make sure my priorities were in the right place.

Ashton burst out of the bathroom in a cloud of billowing steam and the waterfall scent of his cologne. His jeans fit just right and a T-shirt clung to his damp chest. His hair was dripping and dark and oh my God, yes.

"Is this better?" he asked.

"Much. Get over here." I yanked him toward me and kissed him deeply. We sank into the chair together and let ourselves get carried away. We kissed and kissed... until my stomach let out its trademark monstrous growl. We pulled apart and cracked up.

"Jesus, Devon," he said between snorts. "Let's go eat."

After lunch, we headed to the entertainment room. Ashton had a retro video gaming system, so we played old games and laughed at the cheesy graphics. "Her boobs are literally triangles," I said. "Look at that!"

"Hey, they did the best they could with what they had."

"There is nothing good about triangle boobs. Ever."

Sadly, it didn't matter that the games were old. I still sucked.

After old-school Lara Croft fell off another cliff with a bloodcurdling scream, I gave the controller to Ashton. "You do it. And you know what? I think you're so good because you own the system. You have home team advantage."

He shook his head. "Nope. You're just the worst."

"I'm not *that* bad."

He looked at me as if I were the cutest thing ever. "Yeah, you are."

"Keep on with the trash-talking!"

He threw the controller aside and tickled me until I was shrieking in delight. "Admit it," he said. "I'm the video game champion!"

"Never!"

"Then I'll never stop tickling you!"

"No!" I wiggled out of his grasp and darted for one of the luxury theater seats. He caught me, but his phone buzzed as he was moving in for more torment.

He glanced at the screen and frowned. "It's my mother. I should take this." He jumped up, already starting to pace.

After a moment, he hung up and ran to the window. "Holy shit," he muttered. "Come look at this."

I joined Ashton and had to blink several times. So much snow whipped through the air, I couldn't even see the tree right outside the window. Complete whiteout.

"You should call your parents," he said. "Tell them you won't be coming home."

"It's supposed to do this all night?"

He nodded. "My parents are staying upstate." He glanced out the window again. "I really don't want to drive in that."

I was already pulling out my phone. "On it."

"Stay exactly where you are, Bun," Mom said a few minutes later. "I don't need you risking your life out there."

"I've never seen anything like it."

"We're supposed to get at least two feet," Mom added.

"Well, we're in for the night."

"You've got food and bottled water? Blankets? Flashlights in case the power goes out?"

I looked at Ashton. He nodded.

"We have everything," I said to Mom.

"Condoms?"

"Mom."

"Do you have condoms?" she asked firmly.

"Yes!"

"Okay, then. Have a good night. Be careful," she said.

I didn't think she was talking about the snowstorm.

The atmosphere got super charged when I hung up. Ashton gazed steadily at me, his expression making my heart pound.

"Um, we should probably gather up the emergency stuff. In case the power *does* go out," I said. "Flashlights, blankets, bottled water—"

"Devon, we don't need to gather up all that stuff. We have a generator, so if we lose power, we have backup."

"I'll feel better if we have something close by. It's the Girl Scout in me."

He blinked rapidly. "You were a Girl Scout?"

"Once upon a time. Then we had to sell cookies. My troop took things way too seriously. I couldn't deal with the pressure."

He took my hand. "Let's go get all the stuff. Everything's in the mudroom. Except the blankets. Those are upstairs."

Upstairs.

"Okay."

I didn't understand why I was suddenly so nervous, but he picked up on it right away and put his hand on my arm. "It's only a blizzard. It's supposed to be gone by morning."

He had to know good and well that I wasn't shaking because of the weather. He *had* to. We were alone. In his house. Would be all night long. And he was looking so good and smelling so yummy....

Our conversation about having sex seemed like it had happened eons ago, and I was so ready to be with him. But the situation never seemed right. Too much homework. Too much parents being around. Not enough time.

But things were falling into place right now.

I hadn't woken up planning to have sex with Ashton today.

But now that the opportunity was here, I had every intention of it.

He fixed his eyes on mine and we stood there, gazing at each other. Could he tell what I was thinking? Did he have any idea that right now, my mind was filling with images of him and me, as close as we could possibly get?

He brushed a curl from my forehead. "Come on. Let's gather everything, then we can relax."

We dumped everything on the floor in the game room. Extra blankets, extra bottles of water, extra snacks. Of course snacks. I ran my finger along the edge of a pool table that was probably worth more than my mother's car. "Your house seems even emptier when it's cold outside."

"This house," Ashton said, looking around. "It used to give me nightmares. I thought it was going to swallow me." His mouth turned down slightly. "It still makes me feel so small. Like I'll never live up to what it expects from me."

"Can I ask you something?"

"Of course."

"Does depression run in your family?"

"If it does, I don't know a thing about it." He went into an imitation of his mother's clipped voice. "Such things aren't discussed."

"What do you think?"

He picked up a pen and flipped it through his fingers. "I don't know if anyone has it like I do, but I'm pretty sure it's there."

I slid my arms around his waist. Hugged him close. "Did you know that I think you're amazing?"

He squeezed me back. "No. You are."

I gave him a small smile. "There's so much you don't know."

"I know. I want to learn, though. Everything."

"Like what?"

"Does your family have any scandals I should know about?" Now he was twirling the pen like a baton.

"Well... did you know that I'm half *Black*?" I asked in an exaggerated whisper.

The laughter exploded out of him. "You are such a dork!"

"My mom's side of the family looks like a Benetton ad."

He tapped my nose with the pen. "What's a Benetton?"

"Dad told me about it. It was this fashion campaign a long time ago that showed people of all races together. Didn't see much of that back then, I guess, so it stood out."

"What about your dad's side?"

"From what I know, they're all alike. Same chestnut hair. Same blue eyes and pale skin. I haven't had much to do with them, though. I relate more to Mom's side of the family. They never make me feel like I'm less than, or that I don't belong because I'm not full Black."

"You and your mom have such a cool relationship."

"She's the best. Fiercely loyal. She never let me feel ashamed of myself when white people said I was dirty and teased me about how big my hair was, or when Black people were calling me Oreo and zebra."

The color drained from his face. "People called you dirty?"

I nodded. "Yep."

"Fuckers. Let me get my hands on them."

"I get it from both sides. The good and the bad."

He raised his eyebrows. "Your father's family?"

"Most of them flat-out stopped talking to him when he married Mom. It didn't matter that she'd been around since forever. Marrying her crossed some kind of line, I guess."

Ashton frowned. "That's terrible." He paused, then a look of sadness came over his face. "And it explains why my parents didn't surprise you."

I swallowed. "Have you ever wished I was white?"

The sadness turned to confusion. "Why would I wish that?"

"To avoid all of this"—I waved my hand around—"stuff. With your parents. Everyone. You know people have to be talking."

He fixed his eyes on me, steady. Intent. "Do you ever wish you were white?"

I thought about his question for a long moment. There were some things I didn't like about being who I was. Like wondering what people were thinking when they stared at me a little too long with downturned mouths and wrinkles in their foreheads. I didn't like being hyperaware that I was different...or being reminded of it whenever I managed to forget for a few minutes.

But there was so much good that came with being me. My awesome mom and dad. Blair. School. And there were always the stars. So wanting to be someone else? Some*thing* else? I shook my head. "I never wish that."

"Good. Because who you are? Is perfect. I hope you never forget that."

"And you're willing to put up with people's attitudes about...our kind of relationship?"

"Devon, if I have to cuss some motherfuckers out, even if I have to kick the shit out of somebody, I'll do it. I'm not going to let anyone come between us. So to answer your question: No, I don't wish you were white. I don't want you to be anything other than who you are. Because that's who I love. I love every part of your heritage and your history and your *now.*"

My knees shook at the way his fingers trailed up and down my arms. The way he pressed against me. "I love you, Dev."

I kissed him then. Slow. Tender. Intense. I couldn't hold him tightly enough. I couldn't get enough of the taste of him. Slightly salty. Slightly sweet. All him. All mine.

"Dev," he said quietly, "wanna go upstairs?"

I knew what he was really asking.

"Yes."

Chapter 26

ASHTON AND I WERE KISSING NOT EVEN FIVE SECONDS AFTER he closed the door behind us. Ten seconds after that, my sweater hit the floor. Then my bra. His T-shirt. He pulled me close and we kissed again. The feeling of his skin against mine, his strong heartbeat, his breath—I loved it all so much. I loved *him* so much. I let my fingers slide down his chest. His abs. Then I reached down to unbutton his jeans.

He sucked in a breath and covered my hands with his. "Are you sure?"

I drowned in his deep, dark eyes. "Yes."

He led me to his bed. Over and over our lips met, possessing each other, consuming each other, overcoming each other, and it still wasn't enough. Would never be enough. I wanted... needed more of him. All of him.

With trembling hands, we finished undressing each other. I shivered as he looked at all of me.

"God, your skin," he said, his voice shaking. "A real, live sunset. I need to touch you, Devon."

"Do it," I breathed. "I want you all over me."

He moved his fingers lightly over my skin, sending jolts everywhere, making my breath come in short gasps. He trailed kisses down my body, taking me to the edge and withdrawing just in time, leaving me wanting. By the time he made his way back to my lips, I was aching for him.

"Now," I gasped. "Please."

He stroked my cheek with his thumb. "I'm going to go slow. I don't want to hurt you."

I nodded and watched as he put on the condom, his hands shaking.

"You're nervous," I whispered.

His eyes met mine as he moved close to me again. "Yeah."

"But you've done this before."

He put his hands on both sides of my face. "Not like this. Not when it matters so much."

His skin warm against mine. His heart pounding against my chest. His breath tickling my lips.

My body tingling all over.

"Devon," he murmured. "I love you."

"I love you, too. So, so much."

Slow and passionate, tender and warm. Sweaty flesh against flesh, sensation heightened beyond reason. His waterfall scent, his weight, his sweet, salty taste filled my senses, and there was so much of him right now...but it was still not enough. Would never be enough.

Our eyes locked as my body blossomed, little by little, to let him in more and then more. I took deep breaths, getting used to this new sensation. Getting used to moving with him. This was me and this was Ashton and this was *us*. There were no words, but I could feel him. I could feel him in a way that was beyond the physical, beyond cosmic, beyond anything I could understand or had ever experienced. And I could see him. All of him. Raw, vulnerable, naked. *Mine*.

After, we lay tangled up together, trembling and breathing hard. I didn't want to say anything and break the spell we were under, and he seemed to sense that. He traced circles on my arms, and I buried my fingers in his hair. I floated in some sort of in-between place—a land of light dreams. Still aware that his arms were around me, but also on another plane. He held me until my heartbeat slowed and the sweat on my forehead cooled. Then we lay there, looking at each other, his expression tender, tranquil. Haunting.

"Dev? How are you feeling? Are you okay?"

I trailed a finger down his cheek. "More than."

"A little freaked out?"

A small smile. "Yeah. Are you?"

"I never knew it could be so..."

"I know."

"Yeah," he said with a sigh. "It's overwhelming, how much I feel right now."

"Fragile," I said. As if the slightest movement would shatter me.

"Was it really okay for you? I saw you screw up your face when I... when we were first together. Did it hurt?"

"A little. At first."

"I'm sorry. I tried to be gentle."

"And you were. Really. I'm fine." I traced his lips with my thumb. "What about you? How was it for you?"

He didn't answer for a long time. I checked to see if he'd fallen asleep, but he was wide awake, chewing on his lip. "Do you ever worry that things are going so good, something's bound to come along and fuck everything up?"

I stared at him. "What? No."

"I do," he said. "Like right now. I'm too happy. It feels wrong to be this happy."

"You think we're wrong?"

"No! We're perfect. And that's why I'm so scared. The last time I felt this happy was that summer. And you know what happened then."

I traced the scar on his wrist. "Ashton, I want you to be honest with me. Are you thinking about hurting yourself?"

"I just wish the *wrong* part would go away."

"What if you focus on the best parts? About us? About tonight?"

"Okay." He intertwined his fingers with mine. Now I couldn't reach his scars. "Well," he said after a pause, "there was the part where we kissed forever. And the part where you let me take off all your clothes and touch you everywhere. But my favorite part was you being so close to me."

"Can we do it again? Soon?"

"Are you kidding me? We're going to do it again and again and again. I have so much I want to show you." His voice lowered. "So many things I want to do with you."

"And it'll always be messy and awkward? And then . . . wow."

He raised his eyebrow. "You thought it was awkward?"

"At first, when we were . . . when you were . . . Hey, you said it'd be awkward!"

He kissed my forehead. "This is ours, Dev. Awkwardness and all. Is that okay?"

"It's perfect."

Chapter 27

"Something's different about you," Blair said Monday morning.

I shook snow off my coat and hung it in my locker. "I don't know what you're talking about."

She tilted her head back and forth, studying my face. Then she nodded. "You slept with him."

"Keep your voice down!" I glanced over at Ashton's locker, but there was nothing to worry about. He wasn't there to overhear anything, anyway.

Which sucked.

Yesterday morning, I got to be with him again, and I'd loved every minute of it. After, we'd had breakfast, then he took me home once the roads were clear. We talked on the phone last night. But I hadn't seen him since... well, since *Then*.

I was desperate to see him.

Blair squeezed my arm. "My little Devvy is growing up."

"You're being creepy."

She waggled her eyebrows. "What was it like? Was it like in the romance books? Did you see stars? Did he rock your world?"

"Oh my God, I'm not talking about this here!"

"Talking about what?" Tyrell appeared behind Blair and slid his arm around her shoulders.

"Our periods," Blair said.

He nodded. "Cool."

Blair gave him the kind of soppy look I never thought I'd see cross her face.

"Good morning, you lovely people!"

I held back a sigh. The sudden scent of strawberry shampoo and lip gloss could only mean one person. "Yes, Auden?"

She gestured to Tyrell. "So, like, you're okay with him being all up on your girl?"

"We're not lesbians, Auden," Blair said.

"Wait, what?" Tyrell sputtered. "You thought Blair was into girls?"

Auden rolled her eyes. "I'm teasing. God. But to be honest, it would be nice to have some *family* at this school." Then she turned slightly pink. "Pretend you didn't hear that."

I looked at Blair. Blair looked at me. Tyrell looked at Blair. Then we all looked at Auden.

Auden looked at me. "I really came over to talk to you."

I shouldered my bag. "What's up?"

"Calculus. Rumor has it that Professor McJunkin's planning a pop quiz."

What the heck? Girlfriend was never one to give away any intel that could take away her advantage. "Why are you telling me this?"

She grinned her smug grin. "My New Year's resolution is to be nicer to my rivals. But I figured, why wait until some arbitrary date to start? So this is my kind deed to you, my dear rival, Devon."

I blinked. "*Okayyyy.* Thanks, I guess?"

"See ya at Yearbook!" And then she was gone.

"This is such a weird day," Blair said. "So many revelations. I need coffee."

"Then let's get you some coffee," Tyrell said. "Catch ya later, Devon."

Blair pointed to me. "We are definitely having a talk later, young lady."

Young lady. Okay, Blair. I waved them off. Glanced at Ashton's locker again.

He'd never shown.

Chapter 28

THE VIBRATING OF MY PHONE JOLTED ME FROM A SOUND sleep. I rubbed my eyes and focused on the display. Four in the morning. Christmas Day. A text from Ashton telling me he was on my front porch.

What the hell? I jumped out of bed, yanked on my yoga pants, and tiptoed to the front door so my parents wouldn't hear me. "What are you doing here?"

"Can I come in?" he asked, his voice a fervent whisper. "It's kind of cold."

I pulled him inside. "You're not supposed to be here until ten."

He dropped the bag he was carrying and wrapped his arms around me. Buried his face in my neck.

"Hey." I stroked his back. "What's going on?"

He pulled away and stared at me. "I had to see you."

"Everything okay?"

He didn't answer. Instead he looked around, taking in the stockings hanging on the fireplace, the Christmas village on top of the entertainment center, the twinkling lights on the tree. Then he inhaled deeply. "Is that a real tree?"

I regarded the soft, fragrant needles. "We cut one down every year."

"It smells so good." He inhaled again. "This place is a Christmas wonderland."

My dad grew up Catholic, but my family was not religious at all. Mom and Dad were spiritual and believed that every spiritual leader, and therefore every holiday, was important.

But Christmas was their favorite.

They were like little kids, tearing a ring off the countdown chain every day. Shaking presents under the tree and baking dozens of cookies. Watching *A Christmas Story* again and again while sucking on candy canes and snuggling in front of the fireplace.

"My parents go kind of overboard," I said.

"It's perfect, Devon." He nibbled his bottom lip, eyes darting all around.

"Ashton?"

A shrug. "It's all manufactured at my house. Decorators and catered food. But here, it feels real. Like on TV." His forehead wrinkled. "Wait, that makes no sense."

I slipped off his beanie. It was damp from melting snowflakes. "I'm glad you're here."

Finally, he met my eye again, his expression soft. "I swear, just looking at you makes me feel like everything might be okay again."

"Is everything not okay?"

"No. But I'm here."

"Want to talk about it?"

"No. I want to kiss you."

I squeezed his hands and planted a kiss on his lips. His skin was frozen, but he warmed up fast.

"*Mmm*, you're all tousled and sleepy-like. Sexy," he murmured.

His mood swing made me nervous. How he could go from dark to light. But before I could think too much about it, his lips brushed right below my ear, sending delicious tingles all the way through me. "We could get in so much trouble right now."

"You got a stocking," I said, trying to distract him. And myself.

He raised his eyebrows and slid his hands down my body. "We should go to your room."

"Ashton." I caught his hands and intertwined our fingers. "If we go there, we have to behave. I'd feel weird doing *that* with my parents right next door."

He nodded. "Okay."

"I mean it."

"I'll be good. I promise."

Being good meant long, tender kisses and gentle caresses. Holding each other close until he fell asleep in my arms. I did not mean to be that girl watching her boyfriend sleep, but I was totally that girl watching her boyfriend sleep.

I told Ashton I loved him at least twice every day. But in this quiet moment, the love overwhelmed me. What in his dreams made his lips curve like that? I wanted to know that like I knew his breathing. His scent. His passion. His pain. His life.

I buried my face in his hair while he slept on. At some point I dozed off, dreaming of fresh waterfalls and warm breezes. The dream changed. A supermassive black hole, sucking away everyone I loved. Blair, gone in a swirl of cigarette smoke. My parents, whirling around and around like water spinning down a drain. Then Ashton, desperately reaching for me. Calling for me, his face chalky white. But I couldn't save him. My hands, slippery with sweat, lost their grip on his fingertips.

And he was gone.

Bright sunlight yanked me back into the real world. No, not sunlight. Ashton was staring at me, his eyes wide with concern. It was his voice I'd heard in the dream, only it had been real.

I shot up and stuck my thumbnail in my mouth. Started to chomp.

"Devon." Ashton's voice was quiet. His fingertips gentle on my cheeks. "You had a bad dream." He pulled me close and stroked my hair. "You were crying. I wanted to jump in and snatch the nightmare away."

"I wish you could've. It was awful."

"Do you want to tell me about it?"

I shook my head. "I want to forget about it."

"What can I do?"

"Hold me."

"Okay." He tightened his arms around me and rested his chin on the top of my head. Eventually the nightmare faded, and it was just us.

"I'm so glad you're here," I said.

"Can you imagine?" he asked, his lips against my temple. "Waking up like this every day?"

"Is that something you want?"

"Not the nightmares."

I puffed out a snort. "Yeah."

"But the waking-up-beside-you part? I do want that. Very much." His voice grew quiet. "You make me excited about the future, Dev."

I looked up at him. His expression was faraway.

"Gives me something to focus on when things get hard," he added.

"I know they're hard now. Do they get hard a lot?"

"Most of the time, thinking about the next hour is overwhelming. So I think: *If I can survive the next five minutes, it'll be okay*. And then another five. And then another. Some days, that's all I can do."

"Even on the good days?"

"Sometimes the good days are even worse. I'm constantly waiting for everything to fall apart. And what's messed up is I don't even know what that looks like. I just know it's bad."

"The Dark?"

"I'm scared it's going to wake up again. And I won't be able to stop it."

I brushed some hair from his forehead. "You know you can always talk to me, right? You don't have to give in. I'm here."

He nodded slowly. Then he gave me a bright smile. He was like a Ping-Pong ball. Back and forth and back again. "Will you please tell me about Christmas dinner? What can I expect tonight?"

I watched him closely, but he looked fine. "Turkey and Honey Baked Ham."

"I don't think I've ever had Honey Baked Ham," Ashton said thoughtfully.

"You're kidding."

"Nope. Judging from your expression, I've been missing out. What other foods will you make that I've never had?"

"Greens. I doubt you've had those."

"Greens? You mean like kale?"

I snorted. "Uh, no. Hell no. Mustard and turnip. We cook them with smoked ham hocks or turkey necks."

"Turkey necks?"

"For flavor. You're going to try them, right?"

He raised his eyebrows. "The turkey necks or the greens?"

I gently shoved him. "The greens."

"I'm going to try everything. I'm already hungry thinking about it. Please tell me sweet potato pie is involved, because I had some a long time ago and it was the bomb dot com."

"The bomb dot com? How old are you? That's the kind of thing my parents would say."

"I actually did hear your dad say it. What other things will we have?"

My stomach grumbled. "Mashed potatoes. Macaroni and cheese. Dressing."

"Dressing?"

I tapped his chest. "You white folk call it 'stuffing.' Only we don't actually put it in the bird. And we use cornbread to make it. But Mom makes stuffing, too. Dad and Stephanie's family insists on it. You remember Stephanie, right?"

He nodded.

"And you'll get to meet my grandmother Mama Lee, and my uncle Ricky."

He squeezed me. "I can't wait."

"I think you'll like them. And I think they'll like you."

He grinned. "I haven't been this excited about a holiday in forever."

"Is that why you showed up so early?"

His grin faded. "Truth?"

"Tell me."

"Last night, my mind went to a billion dark places. I didn't want to be alone."

"You never have to be again."

He nodded thoughtfully. "Thank you."

"You don't have to thank me."

He kissed my temple. "Did you know you're my favorite person?"

I sent him a mischievous smirk. "I had a feeling, but you can keep telling me if you want. I don't mind."

He poked my shoulder. "You. Are. A. Dork."

"You love me."

"I do." Another temple kiss. "More than anything. I'm so lucky to have you."

"Yes, you are. Never forget it."

He let out a soft laugh, then gave me a quick kiss. "I won't. Promise."

We lay together a while longer, then he headed to the living room while I snuck in a short yoga practice, showered, and dressed. When I joined him, he was grinning at his phone.

"What are you doing?"

"Talking to my grandma on FaceTime." He'd already pointed the phone toward me. "Come say hi."

There she was, wearing an ugly Christmas sweater and big bauble earrings, her smile wide and her eyes twinkling. "Devon!" She clapped her hands. "I'm delighted to finally meet you. You're even lovelier than your photos."

Her voice sounded like pink cotton candy, soft and sweet. I liked her immediately. "It's nice to meet you, too. Ashton's told me a lot about you."

"Everything scandalous, I hope?"

"She knows all your dirty secrets, Grandma," Ashton said, wrapping his arms around me.

"You didn't tell her I stack the deck when we play cards, did you? Because that's really you, and you know it."

Eyes shining, Ashton let out a joyful laugh. "Busted!"

I rarely saw this side of him. Completely relaxed, guard let all the way down, easy and wide smile. I loved it.

"I hate to cut this so short," his grandmother said, "but my ride is here. I'm off to lunch with some close friends. We're all wearing our ugly Christmas sweaters."

"Nothing could ever look ugly on you," Ashton said.

"Such a charmer." She beamed. "I'm so glad I got to talk to you both. I hope to see you soon, Devon."

"Same."

"Don't get in too much trouble, Grandma," Ashton said.

"Who, me?" She winked, then disappeared. Ashton's home screen—a picture of me—came back up.

"Okay, she's awesome. I can't wait to meet her in person someday."

"Well. It just so happens that my family is hosting a New Year's Eve party. I'd love for you to be my date."

"Your grandmother's gonna be there?"

He nodded. "Normally, I'd be visiting her in Monaco, but I wanted to stay here with you. She's flying over on the twenty-seventh."

The thought of ringing in the New Year with Ashton's parents filled me with trepidation, but I really wanted to meet the family member he loved the most. "In that case, I'd love to be your date."

The corners of his eyes crinkled as he grinned. "Awesome. Keep smiling like that." He pointed his phone at me again and snapped a photo. "Perfect."

I gestured toward his phone. "Can I see?"

He handed me the phone, then turned to the fireplace. "Can I open my stocking now?"

"Go for it."

While Ashton dug into the velvety-red stocking, I scrolled through his camera roll. All the pictures were artistic. Deliberately framed or meticulously staged. Evergreen trees coated with snow. A frozen pond, the smooth surface sparkling in the sunlight. Even the candid pictures looked beyond. None of the stuff that filled up most people's camera rolls, like Blair's endless selfies or pictures of her various lipsticks. Or selfies of her *wearing* the various lipsticks. Or my pathetic attempts at astrophotography that usually ended up a blurry mess. "Ashton. These are so good."

"Hmm?" He'd shoved half a sugar cookie covered in M&M's into his mouth.

"Oh my God. Do you have any self-control?"

He swallowed. "I lose my mind when M&M's are involved."

I handed him his phone. "Your photos. They're gorgeous."

His cheeks turned pink. "Thanks."

"I think you could do this professionally."

"I love it too much for that. I want to keep it fun." Then he pointed the phone at me again. "Smile!"

By the time my parents joined us, Ashton had eaten half his cookies, and a snack-size bag of M&M's, and was sucking on the end of a candy cane. Mom's eagle eye went straight to him, then a side-eye to me. "Hello, Ashton!" she said. "We weren't expecting you until later."

"I couldn't sleep," he said.

She gave us both a knowing smirk. "Excited for Santa?"

He and I glanced at each other. "You could say that," he said, the tips of his ears turning pink.

Dad turned from the fireplace, where he'd just lit a crackling blaze. "When can I open my new watch?"

Mom stared at him, her hand on her hip. "Who said you're getting a watch?"

"I have a feeling."

"Or you listened to all of the packages until you found one that ticked," I said.

He put his hand on his chest and had the nerve to look offended. "Well, I never."

"Suuuuurrreeee."

Mom handed Ashton a small gift bag. "This is for you."

Ashton froze in place, a wrinkle between his eyebrows. "What? You didn't have to—"

She shook her head. "Open it."

Face flushed, Ashton pushed aside sparkly green tissue paper and pulled out a game controller ornament inscribed with his name and the year. His mouth opened slightly, and the pink in his cheeks deepened. "Oh wow."

"We want you to hang it," Mom said.

"Are you sure?"

"Pick your spot." Dad gestured toward the tree.

The grin that covered Ashton's face warmed the room even more than the blaze in the fireplace.

My parents squeezed each other's hands as Ashton searched for the perfect spot to place his ornament. Then he turned to us, his cheeks still pink, but this time, with pleasure. "Thank you."

"Come sit with me," I said, pulling him onto the couch. "There's more where that came from."

Ashton grew quiet after we passed around the gifts. He stared ahead, his eyes muted. He was suddenly so pensive, so... still. Something in his expression frightened me, and I glanced away, focusing on the fireplace. The flames danced and retreated, wrestling with the wood as if it were their destiny.

I turned back to Ashton and glimpsed that same struggle in his eyes. What was *he* wrestling with? I gingerly touched his arm, and he turned to me, his face breaking into a smile. The angst melted like a snowflake on hot asphalt. Gone. Just like that.

He must have sensed my concern, because he leaned close and whispered, "I'm fine. Really."

I didn't believe him, not with that guarded look in his eyes.

Mom was organizing the opened boxes under the tree when Ashton nudged my foot with his, a clean white sock bumping against a candy cane–patterned novelty holiday sock. I glanced up to find him holding another box out to me.

"What's this?"

"Open it." Was it my imagination, or did he look nervous?

"It's heavy." I ripped the wrapping paper and my heart stopped. "Are you kidding me right now?"

He stared at me. Hard. "Do you like it?"

"Ashton." My eyes were prickling. I was getting lightheaded. Because there was no way, no absolute way he'd done this for me.

"Wow, that looks expensive," my father, Captain Obvious, said.

"This is... it's a Celestron NexStar...." I managed to choke out. "Oh my God. I can't even believe you got me this. I mean, I can't... I've wanted one for so long."

"What is that, exactly?" Dad asked.

I started nibbling my thumbnail. "It's a catadioptric telescope."

Dad stared at me, a blank expression on his face. "Should I know what that means?"

"I'll be able to see Cassini Division and the Great Red Spot and galaxies and nebulas...."

"Yeah, I'm lost."

I took three breaths and turned to Ashton. "How did you know which one?"

"I talked to Professor Trask."

"But, Ashton..." The enormity of what he'd done was sinking in, making me dizzy. I'd gotten him his own copy of *Tidal Destruction III* and a DLC card to go with it, but that was nothing compared to this. My mouth opened and closed, opened and closed. Speechless.

"Don't you dare say you can't accept it," he warned. "This is too important to you. To both of us."

I threw my arms around him. "Then I'll tell you 'thank you.' So much. I love it. And I love you. So, so, *so* much."

He buried his face in my hair. "I love you, too, Dev."

Dad coughed, pulling Ashton and me out of our bubble. "Enough with the mush already. I need to wash my eyes out with some of that *Tidal Destruction*." He turned to Ashton. "You in?"

With reluctance, Ashton pulled away. "Okay?"

"Yeah."

Ashton grabbed a headset and sent Dad a thumbs-up. "Then I'm in."

"Come on, Bun. Let's make breakfast," Mom said.

In the kitchen, she pulled a carton of eggs and a packet of bacon out of the refrigerator. "Take the strips of bacon and lay them in the glass baking dish. Set the oven to three fifty."

"We're baking the bacon?"

"Why do you think they call it 'bacon'?"

"Um, I don't think—"

"We need to talk about you and Mr. Ashton."

Oh. "What do you mean?"

She pulled on her apron and threw me a look that said *You know damn well what I mean.* "I know he's loaded, but he bought you a very expensive gift. Devon, that's not normal high school romance stuff. Your dad gave me candy bars and bought me chocolate milkshakes."

"Yes, but high school for you was a thousand years ago."

I ducked as she swatted me with a dish towel. "I am not that old, and I look even younger."

This was true.

"You guys are moving extremely fast," she said. "He's buying you expensive science equipment and looking at you like you hung the moon. How long have you been dating?"

I concentrated on separating the bacon strips. "Six months, if you count that summer."

"I'm not sure I do." She stared at me, her eyes narrowed in

thought. "The thing is, I don't want you to get so wrapped up in him that you don't even realize who else might be out there for you." Then she smiled. "But when I see how you two are around each other, it reminds me of your father and me when we were your age. I'm happy for you, but I can't help but worry. No matter what happens, he's going to be okay. His family's wealth will make sure of that. But you can't afford to get distracted. I don't want this romance to derail any of your plans."

"Mom, school is my number one priority. That will never change."

She gave me a long look. As if she couldn't decide whether to believe me or not. "Okay. But make sure you come to me with everything and anything. I'm always here for you."

"I know. And I appreciate it. I really do."

She hugged me, then got down to business. "I really am starving, so we need to get cooking. What should it be? French toast or waffles?"

"French toast," I said. "The cinnamon kind."

I watched as she cracked eggs into a bowl. Added milk and vanilla. Whisked it all together. "What was it like with you and Dad? Did you always know? Did you ever doubt?"

"Of course I had doubts, Bun. But they weren't coming from me. I was so busy worrying what everyone thought about me falling in love and getting married so young that I forgot to listen to my own heart. Once I did that, it was easy." She dipped the bread into the eggs, coating both sides. "Are you listening to your heart? When you envision your future, do you see him there? And are you happy about it?"

I nodded and smiled. "He belongs there."

She wiped her hands on her apron and hugged me again. Then she held me at arm's length, studying me. "I hope he keeps making you as happy as you look right now."

My grin spread. "Me too."

"And for the record, yes, I did always know with your dad. When we were five, I told him I was going to marry him. He threw a worm at me and ran away." Her expression became dreamy. "That's when I knew it was meant to be."

"You're kidding."

"Not one bit." She gave me a wink. "I've always liked worms."

Chapter 29

"I can't even believe you're abandoning me to hang out with your boyfriend." Blair smoothed moisturizer onto my cheeks. "I mean, I know it's New Year's Eve, the night when that all-important kiss sets the tone for the whole year, but jeez, Devon. Whatever happened to hos before bros?"

"I think you have that backward," I said. "And it's not like you aren't going out with your own bro."

Things were *seriously* progressing with her and Tyrell. She'd run into him while skiing in Aspen over winter break, and they'd spent a lot of time "keeping each other warm."

"Now I get why you look so happy-silly all the time," she'd said when she'd arrived earlier today.

"How do you pull *it* off with your family hovering?"

She had smiled mysteriously, her eyes twinkling. "Where there's a will, there's a way. And believe me, I have the will."

I believed her, all right. Especially because she gave me a detailed play-by-play of the Event. It was something I'd have been better off not knowing.

I wasn't going to be able to look at a jar of Nutella the same way ever again.

"When is Tyrell picking you up?" I asked.

"Ten," she said, then shook her head at me. "You are hopeless with makeup."

"I can't help it that I'm a natural beauty," I said. The actual truth was that I didn't see any need for makeup. After my mom spent a hundred dollars on makeup to make it look like she wasn't wearing any, I figured I'd skip the whole thing and not wear any at all.

Besides, I had a hard time finding colors that went well with my complexion and eye color. But Blair didn't seem to have that problem. She studied my face, the gears in her brain turning, then went into her makeup kit and pulled out colors that complemented me perfectly.

She bopped me on the head. "It's not about making an ugly girl pretty. It's about taking all this beauty and making it pop."

"Remind me where you and Tyrell are headed," I said.

"The President's Club." She grabbed a water bottle.

"*Ooh*, swanky!"

Her brows furrowed. "A cocktail party and dinner at the Founder's Mansion is pretty swanky, too."

"I know. A ton of important people are supposed to be

there, and Ashton said he would introduce me to all of them. But you'll get the real VIPs. The President's Club is big-time. They televise the local countdown from there." A thought occurred to me. "Maybe you'll be on TV!"

"Ha. I wonder how my father would react if he saw me dancing with Tyrell on TV."

"His innocent, precious daughter out on a date? With a *boy*? I can only imagine," I said.

Blair spit out her water. *"Innocent. Okaaaaay."*

"Just sayin'."

"Yeah, *stop sayin'*. I need to do your lips."

"Knock knock." Mom popped her head in, then came over and ran her fingers through my hair. "I'm here to do your bun, Bun."

I groaned. "Mom."

Her strong fingers massaged coconut oil into my scalp before she started gathering and twisting the springy strands.

"Doesn't Devon look pretty, Mrs. K?"

"She always looks pretty," Mom said, ever so loyally. "But you did an incredible job on her makeup."

"And her dress, too," Blair said. "I'm especially proud of it."

"I still can't believe you designed this for me." Dark-green, sparkly on top with a sweetheart neckline, flowy chiffon bottom. "My first-ever couture piece. It's stunning."

"I'm glad you like it." Her cheeks flushed with pleasure.

"Like it? I'm obsessed!"

At precisely nine, the doorbell rang.

"Your date is here," Dad called.

I swallowed down the panic rising in my throat. "I'm nervous."

"You're going to blow them all away," Blair said.

I squeezed her hands. "Thank you. For everything."

She hugged me and pushed me ahead of her.

And there was Ashton, his gray suit fitting him perfectly, his smile radiant.

"How do I look?" I asked, modeling my dress.

"You're beautiful," Ashton said, his eyes filled with longing. The way he looked at me always affected me all the way to my core.

He took my hand and heat shot through me. "Ready to go?"

I nodded.

"Pictures first," Mom called.

"Mom, it's not prom."

"Humor me," she said. "You're both dazzling. I want to document it."

After the paparazzi session ended, Ashton took my hand again. "Come on, gorgeous. Let's go ring in the new year."

"Have fun, be safe, yada yada," Mom called.

"Don't wait up," I said.

"Wasn't planning on it."

I grabbed my peacoat and tiny purse, and we went out into the crisp air. Then I stopped dead at the sleek maroon vehicle. "Are you serious?"

He grinned. "I thought you'd like it."

"Your father let you take the Maserati?"

Ashton opened the door for me. "I'm allowed to drive any of the cars, Devon."

I sank into the buttery leather seat and inhaled deeply. *Mmm.* "I can't believe I get to ride in this thing."

He climbed in, pulled on a pair of driving gloves, and started the car. "If you're good, I'll let you drive it home tonight."

"Don't even tease me."

"I'm not. You can drive home tonight."

"The Maserati?"

He waggled his eyebrows. "*This* Maserati."

The growl of that engine. The power in that rev. Chills. Everywhere. "You are the best boyfriend ever."

He gave me a smile that made every part of me smolder. "Can I tell you that you look really, really hot tonight?"

"You can always tell me that."

"You look so hot," he said. "And as soon as I get you alone, I'm going to kiss you until your knees buckle."

I shivered. "Tell me more."

"I'm going to get you out of that cute little dress," he murmured. "Then I'm going to taste every inch of your body and touch you until you can't breathe."

"Then what?" I asked softly.

He looked at me meaningfully. "What do *you* think should happen next?"

"I think we should make love," I whispered. "All night long."

"Yes, yes, a million times yes. I wish we could skip dinner

and go straight to bed. Wouldn't that be a way to ring in the new year?"

"The best."

We rode in silence for the rest of the trip, our eyes meeting from time to time.

"Come here," he whispered after we parked. "I need to kiss you. Now."

I ripped off my seat belt. "I'm always good with that."

Our lips came together in a fevered rush. Ugh. Who put this console and wheel in the way? I wanted to be on his lap, straddling him. Claiming him. Loving him with all of me. We kissed for a good ten minutes. At least, it felt like ten minutes. Losing track of time while kissing him was a regular thing, though, so who knows how long we were out there?

"We're making out in a Maserati," I said with a small grin.

"Damn right we are," he said, then kissed me again. Hands everywhere.

"We're going to be late," I murmured after another indeterminable amount of time.

"I don't care," he said breathlessly, his eyelids lowered with desire.

"We're going to get in trouble."

His lips tickled mine. "Worth it."

"Ashton."

Another long kiss. Then he pulled away and let out a deep breath. "I have to tell you something."

"Why does this sound ominous?"

"Rochelle's here. I didn't even think about it until my mother said something to me today."

Of course. The universe decided to thrust Rochelle right in my face. Nice. "So, basically, it's going to be awkward."

He winced and nodded. "Basically, yeah."

"Great." I grinned so much my face stretched. "Fantastic."

"I guess we'd better get inside and face the music." He shook his head. "But don't smile like that."

"Hold on, you have lipstick all over your face."

"Whoops." He pulled out a handkerchief and fixed himself up. "Better?"

"Much. How do I look?"

"Like you've been making out forever and thoroughly enjoying it."

"I mean, I have been, so..." I pulled out my compact and fixed my own mouth.

"Ready to head in?" he asked when I was done.

I took a fortifying breath and nodded. I could do this.

"Hello, Mother."

Mrs. Edwards wore a sleek, long black dress and a diamond choker that shot bolts of lightning right into my eyes. *Her* eyes swept over my own dress, and finding no fault there, she leaned in to kiss my cheek lightly. The scent of her Chanel No. 5 filled my nostrils and tickled my throat.

I could do this.

"Hello, Ashton. Devon, you look lovely as ever."

I had to do this.

"Thank you. So do you."

She chuckled and ran her hands over her hips. "You're too kind. Ashton, dear, will you take Devon's coat?"

He gave her a stiff smile. "Of course."

Mrs. Edwards hooked her arm through mine. "I'm delighted you're here. I must show you the new piece of art we got yesterday. I know you liked to look at the paintings at the beach house."

This woman had some nerve, I had to give her that. Referencing that summer as if it were yesterday. As if there hadn't been more than a year of pain and betrayal between then and now. Phony people truly amazed me.

I wasn't really into art. I liked pretty pieces, but an aficionado I was not. I couldn't tell you if the artists used acrylics or oil or watercolor paints, or even if they used paint at all. Looking at the artwork at the beach house had been something to do while waiting for Ashton's parents to go to bed.

"Here is a piece by Liudmila Kondakova," Mrs. Edwards said. *"The Magic Hour."*

I took in the whimsical pinks and purples, the fluffball trees. The depth of the painting as the rooftops accentuated the focal point: the Eiffel Tower. "It's really pretty."

"Of course, it's Paris, your favorite, no?"

How did she know this?

"Everyone should spend some time outside the US, in my

opinion," Mrs. Edwards said. "Get a better perspective of the world. Have you ever been to a foreign country?"

"Not yet." The Paris Observatory continued to call my name. Not as loudly as McCafferty did, but the whispers were always there.

She trailed a finger around the rim of her wineglass. "I'm sure you know that Ashton brought you here tonight with the intention of formally introducing you to our circle. It seems that you and he are getting very serious."

"I love him," I said, my voice soft.

"I know," she said. "And it's evident that he loves you. But I have some concerns. Today, I overheard Ashton asking his grandmother about rings."

I froze. "Engagement rings?"

She made me nervous, the way her eyes bore into mine, as if she were trying to unravel my every secret. "You seem nonplussed. He hasn't talked to you about this?"

"Only in passing, Mrs. Edwards. A someday-maybe type of thing."

She kept those eyes on me. "But he's thinking about it enough to ask. Which raises some serious alarms with me."

With me, too. Why hadn't he mentioned this to me? And why wasn't he a part of this dialogue right now?

"First of all, you're moving very quickly," she said. "Too quickly. To talk about marrying a girl he's only dated a couple of months—well, that's downright foolish."

I had to admit that I partially shared that concern. Just

like that summer, my relationship with Ashton had become intense very fast. And I was okay with it. Most days I was able to push aside the niggling worry that he could turn on me again. Walk away, like he did before. But it was there: I loved him very much, but did I trust him? I wasn't sure.

I stood there, letting that sink in.

After all this time, even after sleeping with him, I still didn't completely trust Ashton to not hurt me again. And if I couldn't trust him, I had no business entertaining, even in a fantastical way, the idea of marrying him. Not that I was, anyway. So Mrs. Edwards needed to calm the hell down.

"Second, you're so young," she continued, pulling me out of my trance. "You may not be the same person in three months, let alone in three years. But if you marry him, it's for the rest of your life. The Edwards family does not divorce."

She made it sound so final. Like a death sentence or imprisonment. That's not what marriage represented to me. My mom and dad were each other's favorite person—it was obvious in so many tiny ways, and so many big ways. How her face lit up as soon as he walked in the door after work. The way they danced together when one of their songs (and believe me, they had a lot) popped up on a playlist. When he brought her tea every night, exactly the way she liked it.

But Ashton said his parents fought constantly. They wanted him to marry a girl who could make him even richer, instead of the girl he loved. Maybe that's what happened to his mother. So maybe marriage *was* a prison sentence for her?

"Most important, my husband's family is very powerful.

We have an image that we need to uphold, not to mention the responsibilities of being a part of the Preston-Edwards empire. If we were to allow this marriage to happen, there would be things expected of you that I'm not sure you're equipped for."

Allow?

Like a betrothal? Blessings and courting and calling cards? He'd said his parents were old-fashioned, but this was beyond what I ever pictured.

She smiled and shook her head. "You make my son happy. He lights up when he talks about you. But I'm not sure that's enough, with your backgrounds being so different."

"How *do* you know so much about my background?" I asked cautiously.

"We researched you to the hilt that summer, Devon. The first time he brought you to the beach house, I knew you looked familiar. You're in the running for valedictorian at Preston Academy, which you're attending on a full scholarship. I was one of five adjudicators who made the decision to accept you."

Wait, what?

No, seriously.

What?

She went on, oblivious to my shock. "Those of us who endow Preston get letters every year outlining the progress of its recipients."

I should not have been shocked. His family *founded the freaking school*, so of course they had a say in who got accepted into the academy and who got the money. Then something dawned on me. "Once you realized who I was, you pushed for Ashton to break up with me."

"You have to understand where I was coming from," she said. "Here was my only son, ready to risk it all for a girl he'd only known for a few weeks. At age sixteen. Don't get me wrong—I was thrilled to see him so happy. But there were far-reaching consequences he wasn't even considering. Someone had to set his head straight."

"But it was only a summer romance."

"You and I both know it was more than that," she said. "And if you were to marry Ashton, you'd be set beyond your wildest dreams."

The implication kicked me in the gut. "You think I'm a gold digger."

"Maybe you didn't start off that way, but it would give you a reason to hold on, wouldn't it?"

I fought to keep from clenching my fists. Here's the thing: Mrs. Edwards knew everything about my family's financial situation; we'd had to disclose so much information to be in contention for scholarship funds, even the merit-based ones.

"That's not fair," I said. "First, I had no idea that he was part of this massive empire when we were together that summer. Second, you know so much about me, so you should know how hard I work."

"But marrying into this family would make things so much easier for you. My son is going to inherit a legacy beyond comprehension. Our money and connections would open so many doors for you. Including a spot at McCafferty."

My heart nearly skidded to a halt. I'd practically give up my firstborn to secure a spot at McCafferty. But she couldn't know that. No one could know that, because to broadcast it would be to broadcast weakness. I could not afford to be weak right now.

"I can't say I've been sitting around thinking about it," I said, struggling to keep my voice steady. "I just want to be with Ashton."

"In addition, we've never had people who are—diverse, for lack of a better term—in our family," she continued. "Ashton marrying you would introduce a whole new dynamic, and the senior members of the family will push hard against you, knowing that you're not like us."

Not like us. Did she even hear the words coming out of her mouth? How could she be so composed, standing there sipping her wine, when I was about to burst into cold flame?

"I'm the same as you are," I said in a small voice. "How could you say I'm not?"

She sighed. "I like you. And I like what you do for Ashton. But I'm afraid it's not so simple." She regarded me then, her expression thoughtful. "Your family is important to you, right?"

I nodded. My family meant everything to me.

"And you'd do anything for them."

"Yes."

"So you should see where I'm coming from. I have a legacy to protect. *His* legacy. *My* family. You'd do anything to keep your family from harm. That's what I'm doing."

"I don't want to harm your family," I said quietly. "I just want to love your son."

"And I want to believe you," she said sadly. "I truly do. But too much is at stake. If you want to become a part of this family, you need to prove you deserve it."

We stared at each other for what felt like an eternity. Then a soft bell tinkled.

"Dinner is soon. Let's go join the others." Ashton's mother squeezed my arm and went into the dining room.

Chapter 30

What. The. Hell. Who picks a party to have a conversation like that? Especially one she was supposed to be hosting? I dug my fingernails into my palms. How dare she?

Prove you deserve it. Except most of the people chattering in the next room had been born into this. Why should I have to prove myself when I had the same right to be here—the same right to *exist*—as they did?

Prove you deserve it. Anger flooded my veins. I trembled so hard my bones rattled. I was so done with people shaming me, my family, our values, our life. The desire to walk out the door and let this family rip itself apart over power plays and politics grew with each breath. But that's exactly what she wanted, and there was no way in hell I was giving it to her. Even with the amount of scrutiny I'd been under and would be under as long as I was with Ashton.

Ashton. Always Ashton. With his gentle support and fiery touch and all-consuming love. Ashton, who I discovered in the dining room chatting with a stunning girl. Flawless dark-brown curls. Even, smooth complexion. Curves that made me look like a twelve-year-old boy. And she wasn't wearing tiny high heels like I was. She had on stilettos, because of course someone like her would be wearing grown-up shoes.

Rochelle.

She embodied everything about this world: fancy cars, expensive champagne, designer clothing, and sparkling diamonds. The opposite of me: wild hair, clothes from the mall, and grades that I had to work my ass off to earn. She looked as if life was effortless for her. And it probably was.

What was I doing here? There was no way I could compete with Rochelle. With any of these people.

I was crumbling. I was not okay. I rushed to the bathroom to compose myself and caught my reflection in the mirror. Flushed cheeks. Silvery eyes shining with unshed tears. Trembling lips. Whirling nausea.

Inhale . . . two . . . three . . . four.

Exhale . . . two . . . three . . . four.

I refused to fall apart. Because if I couldn't keep it together tonight, how in the hell could I expect to do so when his family started really putting the pressure on me?

I could do this.

I *would* do this.

But the bigger question: Was Ashton worth all this?

All I wanted was to love him. Go to McCafferty. Study the stars.

Mrs. Edwards said it wasn't so simple, but why couldn't it be?

I could stay in here all night, sitting on the cozy settee, sniffing the pretty soaps and perfumes. Hiding from the pretty people milling around, waiting for their pretty dinner.

But I was better than this. *So get out there, Devon.*

Now.

I splashed my face with cold water. Wiped my eyes. Redid my lipstick. Then forced myself to leave the powder room.

And there they were.

She leaned close to him and whispered something that made him laugh. God, they looked like a perfume ad. I wanted to chuck something at them.

Instead, I swallowed hard and made myself walk over to them.

I tickled Ashton's hand lightly. He turned to me and smiled, his entire face lighting up. Even with his gorgeous ex-girlfriend standing right there, he still managed to make me feel like the prettiest girl in the room.

Feeling bolder now, I turned to Rochelle. Her gaze swept over me, making me feel like a little kid playing dress-up. The urge to run and hide came again, but I clamped it down. I refused to leave him again with this girl who was the perfect fit for his perfect life. The girl he'd have married, if I hadn't come back into the picture.

Breathe.

"You must be Devon." She was smiling, dimples flashing, but there was something behind her eyes that I couldn't quite read. "I'm Rochelle," she added.

"Hello." Her handshake was firm, which disappointed me. But I shouldn't have expected someone who looked like a Victoria's Secret model to have a wimpy handshake.

Ashton's mother beckoned to him, and with an apologetic look at me, he went to meet her across the room. Leaving me with Rochelle. The ex-girlfriend. Oh my God. Why.

"So you're Ashton's sunset girl," she said. Her eyes swept over me again, then she nodded. "I can see it."

A sudden rush of love—and possessiveness—for Ashton almost knocked me over. I looked over at him. Whatever his mother was saying to him was pissing him off, making his jaw twitch like mad.

"He told me about you a long time ago," Rochelle said. I forced my eyes away from the mother-son exchange and turned to pay attention to her. "The look on his face when he talked about you... the way he said your name, even. I knew if he ever saw you again, I'd be history. Never thought it'd actually happen."

Again, what was I supposed to say to that?

She glanced over at him again. "He's kinda fragile, but he's special. Don't break his heart, okay?"

I snorted. "He's more likely to break mine." Whoa. What was wrong with me, trading intel with the ex? *Abort, Devon. ABORT.*

"He does kind of have a track record in that department," she said. "What he did to you was shitty."

"You know about that?"

She fluffed her hair. "I had to drag it out of him. He was miserable over it for a long time."

"So was I."

"Understandably so." She sighed. "Listen, take care of him. Unless he hurts you. Then you should kick his ass. I'll help."

Huh. I liked her. In another life, we probably could've even been friends. "Is that his grandmother who just joined them?"

Now Rochelle offered me a full, dazzling smile. "His favorite person ever. I'm going to leave so he can introduce you without it being all weird." She gave my arm a reassuring pat and sauntered away.

Ashton's grandmother was tall, with impeccable posture, a severe bun, and an air of quiet authority. She wore a long, elegant gray dress accented with a diamond brooch. She glanced over and saw me staring. Her face lit up with delight, and she leaned over to whisper to Ashton.

Ashton's face softened as his grandmother spoke to him. As they walked over, his posture relaxed and the wrinkles on his forehead smoothed out. But the fists at his sides and the way he kept cutting his eyes at his mother showed me he was barely holding it together.

Up close, Ashton's grandmother's eyes twinkled. A small smile played around her mouth, suggesting a secret mischievousness. My heart pounded as if I were in the presence of a celebrity.

Ashton slipped his arm around my shoulders. "Devon, I'd like you to officially meet Harriet Edwards, my grandmother," he said. "Grandmother, this is Devon Kearney, my girlfriend."

She clasped my hands in both of hers. Warmth and acceptance poured out of her like fine wine. "Devon. It's wonderful to officially meet you."

All my tension faded away. "Likewise."

The dinner bell rang a second time.

Ashton looped one arm through his grandmother's and the other arm through mine, and led us to the dining room. After everyone settled at the table, he threw his mother a hard look. Then he leaned over to me, his face pinched, his mouth a straight line. "You were upset earlier. What did my mother say to you?"

I shook my head. "I'll tell you later."

He nodded. "Later, then."

During dinner, I watched Ashton and his grandmother. Their easy conversations, their inside jokes. The way his face was smooth around her, happiness radiating off him. He included me in their conversation as much as he could, but I kept fading out, content to watch as they interacted.

After dinner, the adults headed to the sitting room. A four-piece jazz band played bouncy tunes while a steady stream of people took advantage of the open bar. Some of the older couples whirled around the dance floor to classics like the fox-trot. Most of the younger people gathered in a corner. Ashton had explained that they were his peers: people he hung out with because their parents were all Very Important People who hung out together. Played golf together. Hosted charity fund-raisers together. Did business together.

More guests arrived in a whirlwind of fur coats, expensive perfume, and flashing jewelry. Ashton spent time greeting these new arrivals, then spent the next hour making nice with everyone who had come to the party.

"This is my girlfriend, Devon Kearney," he said proudly to the press, to his friends and family, to anyone who would listen. Ashton's arm stayed around me the entire time. Almost defiantly, as if he was daring someone to say something out of line.

"Smile," photographers from society publications called as shutters clicked and the flashes popped.

Once the articles were printed, Ashton explained, it would be official. I'd be a part of society. The funny thing was, these people weren't so very different from those in my world. They simply had bigger bank accounts, wore fancier clothes, and drove expensive cars. But those things were important in his world, and for now, I had to play the part.

Watching Ashton play the part was both fascinating and unnerving. The perfect blend of formal and charming, he knew exactly how to flatter, and they ate it right up like lions feasting on gazelles. He stood tall and proud, embodying his family's power in a way that impressed and intimidated me.

This was nothing like the passionate, vulnerable boy he was when we were alone. Were all wealthy people like this, able to shed one skin for another when it suited them? Conflicting feelings about his family's legacy caused him constant angst, but you wouldn't know it tonight. It troubled me in a way, seeing him slip into this act so easily. How much of it even was an act? I didn't know. But I did know this: Ashton fit into this world in a way I never would.

A gentle hand on my shoulder made me nearly spill my sparkling cider. "You're doing well for your debut," Ashton's grandmother said.

"Oh, hi." I put my hand on my chest.

"Oops. Didn't mean to startle you. Although I should have noticed how hard you were staring at my grandson."

My face warmed. "I'm glad you came to talk to me, Mrs. Edwards."

"Please call me Harriet," she said, looking around. "I know this must be a lot. All these people staring at you, asking you questions, taking pictures."

"It's a little overwhelming, yes."

"But you'll get used to it. I know you will."

My hands trembled, making the cider slosh. "You think I'll be around long enough for all this to matter?"

"Ashton looks at you like you're his whole world. Even if no one else believes it, he does. And for the record, I do, too."

I let out a long breath. "Thank you."

"Listen. I know his mother is kind of a"—she leaned down to whisper—"hard-ass."

I bit back a snort.

"She takes things like class and lineage very seriously."

"Believe me, I know."

"I used to be the same way. But I've learned there are things more important than how blue your blood is or how much wealth your ancestors have accumulated. Love. That's what's important. And if you have one person you truly love and who truly loves you, then that's all the wealth you need."

Beautiful sentiment, but she was filthy rich, so I wasn't sure I completely bought it.

Still. It was a nice thought.

"What about his father?"

We watched as Mr. Edwards beamed and gave Ashton a hard pat on the back. He *acted* proud of Ashton, but honestly, it didn't seem as if they liked each other one bit. Ashton was smiling, but there was a subtle strain there. Only someone who knew him well would be able to tell that he was uncomfortable.

The sides of Harriet's mouth turned down slightly. "Tristan is very conservative. He thinks things should stay a certain way, and nothing should ever deviate from it."

"So, his son dating a middle-class biracial girl—"

"Is definitely deviating from what's normal. For him. My influence only goes so far. His father was hard on him, and, unfortunately, I didn't stand up to him much. Big mistake on my part, I realize that now. Naturally he doesn't think I have a right to tell him how to run his life. But when I try to point out the same thing about Ashton—"

"He gets loud."

She gave me a sideways glance.

"So I've heard," I added.

"Sometimes I feel like Tristan resents that I give Ashton

the attention I should've given him as a child. I don't want to believe that of my son, but that's the way he treats him. All the restrictions and the demands, then making Eleanor do all the dirty work. It hurts my heart. I imagine it hurts Ashton's, too." Regret etched itself into the lines on her face.

"So, what do I do?"

"Love Ashton. Be by his side. Fight for him. I'll do what I can, but it's ultimately up to you two."

"How are you holding up?" Ashton asked once the cameras were turned off, the recorders put away.

"Hanging in there."

"I'm glad you're here."

I caressed his cheek. "I'm glad I'm with you."

Thirty minutes before midnight, the party kicked way up. Loud laughter, free-flowing champagne, and *oh my God* some of the dancing the parents were doing. And this, after living with *my* parents, poster children for PDA.

During the countdown, Ashton pulled me aside and gave me a long, gentle kiss. His lips felt so good against mine that I didn't want to let him go.

Maybe I didn't fit in his world, but he and I did fit together.

While everyone sang "Auld Lang Syne," Ashton and I slipped out of the sitting room. He studied my face, then brushed a curl from my forehead.

"Something's bothering you," he said. "Talk to me."

"I love your grandmother," I said. "She believes we have a

future together. But your mom doesn't." I froze. "I shouldn't have said that."

His expression turned stony. "No. Keep going."

At first I held back. This wasn't the time or place. But he'd asked, so I let him have it. When I got to the part about his mother calling me a gold digger, he froze, stone-cold anger hardening his features. By the time I got to the diversity stuff, he was clenching and unclenching his fists and his jaw. Then he exploded.

"I find the one thing, the one damn thing that makes me happy, and she wants to snatch it away? To hell with her."

I shook my head. "No, I mean, I get it. There's a lot at stake." And now I sounded like his mother.

He shook his head, his jaw set. "No, there isn't. We have a whole royal family with a biracial duchess existing in this world. That's real. The crap Mother's saying to you? It's bullshit." His forehead furrowed. "Did she threaten you?"

"Not exactly, but—"

"Come on."

He pulled me into the sitting room. Right to his mother and Rochelle... and another woman, who had to be Rochelle's mother. She had that same thick curly hair, those same deep dimples. The same effortless glamour.

They were all holding half-empty champagne glasses and laughing together. Carefree. Privileged. Shiny-perfect.

"Oh, look, it's Ashton." Mrs. Edwards squeezed his shoulder. "And his little friend Devon."

"My *girlfriend* Devon," he corrected, his voice ice-cold.

Rochelle's mother whipped around to stare at her daughter, sculpted eyebrows nearly jumping off her forehead. "Girlfriend?"

Rochelle rolled her eyes. "We've talked about this. God. Devon, this is Janelle Ryan, my mother."

"Pleasure to meet you, Ms. Ryan." I held out my hand, but she didn't extend hers. Instead, she clutched her glass more tightly.

Okay then.

"This is the girlfriend?" Ms. Ryan said. "He picked *her* over you?" Then her expression changed. "Oh, I get it."

"Do you have a problem?" Ashton asked quietly.

"Ashton!" Mrs. Edwards grabbed his shoulder, but he was unmovable.

Ms. Ryan gave him a wan smile. A knowing smile. "Not at all."

Whatever. I could tell by her sideways smirk, the way her eyes swept over me and skipped away, that she figured I wasn't any sort of threat. As if I wouldn't be around long. Then things could get back to the status quo.

Rochelle's face was a mask of utter exasperation mixed with horror. But she didn't say anything. So did that make her just as bad?

"Mother, I need to speak with you," Ashton said.

"Ashton, this is really not the time or place—"

But Ashton had already turned and was dragging me away. I heard Mrs. Edwards murmur an apology, then the click of her heels behind us. "Ashton Edwards. How dare you embarrass me in front of my guests?"

He snorted. "Oh please. Janelle is so blitzed it'll be a miracle if she remembers anything ten minutes from now."

Mrs. Edwards sighed and pursed her lips. "What is this about?"

"How could you say those things to Devon?"

Mrs. Edwards flashed those icy blue eyes at me. "I'm looking out for our family. You, more than anyone, should know that."

"Mother—"

She slashed the air with her ring-laden hand, the diamonds painfully brilliant. "We will discuss this when it's appropriate."

Ashton stood tall, face-to-face with his mother. "Devon's my girlfriend. I love her, and I'm not letting anything come between us again." His voice was a deadly calm that made my hands tremble. "Not even family."

Mrs. Edwards's smooth skin turned blotchy. "You'll see the choices you have to make when you become a parent." She glared at me again. "I need to get back to my guests." She spun on her heels and left Ashton and me in the foyer.

He stood stock-still, fury flashing in his eyes. "Like later is ever going to come," he muttered. "This family is a joke." Then his shoulders slumped. "I shouldn't be dragging you into this mess. I don't even know why *I* stick around."

"Because it's your blood. Because you have a legacy."

"Yeah, well, maybe we should start our own legacy."

I stared at the floor. "I don't know. Sometimes I feel like I don't belong anywhere."

His face softened, the sternness—and maybe a touch of hurt—melting away. "Dev..."

I wrapped my arms around myself. "Most of the time I can push it aside. But then your mother said all that stuff, and those bad feelings came rushing back."

He gripped my shoulders and held tight. "Listen to me. You belong here. More than anyone. And you sure as hell belong with me."

"You asked about engagement rings," I blurted.

"Because I'm seriously imagining a future with you. I know you don't need me to take care of you, but I want to. I think about it all the time, Dev. But... I shouldn't have done it. Not without talking to you first."

"You could be with Rochelle and avoid all this drama. She's perfect, and your mother obviously loves her." I glanced into the sitting room, where Mrs. Edwards and Rochelle were laughing together again. "I can't compete."

Ashton moved close to me and buried his fingers in my hair. My bun came loose and curls tumbled around my shoulders. "There is no competition. There never was. I broke up with her because I wanted to be with you. Because I *needed* to be with you." He fixed those eyes on mine, searing me with his intensity. His urgency. "I need you."

I shivered as his lips covered mine. Now I was messing up *his* hair, but I didn't care. Not one bit. I leaned against the wall as we kissed again, deeply and passionately. The whole length of his body pressed against me, showing me his need more than anything he could say. I shivered again, aching for him in the most carnal way.

"Come upstairs with me," he whispered against my lips.

"Leaving your own party?"

"I have to be alone with you. Right now."

This was Ashton. My beautiful, complicated boy. The boy I loved more than anything. Was he worth it? Yes, and then some. To hell with everything and everyone else.

"Let's go."

Chapter 31

January 25. Blue Monday. Some said it was the most depressing day of the year. The holidays over, the reality of the long cold winter ahead. The Christmas bills rolling in. The failed New Year's resolutions.

But for me, it was the day my boyfriend's world shattered.

The chef had prepared minestrone soup, and Ashton and I were about to tear into it when the vibration in the kitchen changed. I glanced at the doorway, and there was Ashton's father, his expression grave.

"Do you want sparkling or still water?" Ashton asked, his voice muffled by the thick refrigerator doors.

"Ash." I nudged him gently.

"Hmm?"

I didn't say anything, which made him pop out of the

fridge. "What...?" Then he saw his father. Immediately went stiff. "Father."

"Ashton and I need a moment," Mr. Edwards said.

"Of course," I answered, my voice quiet.

Ashton touched my arm, his fingers tightening just a little bit. "I'll be right back."

I nodded, and they disappeared, leaving me alone.

An eternity passed before Ashton came back and gripped my hand. I could tell he wanted to say something, but the words would not come. It was the way he kept opening and closing his mouth. The shallow, hitching breaths. The look of devastation on his face.

"Ash...?"

"It's Grandma," he blurted out. "She's gone."

In the movies, funerals always happen on rainy days. People dressed in black and holding black umbrellas, standing around a coffin while a preacher says prayers. People throwing dirt on the coffin before walking away from the gravesite, their expressions solemn.

This day was not rainy. It was bitterly cold, and I nearly froze in my black dress and tights. I'd almost slipped on the ice twice in my heels, but I didn't even care.

My boyfriend was grieving, and it was breaking my heart.

I met him at his house that morning. The atmosphere was gravely quiet except for the ticking of the grandfather clock. Mrs. Edwards's eyes bore into me, but my eyes were only for

Ashton. He didn't talk, even when I straightened his tie, which didn't really need fixing. He just stared at me, almost as though he was trying to draw strength from looking into my soul.

"It's time," his mother said, pulling on her coat.

"Ready?" I asked him. He shook his head, but then took a deep breath and slipped his hand into mine.

The service was stiflingly formal. Sadness was prominent here at Holy Name Lutheran Church, of which, according to the obituary, Ashton's grandmother had been a part since she'd been a little girl. She'd kept in touch with the parish after she'd moved to Monaco, making generous donations and visiting whenever she made her way stateside. A home base, so to speak, in our small town. So many people had come to pay their last respects, dabbing at their eyes with silky handkerchiefs. And the flowers. Beautiful greenhouse ones that made my eyes water and my throat itch.

Pancreatic cancer took Harriet Edwards's life. She'd refused chemotherapy and radiation, as the disease had been too advanced by the time she was diagnosed. She hadn't shared the details of her diagnosis with any of her family, instead choosing to live her life as fully as she could, until the end.

She was eighty-two years old.

I wish I'd gotten the chance to talk to her again, but my sadness was nothing compared to what my boyfriend was feeling. The storm brewed in his eyes, showing me the barely contained grief, the hopelessness.

I sat with Ashton and his parents. He squeezed my hand

so tightly I was afraid my circulation would get cut off. But I didn't let go.

★ · • · ✕

Ashton wouldn't let himself cry. He also wouldn't eat. He barely acknowledged the people who had come to pay their respects. Even his best friend knew to steer clear. And when the after-service talk at his house went from somber to jovial as they started to share memories, Ashton dragged me to his room. "I couldn't take the laughing," he said. "I couldn't take any of it."

"Even if they're sharing good things?"

"It's all an act, Devon. Wait until the will is read." His face crumpled. "We'll see if they're laughing then."

The threads holding Ashton together were snapping right before my eyes. He sank onto the floor and buried his face in his hands. I pulled him close as he shook with silent sobs.

I stroked his hair and kissed his forehead. I brushed the wetness from his cheeks. I let him take as long as he needed, until he looked up at me, his eyes red and swollen.

"I wanted to take you to Monte Carlo with me," he said in a choked whisper. "For spring break. The stargazing there—it's supposed to be unreal."

I had no idea what to say.

"A few weeks after...that summer, she was the only one who didn't treat me like I should have been ashamed to screw up like that. She was the only one who understood how desperate

I was to get away from the Dark. And she told me...she said as long as she lived, she would protect me from it. I knew she really couldn't, but it was a nice thought. Except now she's gone."

He let out a hitching breath and leaned his head on my shoulder. "Who's going to protect me now?"

The pungent cloud of Chanel No. 5 reached us even before the click of heels made us jump apart. Guilty conscience, even though we weren't doing anything wrong.

"Why aren't you downstairs with the family?" Ashton's mother asked him, her voice sharp enough to cut glass.

"I needed some time. Alone."

"Except you're here with your girlfriend, which is highly inappropriate." Her eyes cut to me. "As you both know."

Her son was a wreck, and she could only focus on propriety?

"We were talking." Ashton stood and pulled me with him. "Since when is that a crime?"

She pressed her lips together. "You're dishonoring your grandmother's memory. Couldn't you have braved it out for one more hour? People are leaving now."

"I. Couldn't. Stand. The. Bullshit."

"Language."

Ashton grabbed his hair and yanked. "We just buried the only person in this family who gives—*gave*—a damn about me. I don't—" He stopped and rubbed his forehead. Then he took a deep breath, stood up straighter, and looked Mrs. Edwards in the eye. Like magic, the flush in his cheeks and the tremor in his hands disappeared. The emotional breakdown had somehow been diffused, and now he was as polished as a politician.

How the hell did he do that?

"You're right," he said, the passion in his voice gone. "I'm sorry. We both are."

Wait, what? I had nothing to be sorry for, so why was he saying this stuff?

"Apology accepted. I understand that you're upset. Don't let it happen again," she said briskly. "Either of you."

"I'm taking Devon home." He swept past her, pulling me with him.

"Ashton," she called.

"Yes?"

"She's not the only one."

He stiffened.

"Your grandmother. She wasn't—she's not the only one in this family who cares about you."

My parents were out. I took Ashton to my room and switched on the Christmas lights. He watched as I yanked off the stiff dressy clothes and got comfy in my yoga uniform. Then I plopped on the bed and let out a long sigh.

"Better?" he asked with a small smile.

"Much." I reached out my hands. "Join me."

He climbed in beside me and played with my fingers.

"What was that all about? At your house?" I asked. "It was like Dr. Jekyll and Mr. Hyde."

He laughed then, bitterly. "Sometimes it's easier to let her believe she's right than to fight it."

"You totally could have won, though. She had guests to save face in front of."

He let out a snort. "She said she cares about me. She's sure got a fucked-up way of showing it."

"I'm sorry. I wish I could fix it all for you."

He shook his head. "Whatever. I'm done talking about it."

He wasn't done thinking about it. His pinched forehead showed me that. I ran my fingers across the wrinkles until they smoothed out. Until he let out a sigh and lay on his back. "Come closer. Please."

I snuggled up to him and buried my face in his neck. Inhaled his scent. Let the events of the day fade away.

He squeezed my shoulder. "I love your ceiling. Are the stars arranged by actual constellations?"

"They are. I put them up when I was eleven. I was a colossal brat about it because I wanted it to be perfect. My parents were so done with me."

He chuckled. "I can't see you acting that way."

"Ask Dad. He'll be happy to tell you all about it." I stroked Ashton's cheek so he'd turn to look at me. "Do you want to stay with me tonight?"

He rubbed his nose against mine. "I don't want you to get in trouble."

"I don't care about that right now. I only care about you."

"I do want to stay. Today sucked. I want to forget all about it."

I fiddled with his tie. "Maybe I can help you take your mind off things. If that's . . . if it's okay."

He sucked in a breath. "Yeah, I think that'll be okay." His voice shook and his hand trembled as he reached up to touch my face.

I kissed his fingertips. "I love that you still react like this."

"It'll never not be special, Devon," he said. "Twenty years from now, I'm still going to react this way. Every single time."

"I like when you talk about our future," I said. "I worry about you."

"Don't worry right now, okay?" he said, closing his eyes. "Let's just love each other."

I kissed him then, and we didn't speak for a long time.

Chapter 32

"You wanted to see me, Professor Trask?"

He nodded, eyes grave. "Please sit."

I knew why I was here. I'd nibbled my fingernails down to the quick, waiting for this moment. Or one much worse.

Winter had descended full force. Every day we got pounded with freezing winds, blowing snow, and frigid temperatures. The weather was definitely getting me down.

So was Ashton's sudden distance from me.

We'd had the best Valentine's Day ever, holed up in his house watching movies and eating junk food. I wore the heart-shaped Tiffany earrings he'd given me every day since. But it had been a month since then, and these days, he was quiet. Withdrawn. Mysterious, but not in a good way.

I'd texted him three times today with no answer. And he'd skipped school again.

"Some of your professors are concerned about you," Professor Trask said. "You're missing homework assignments, and you didn't score as highly as usual on your last few quizzes. Is there anything you want to talk about?"

Yes, Professor Trask. Where should I start?

1. My boyfriend's depression was taking over and he was shutting me out.

It was the first time I'd admitted it to myself. But the signs were there. The withdrawal. The exhaustion that bruised the skin under his eyes. The eerie silence that was nothing like our usual comfortable quiet. Instead, he was engaged in some private war within himself. Even on our good days, he'd been distant. His mind, a million places, but not with me. And now he wasn't talking to me at all.

2. I still had a month until I got a final answer from McCafferty. Knowing the date probably should've calmed me down, but it only made me more anxious.

3. Therefore, school didn't seem quite as important as keeping my boyfriend from doing something desperate. Except he wasn't talking to me.

4. The complete lack of control I felt about *everything* in my life right now.

I didn't want to flunk out of school. But I was exhausted from caring so much about so many things that there was no room in my brain for calculations and research and hardcore studying. And this was how I knew something was terribly wrong.

Since when did I not have time for the stars?

"Devon?"

"I'm fine," I blurted.

Of course Professor Trask didn't believe me. *I* barely believed me.

"Devon, you're our top student, but if you keep performing like this—"

"I know."

He shook his head. "I don't think you do. You're obviously having a hard time, but I can't help you if you won't let me. You have too much to lose here, so please, think about what you're allowing to happen. And please get help, even if it's not from me."

I stared at my lap.

"You still have time to get back on track," Professor Trask said gently. "It's up to you how you're going to proceed."

"I'll do better," I said, my voice raspy. Husky.

"Don't tell me. Tell yourself. Then actually do the work."

Chapter 33

THE WEEK RACED BY IN A FLURRY OF PROJECTS, REPORTS, and assignments. I was on autopilot. The only thing that pulled me out of my stupor was getting a D on an Astronomy pop quiz. A *D*. In *Astronomy*, of all things.

I stared at the paper, the words swimming, the red D blurring into a bloody smear on my academic career. And at that moment, I hated everything. I hated Professor Trask's look of concern and disappointment. I hated Ashton for making me worry so much. And I hated myself for giving in and screwing up my grades. My *life*.

Voices rattled around my head constantly. Professor Trask, the disappointment evident as I was late with yet another homework assignment. Auden, "touching base" with me for the millionth time about the invoicing for the yearbook. Blair, her forehead wrinkled as she asked a million leading questions, trying to make the dam burst.

I had to stop staring at Ashton's empty seat during lunch. I had to stop checking my phone every ten seconds. I had to stop jeopardizing my future for a boy who refused to let me in.

Time to make a new plan.

What do you want? I mentally screamed at myself.

I wanted, no, *needed* my drive and ambition back so I could go back to kicking Auden's butt.

What's standing in your way?

Worrying so much about Ashton.

So what's the solution?

Eliminate the worry, regroup, and refocus.

But for now, I balled up the quiz and sat blankly through Professor Trask's lecture.

Chapter 34

I LOVED THE STARS. THERE WAS NO DENYING THAT.

But sometimes I needed a break from them.

I loved Ashton. There was no denying that, either.

But I needed a break from him, too.

(It wasn't like he was answering my texts, anyway.)

Friday night. Not out and about, but home, where it was warm and quiet. Green tea incense cleared my mind as I pulled up the yearbook-builder website on my laptop. Logged in. And clicked through.

Analyzing hundreds of photos probably shouldn't have been as satisfying as it was, but there was something meditative about finding that perfect shot, then tweaking it so it was sharper, more colorful, more alive.

As I flipped through, I had to laugh at how Colton managed

to photobomb every club's group photo. Like his steak-loving self would be caught dead as an actual member of the Vegan Club. But there he was, standing in the back and grinning like a maniac. I marveled at Tyrell's talent to tell stories with the way he laid out the pages. I even had to begrudgingly nod at Auden's foreword, and how it managed to capture perfectly the theme of the book, and of our school.

There were photos of our dinner out—a special treat from Professor Wilcox for managing to sell all the yearbooks before spring.

She'd probably regretted taking us out in public. Auden and Tyrell snapping at each other like they always did. Colton sneaking bites from everyone's plates. Me picking at my food because my mind was in a million places at once.

And now my face was wet. Seeing these photos—batches from every grade—brought back a boatload of memories. Blair taking me under her wing my first day of school, when I was scared and lost. Auden's smug smile on my second day, declaring our Unofficial Official Competition. Professor Trask with his warm belly laugh, further encouraging my obsession with all things cosmos.

Afternoon teas, thrown by Dr. Steelwood to help new freshmen get more easily acclimated to the school. Sophomore year finishing classes, where we learned how to hold our forks and properly eat bread at a formal dinner. Junior year standardized testing prep. Stress magnified.

And now senior year was flying by. Preston was full of so many personalities, and even though I didn't spend a lot of time outside my little circle, it still hurt that soon we'd all be separated. I would miss them all.

Even Auden.

With my time at Preston Academy nearing its end, with Ashton being so distant, with my future studies uncertain, I felt like a broken butterfly, being tossed here and there by the wind. Everything that held me together was unraveling, and I wasn't sure what was next. For the first time, I wasn't ready for the future.

I was terrified of it.

Chapter 35

Saturday morning, I called Ashton first thing. "Dad lent me his car. I need to go to Happy Paws. Do you want to come with me?"

"I think I'm going to stay home." His voice was dull, flat.

"But our brunch date?"

A long pause, then, "That's today?"

"We were going to try the new waffle place. Remember?"

Another pause. "Can I take a rain check?"

"Ash, we don't have to go out. I can come over when I'm done at the shelter."

"No, Dev. You should enjoy your Saturday. Don't worry about me."

"I'll always worry about you," I said quietly.

"Well, don't. Okay? I'll talk to you later."

He hung up. Stung, I sat frozen on my bed. Heartbreaking scenarios raced through my head. What if it wasn't his depression at all? What if he didn't love me anymore? What if we were over? God, I hated this limbo. I needed to get answers out of him, but how could I do that when he wouldn't talk to me?

No. Sitting here feeling sorry for myself wasn't an option. I had too much to do. I swallowed the lump in my throat, grabbed the car keys, and got the hell out of the house.

I hadn't been to Happy Paws since I finished my volunteer hours in September. I probably would have never come back, except they'd needed me to fill out one more piece of paperwork so my hours would actually count. The bright lobby was warm and welcoming, a stark contrast to the bitter cold outside.

"Hi! Devon, right?" There was Angelica, as chipper as the first time I'd met her. This time, her hair was dyed to mimic a rainbow.

I tried to make my smile radiate like her curls. "That's right."

"Great. I'll have your form in a bit. In the meantime, do you want to say hi to Buddy? He's our official mascot now."

"He's still here?" I frowned. "That makes me so sad."

"He's pretty sad, too. His friend hasn't been by in a while."

I froze in alarm. "Ashton?"

She nodded. "It's been at least four weeks."

What the hell. Ashton loved that dog. But then, he said he loved me, too, and look where we were.

I sent him a text, asking what was up. No answer. Seriously, *what the hell*, Ashton?

Buddy had been moved to a smaller room that housed older dogs who lay curled up and watching me with sleepy eyes. I sat on the floor, and Buddy padded over and laid his head in my lap. I scratched behind his ears and he let out a content sigh. How could so many people come through this shelter every day and pass up this awesome creature? How could Ashton abandon him? I sat with Buddy and pulled out my phone.

Depression: Supporting a Family Member or Friend.

Symptoms:

Irritability?

Check.

Loss of interest in hobbies?

I looked sadly at Buddy. Check.

Forgetfulness?

Yup.

I knew them well by now. What I needed to know was how to help him. If I could help him. Except the site was no help, either. *Talk to the person.* Okay, right. Not useful when the person wouldn't talk to *me*. Frustrated, I shoved my phone into my bag and buried my face in Buddy's fur.

After I filled out my form, I drove around town, trying to decide what to do. Ashton had said for me to enjoy my day, but how could I when my brain kept playing the worst scenarios over and over? And yet, I wanted to respect his boundaries. Give him space if that's what he wanted. Except I didn't know if that's what he actually wanted, or if the Dark was telling him that being alone was what he deserved.

I parked at the grocery store and leaned my head against the steering wheel. I hated everything about this. I hated depression. I hated its lies and its darkness and its all-consuming power. I hated how powerless it made me feel. And if *I* felt powerless, how was Ashton feeling?

My fists clenched. Screw this.

I put the car in gear.

Chapter 36

I DROVE TO THE GATE AND PUNCHED IN THE CODE. CIRCLED the fountain and parked right in front of the main door. Marched directly upstairs and burst into Ashton's room.

He was sprawled on the floor, holding a video game controller and staring at his TV. He looked like a hot mess, and didn't seem surprised to see me when he gazed up at me with dull eyes. Pajama pants. Shiny face. Greasy hair. Junk food wrappers everywhere.

"Hey," I said. "Can I sit with you?"

He didn't say anything. Just handed me the other controller.

The quest was to retrieve a chest of gold before the ogre woke up. But there were traps and timers and tricks, and they got me every time. We played until I lost all our lives.

"Sorry," I said.

He dropped the controller and offered me a tiny smile. That little sign of life filled me with relief, albeit short-lived.

I dropped my controller, too, and wrapped my arms around him. He closed his eyes and nestled close to me, burying his face in my neck. And we sat like that, so still, so quiet, for what felt like hours.

"Ash," I said against his temple, "are we okay?"

He stared right into my eyes. Then he nodded.

"Are *you* okay?"

No answer this time. Just his arms, tightening around me.

"How can I help?" I was asking this even though I felt as helpless as he looked.

He let out a long, trembling sigh. "I don't know if you can."

"I can try. I don't pretend to know what you're going through, but I'm here. I'll always be here. I love you."

He squared his shoulders and gave me a bright smile. One that didn't quite reach his eyes. One that crackled, its intensity was so high. "Don't worry, Dev. I'll get through this. I'll be okay."

Who was he trying to convince? Himself or me?

And why couldn't I believe him?

Chapter 37

Celestial coordinates: the positions of stars, planets, and galaxies. There were five different celestial coordinate systems to determine these positions, and I had to learn them all. This should have been right up my alley. It amazed me that these complicated calculations could tell me so much about something so far away.

Except I couldn't bring myself to care about any of them right now. I stared hopelessly at my Astronomy textbook, watching letters and numbers and symbols spiral into an indecipherable mess.

I'd wanted to glue myself to Ashton's side last night. But my phone had started blowing up with messages from Mom.

Where u at?

I'm starving! U ok? Been here 10 mins.

If I don't hear from u by the time I count 2 thirty I'm calling police.

& eating ur bacon.

Ashton had practically shoved me out the door, telling me I should enjoy my Mom-Daughter time and not worry about him. Why did he always say that? He had to know that I was going to check my phone over and over. That Mom would snatch it away so I could be present and enjoy our breakfast for dinner at the old-fashioned diner.

"Bun, you aren't eating," Mom had said last night. Dark-brown eyes scrutinized every bite I pushed around the plate. "You've barely touched your blueberry French toast."

"Not that hungry."

"But you love breakfast for dinner. Is everything okay?"

I twirled my fork, mangling my toast and ripping it to shreds. "Everything's fine."

"How are you feeling?"

Like a jumbled-up, mixed-up mess. But I swallowed those emotions and forced a bite. The French toast really was delicious. "Just tired."

There was no way she believed me. I could tell by the way her eyes narrowed, the way her lips pursed. But as I said, Mom always knew when to give me space, even when she really didn't want to. Even when I wasn't sure I wanted her to.

"Then you should hit the sack early tonight," she said. "You can't afford to get sick now."

No, not with second semester midterms coming up.

Which was why I was studying right now. Trying to, anyway. Ashton had some serious stuff going on, and despite my best efforts—which, let's be honest, weren't that great these days—it was still affecting my grades. Professor Trask's warning had simply floated away, like those thought clouds yoga teachers were so fond of talking about during meditation. Every day I sat in class, nibbling my nails, anticipating a call to the office where Dr. Steelwood would tell me I'd been kicked out. My concentration was festering in hell, and instead of formulas and solutions, I saw Ashton's face. The desperate look in his eyes. The strain around his mouth.

I pushed my book aside and flipped to a new page in my notebook. Then I pulled up the calculator on my phone. Because I needed to concentrate, but I also needed to obsess over Ashton. It made no logical sense, but I knew I wouldn't be able to study until I got him out of my system, at least for tonight.

Calculations, calculations. I loved calculating. But no matter how I rearranged the figures, no matter how many charts I drew, I could not work out a good balance. And this was a problem.

I slammed the notebook shut and marched over to the mirror. This is what stared back at me: frizzy golden spirals, pale cheeks, and dark circles under my eyes. No more stars.

But my voice was strong.

"Devon Kearney, you are better than this. This is your future. Yours. No one else's. Get yourself together and do it *now.*"

I needed to be more forceful.

"This is serious. This is your life. Your dream. Now act like you have some sense, and get your priorities straight!"

My reflection stared back, her mouth set in defiance. I had to get out the big guns.

Deep breath.

And go.

"If you don't straighten up, then you'll need to choose. School or him." I swallowed. Hard. "Do you want to give up Ashton? Because you'll have to if you don't get it together. And that's not an option."

I gripped the dresser. Even saying it made my head spin. I was so scared of losing him. I absolutely did not want to give him up. But I had to stop this foolishness.

My eyes hardened. Who cared about those silly calculations? I had this. I could keep up with school, and I could keep him, too. It wouldn't be easy, but nothing worth doing ever was.

Bring it.

I picked up my phone and shot him one last text:

I'm here whenever you're ready.

Then I forced myself back to my textbook and my notes.

I'd just finished an equatorial-to-ecliptic conversion when the doorbell rang. I dropped my pencil and ran to the door, and there was Ashton, standing in the cold. "Hey, you!" I threw open the door and pulled him inside. Then I noticed his expression. Helpless. Hurting. Devastated. "What happened?"

"We have really awful fights all the time, you know?" His voice was low and thick. "My father and me. But he's never gotten physical."

"What?!"

"He grabbed me. Threw me. I fell and knocked over his drink cart. He—" Ashton let out a shuddering breath. "I can't talk about it anymore. I can't even believe it happened."

I clenched my fists and closed my eyes.

Inhale... two... three... four.

Exhale... two... three... four.

"Why?" I choked out.

He collapsed onto the couch and buried his face in his hands. "He was drunk. Said awful things. He drinks all the time now. And when he starts drinking, I have to get out of the way. And ever since Grandma died... it's a fucking nightmare."

I grabbed his hands. "Oh my God."

He continued as if he hadn't heard me. "He said I was worthless. Called me a waste." His hands started shaking. "I'm not a waste. I'm not a fucking waste." Then he looked at me, his vulnerable expression breaking my heart. "Devon, am I a waste?"

"You're not a waste." I squeezed his hands. "You are not a waste."

He was still for a few moments, gathering himself. Then he sat up a bit straighter. "They read the will yesterday."

"Were you there?"

"I tuned out halfway through, but the gist of it is that everyone's pissed at my father. And me."

"But what in the world did you do?"

He let out a bitter laugh. "Be her favorite."

I could only imagine what that meant.

"Now my father, his brothers and sisters—they're all fighting. He came home last night and got wasted. He stayed home today and got drunk again. I was in the wrong place at the wrong time."

"Holy shit, Ashton." I traced his face, looking for bruises or cuts. "Does your mother know?"

He snorted. "She's no better. All she does is go on about me being with you. On and on about how 'being with Rochelle is more aligned with our family goals.' How she's more equipped to deal with the pressures of being in a powerful family. How she's more suitable. Doesn't matter if I don't love Rochelle, Mother says. Because apparently the Edwards family marries for power, not"—he went into a snooty imitation of his mother—"fleeting, silly things like puppy love."

"Great."

"Here's the kicker: Rochelle's seeing some titled dude in Europe now. I thought telling them that would get them off my back, but no. They still don't want me with you because apparently you're a distraction from me finding the 'right' person."

"The 'right' person," I repeated bitterly.

"Father threatened to cut me off if I didn't break up with you."

I covered my mouth with my hand.

Something in his grandma's will must have triggered this. Therefore, I needed to be dismissed as soon as possible.

Dismissed. My stomach lurched. "Is that why you're here? To break up with me?"

He glanced at me out of the corner of his eye. "If I was cut off, would you stay with me?"

Oh hell no. Family drama or not, this was some bullshit. "I can't believe you would even ask me that. What the hell?"

"No. Dev." He shook his head. "That's not what I meant. It's because of me. Why would you be with someone whose parents don't even like him?"

I was so tired. "Ashton, I'm not dating your parents."

"I know, but—"

I gestured between us. "They have nothing to do with what's going on right here."

He swallowed. "You're right."

"But to be honest, I don't think you'd stay with me."

His face colored. "What the fuck? Why would you say that?"

"Listen. You getting cut off wouldn't be a big deal to me, but you grew up with all that. That's all you know. Can you live like a regular person? Do you even know how?"

He sighed, defeated. "All I know is that I love you and I'll do anything to keep you in my life. What you and I have? It's the best thing in my life, and I'm not about to throw us away. Not for my parents. Not for anything."

"Even your family's money?"

"Especially that."

I could make it easy. I could break up with him. He could keep his money. He'd eventually find some WASP princess to settle down with. There would be harmony in his family, and I wouldn't have to deal with their drama, politics, and scrutiny.

But the thought of doing that made bile rise in my throat. Regardless of what happened in the future, he was my right now and I loved him so much. And call me selfish, but he was mine, and I wasn't about to hand him over. Besides, no matter what choice I made, I would come out looking like the gold digger his parents thought I was. So why break his heart when whatever I did wouldn't make a difference, anyway?

At least this way I'd get to keep him.

"I told my father to go fuck himself," Ashton said. "That's why he hit me."

I couldn't even blame Ashton. I had my own choice words for Tristan Carter Preston Edwards right now. But I kept quiet. The man was still Ashton's father, and I wasn't about to disrespect him.

Not that he *deserved* any respect from me. But still.

"Do you know what it's like to have your father look at you like he's disappointed in you all the time?" Ashton glanced at me. "No, of course you don't know. I'm glad you don't know. Because it's awful. I wish I didn't care. But I do, and I hate it."

"Of course you care, and of course you hate it. And that's okay."

He jumped up and started pacing. "I don't know if I can live like a regular person. But I'm willing to try. I would love to take my place in the family business and show them—show *him*—that I can make it bigger and better than before." He stopped and ran his hands through his hair. "But I have to get the hell away from him, even if it means leaving all of it behind."

"But if they cut you off—" I broke off.

One thing I'd learned about wealthy people is that they made sure they were taken care of, no matter what happened. But I didn't know how it all worked. Could his parents seize all that? Would they leave him destitute? It didn't make sense to me, but maybe there were rules in his world I'd never understand.

I nibbled my thumbnail. Everything was so complicated now. That summer, things had been so simple. Ashton and me: two people in love. Now it felt political. Then adding his depression, plus my own pressures with school...the weariness climbed into my bones and settled heavily there.

"Devon, we'll be okay," he said. "Right?"

I slid my arms around his waist and closed my eyes. "I hope so."

Chapter 38

My parents were the ultimate hippies, and Mom sometimes took mysticism to a whole other plane. Because of my obsession with the stars, I was more pragmatic. Didn't really get into the whole psychic-connection-ESP thing.

Except I couldn't ignore the pang in my gut that told me Ashton was in danger.

He'd skipped school today. Said he was going home. Running right back to the very place he hated so much.

And I wanted to be right there, holding him and distracting him from the darkness taking him over. Convincing him not to do what I was so afraid he was planning to do. I wanted to climb into bed with him and relive last night, after we'd stopped talking about his parents and fell silent, eyes locked. When the need to be close to each other took over, and our lips met as if it were our first and last kiss. When we were naked in each other's arms, immersed in our own world. A world with no pain, no drama, and no demons to torment him. Just me and Ashton, connecting in our ultimate way. Close and raw and passionate and real.

Last night, after he'd pulled on his coat, I'd traced his face and given him a gentle, lingering kiss. Then I rested my thumb on his bottom lip. "I love you, you know."

"I love you, too. So much." Then he'd given me a look that filled me with alarm. It was like he was soaking me in, saving me up for when I wasn't there. As if he was never going to see me again.

And there was no text from him when I woke up.

Now, with every class, every ring of the bell, the foreboding feeling ballooned until it completely consumed me. Auden scribbled away on our Calculus pop quiz, that annoying smug smile on her face. But for me, the questions swam on the paper until they were nothing but piles of black gibberish.

My phone buzzed.

Two texts from Ashton that shot terror clear through me.

Oh.

God.

I had to get to him.

Wait. Failing this test would ruin my GPA and knock me out of the top spot, obliterating any chance of me getting into McCafferty. Leaving school unexcused could get me a demerit, which would jeopardize my scholarship.

Him or my future? What was it going to be?

★ • ● • ✕

Blair met me by my locker. "I'll drive you."

We rushed straight to his house. Straight to his room.

"Ashton." I sank to the floor next to him, aware of nothing except the sick boy hunched over, sweating and shaking, in front of me. I yanked his head up so we were nose to nose. "What did you do?"

But I knew what he'd done. Of course I knew. Why else would I have rushed here?

He raised desperate eyes to meet mine. "I'm so scared," he said, his voice faint, his words slurred.

I swallowed a sob. "Ash..."

"I wanted everything to stop. The fighting, the yelling. I wanted the Dark to go away." His eyelids fluttered. "I thought I wanted to die, but I don't." The look in his eyes turned wild, feral. "I don't wanna die."

"Then you've got to stay awake," I said, my voice firm. The exact opposite of what I was feeling: a meteoric explosion of fear.

"I'm calling 911," Blair said. "I'll take the pill bottles with me."

Pill bottles. There were pill bottles. How had I missed them? "Ashton," I said firmly, "I need you to stay with me."

"I'm sorry," he said, closing his eyes again. And that's when I stopped trying to hold back. It was too hard to stay strong.

"Please don't leave me." Hot tears blazed down my cheeks. "I can't lose you again. Please."

He opened his eyes. Unfocused. Glazed. "Dev. When did you get here?"

I didn't try to fight the sob this time. "Ashton Edwards, you cannot go to sleep, do you understand me?"

His voice hitched. "I'm so scared."

I wiped his forehead. Cold, clammy, and sweaty. "Then don't go. Not now. Not today. Stay with me. Please, please stay with me."

His face crumpled. "I'm going to be sick."

I grabbed the trash can and thrust it in front of him, then rubbed his back as he was violently ill. He was pale and trembling by the time he was done.

"What did you take?" Anything to keep him talking.

"I don't know. Vicodin. Oxy-something." His voice started to fade again. "Some other stuff."

"Where did you get them?"

"Bought 'em."

Which meant that he'd been planning this. How long had he been planning this?

"Stay with me," I pleaded again. "Please."

He was still, except for his lips. Trembling. His fists. Clenching and unclenching.

Fighting.

Yes, Ashton. Please keep fighting.

"You have to make it," I said desperately, because I needed him to believe it, and I needed to believe it. "You're going to survive this. You are."

He focused on me then, and his face softened into that tender look.

"Devon," he whispered. "I love you. And I'm so sorry."

"Ashton, stay awake. Please." I was losing him, and there wasn't a thing I could do but watch him give up his life. All the cracks in me from holding it together for him were splintering. Pieces of me were falling to the floor and shattering. And Ashton's eyes were closed.

I shook him. "Wake up. Please, wake up!"

He was unresponsive. But he was still breathing. Short, shallow breaths. He was here now…but for how long? I buried my face in his hair and sobbed. Where was the ambulance? They needed to get here soon. Oh God, let them hurry.

"They're in here." Blair's voice sounded like it was underwater.

Two paramedics rushed over to Ashton. They checked his pulse. Shoved an oxygen mask over his face and strapped him to a gurney, shouting urgent instructions to each other the whole time. I followed the paramedics downstairs and into the chilly air outside. I didn't want Ashton out of my sight.

The paramedics wouldn't let me ride with him. Blair's strong arms kept me from scratching their eyes out. Anger and desperation rose in me as I struggled against her. Ashton needed me. Why couldn't anyone see that?

I couldn't see a thing; I was crying so hard my head spun. Tiny, frightened, and shaking. My Ashton, my love. Was he leaving me?

The flashing lights. The disembodied voices coming through the radios. The rattling diesel of the engine. How was this happening? How was this real?

"Wake him up," I sobbed. "Make him wake up!"

"Devon, they're going to take care of him," Blair said.

I wanted to believe her. I did. But I watched him give up. I saw him close his eyes, and I heard him say good-bye. *Please, God, don't let this be good-bye.*

I smelled her familiar coconut scent before I saw her. Before she wrapped her arms around me.

"Mom?" I choked out. When had she gotten here? Where was I? What was happening?

"Thanks for coming, Mrs. K," Blair said. "She's in shock, and I'm scared."

"I'm taking her to the hospital," Mom said. "Do you want to come with us?"

My best friend had paled to the point of translucency. "Yeah," she said, her voice wobbly.

"Let's go."

Ashton's parents were in the waiting room when we arrived. His mother screamed abuse at the receptionist while his father paced, his eyes wide and empty. I glared at him, wanting to blame someone, because Ashton was back there having God knows what done to him, and I had to sit here with tears getting in my hair.

I couldn't stop crying.

"Let's sit down," Mom said. Blair sat on the other side of me and held my hand. I couldn't tell which of us was shaking more.

Days passed. Or maybe it was hours. It could have been

minutes. Someone wrapped me in a blanket. Blair, Mom, and I huddled together, waiting to hear something. Anything.

Ashton's mother ended her tirade and joined her husband in pacing. Around and around and around. Hypnotizing, watching them circumvent each other. Watching them treading so carefully. But I could see her. I could see the cold fury flashing in her eyes every time she glared at her husband, and I could see the shame in his.

The doctor came out and took his parents aside. He spoke to them in low murmurs. I was desperate to go over, but it wasn't my place. I loved Ashton more than anything in the world, but I was only his high school girlfriend. Someone who might not even be around in a few months, as far as they were concerned.

Ashton's parents went through the double doors. What did that mean? My heart beat faster and my palms grew damp. Mom held me tighter while I buried my face in her shoulder and tried to keep from imagining the worst.

Another eternity passed, and finally, Ashton's mother emerged from the back and came over to me. I pulled away from my mom slightly as Mrs. Edwards took my hand.

"He's stabilized for now," she said. "They're moving him to intensive care."

"Is he awake?"

She closed her eyes and kept them closed for a long time. Then, slowly opening them, she said, "He's still unconscious."

"I need to see him," I said, my voice raspy.

"You should go home. Get some rest."

"I won't be able to sleep." I shook my head. "Not until I see him."

She nodded and sighed. "I thought you might say that. But they're not letting anyone back there other than family."

"Is he going to make it?"

She swallowed and looked down. "We don't know."

I covered my mouth with my hand.

"He took a lot of pills. They had to pump his stomach. It's a good thing you showed up when you did. My husband and I weren't supposed to be back for hours. I don't know what would have happened if—" She broke off.

"I have to see him." My voice cracked. "Please."

"Devon," Mrs. Edwards said, "I'll be here. And I promise I'll get in touch with you if things change."

If.

"Come on, Bun," Mom said. "It's late. You can come back tomorrow."

NEBULA

Chapter 39

Blair came home with me. We didn't watch movies or experiment with makeup. We sat stone-still, shocked and quiet. At some point, I climbed into bed, but sleep didn't come. I lay awake. Wide-eyed. Empty.

I closed my eyes, but sleep still wouldn't come. Tears did, though. So many tears. So much fear and so much worry. What could I have done to prevent this? I should have helped him more. Why didn't I help him more?

His texts had burned into my memory:

Dev, I did something.

I'm scared.

The fear turned my stomach over and over. The images wouldn't go away. Those terrifying texts. The flashing ambulance lights. His pale face and clammy skin.

I gave up on sleep and stared at the ceiling. Watched my glow-in-the-dark stars fade as the room lightened with the dawn of a new day. Would Ashton ever see a new day?

I squeezed my stuffed bunny and prayed.

When the alarm went off, Blair jumped a clear two feet. Then, without a word, she hopped up, shook her head, then trudged into the bathroom.

My eyes were gritty with fatigue and my head hurt, but I dragged myself out of bed anyway. Skipped yoga. Skipped breakfast. Would have skipped my shower, but Blair drew the line at that.

Mom gave me permission to stay home from school, but I wanted the distraction. I wanted the work and the bells and Auden's obnoxious smile. I wanted the lectures and the slamming lockers and my turkey sandwich for lunch.

But nothing helped.

Weak with worry, I kept my eyes lowered and focused on organizing yearbook orders. Taking notes that might or might not make sense later. Barely hearing any lectures. But the effort only made my head hurt worse. Blair hardly left my side. She stayed quiet during lunch—a miracle for her. I could sense her watching me, even while she tried to pretend to be immersed in whatever was on her phone.

My phone stayed silent. I nibbled my nails, desperate to hear anything. No, not anything. I wanted good news. I *needed* good news.

"I'm sorry, but I can't let you back," the nurse said. "You're not family."

My fists clenched. "Your policy says significant others count as family. I'm his girlfriend."

"The rules are different for intensive care. I'm sorry."

Shaking with rage, I made my way back to the waiting room. I'd rushed here right after school—hadn't even bothered to change—and I wasn't about to turn around and leave. Maybe they could stop me from going back there, but damn if I would leave this hospital without hearing something from someone. I collapsed into one of the orange vinyl chairs and tried to breathe.

Inhale goodness, exhale badness.

My eyes stung.

Inhale goodness, exhale badness.

A sob escaped. And yet, I kept inhaling...*two*...*three*...*four.* Exhaling...*two*...*three*...*four.*

"Devon?"

My head snapped up. Mrs. Edwards stood outside the waiting room, gazing at me curiously.

Her usual polished look was gone. Still wearing her business suit from yesterday, she had runny makeup and messy hair. This woman I'd been so resentful of was a shell of herself, mirroring my worry and my grief and my love for the sick boy down the hall.

"How is he?" I asked.

"He still hasn't woken up."

"They won't let me see him."

"You were going to just sit here?"

"I need to be close to him."

She gave me a strange look. "You really do love him."

"He's my everything," I said quietly.

She nodded and swallowed. Made her way across the lobby and collapsed into the chair next to me. We sat for what felt like hours, the drone of the news in the background. I jumped when she started talking.

"I was raised in a household where we didn't show a lot of affection," she said in a trembly voice. "It just wasn't done. So that's how I raised Ashton. I let the nanny pick him up when he was crying. She raised him until my husband sent him to a boarding school. But Ashton, bless his heart, craves love." A bitter laugh. "If I hadn't been so concerned with doing things the 'right' way... if I'd learned from the first time he tried this, maybe we wouldn't be here again."

Without even thinking, I reached my hands across the cold metal armrest to clasp with hers. I had a feeling she craved love as well.

"I sent him to his grandmother every chance I could because she was different from the rest of us. I pushed him away, then I wonder why he's distant." She shook her head. "Stupid."

I didn't know what to say. Maybe I didn't need to say anything at all.

"My husband hit him and I froze. I didn't do a thing to stop it. I failed my son. Again." She shook her head. "That changes today. That changes right now. If he makes it." Her eyes squeezed shut. "Please let him make it."

The sleepless night was catching up to me. My head began to nod. But it snapped right to attention when the man in blue scrubs came over to us and uttered the two most gorgeous words in the English language.

"He's awake."

"Oh, thank God. Thank God, thank God, thank God." Mrs. Edwards sagged with relief, but then seemed to remember herself. Back was the smooth face, the collected composure. "Take me to him."

"Certainly," the doctor said.

Mrs. Edwards squeezed my hand, and said to me with genuine warmth, "Let's go see Ashton."

She and I followed the doctor through the double doors. I barely noticed the antiseptic scent stinging my nostrils. The nurses in scrubs holding IV bags and rushing into rooms. The blazing fluorescent lights.

A big contrast to the dim lights and gentle beeping of the heart monitor in Ashton's room.

He was collapsed against his raised bed, tubes and wires snaking around him. His skin matched the stark white of the sheets, and there were dark circles under his eyes. He could have been sleeping, the peaceful way his chest rose and fell. But there was nothing peaceful about my boyfriend lying in the hospital because he'd tried to die.

My brain went to war. I wanted to run to him, but I

stayed rooted in place, watching as Mrs. Edwards went to her son. Brushed his hair from his forehead. Let her tears flow.

His eyes blinked open. Then he stared at her, his expression unreadable.

"I'm so sorry," she said to him. Then she buried her head in his chest while he sat, unblinking.

I shouldn't have been seeing this. My instincts screamed for me to step into the hall, let them have their moment. But then she gestured for me to come closer.

"I'll give you some privacy." She squeezed Ashton's hand before leaving and sliding the door shut.

I took his hands into both of mine. He moved over, making room for me in the hospital bed. I climbed in and pulled him into my arms.

"I was so scared," I whispered.

He let out a shaky breath. "I know. Me too. I—I'm going to get help."

"Promise? Because I don't ever want to pick out clothes and flowers for your funeral." I let out a shaky laugh. "I'm sorry. That was morbid."

He gave me a weak smile. "I get it."

"I'd much rather do that for our wedding someday. You know that, don't you?"

That soft look came over his face. "You still want to be with me? Even after all this?"

I smoothed his hair back. Ran my hands down his cheeks.

Over and over and over. He was warm. And breathing. Not cold and stiff. Not dead. "Yes."

He closed his eyes and leaned against me, his fingers curling into my blazer.

We didn't talk anymore. We clung to each other like life preservers. And in a way, in that moment, I think we were.

Chapter 40

Two days after his attempt, Ashton got switched from the ICU to the psychiatric ward. While he was there, I visited him every day after school. He didn't talk much, but he always moved over and made room for me in the hospital bed. He wrapped himself around me while I did my homework, and I kissed his forehead and played with his silky hair in between subjects. He was always so still, so quiet. What was he thinking about? He never said. Instead, he listened. He listened to me when I babbled on and on about school. He laughed when I told him about Blair's shenanigans, and grew indignant when I told him about Auden's latest obnoxious attempts to unsettle me with all her smack talking. And I brought him junk food, which he devoured.

A week later, he transferred to Lucerne Institution and Rehab Center, right outside town. They cut him off from the world so that he could focus intensely on treatment. I counted the days until I'd get to see him again.

★ · ● · ✕

April 16. Decision Day. I sat on the couch between my parents and refreshed my email over and over. Mom flipped through a magazine on one side of me and Dad screamed into his headset on the other, and neither of their activities did a thing to calm my jumping, jittering nerves.

I took deep breaths, trying to mentally prepare myself for the denial from McCafferty. Because, frankly, the chances of me getting in regular decision after being denied early action were very slim. The stats were dismal: less than 3 percent. Not even worth hoping for, really.

So I spent a lot of time psyching myself up to send my offer acceptance to DeKinsey, one of my backup schools. DeKinsey had a good science program. Not a specific astrophysics one like McCafferty, but enough core courses to prepare me for graduate studies at a school that did. Also:

1. DeKinsey cost way less than McCafferty, which meant less student loan debt.

2. They'd also offered me a scholarship, which was always a good thing.

3. I'd also gotten a bunch of private scholarships, and one corporate scholarship. My grades were making their way back to pre-Ashton-meltdown levels, and if I kept it up, the Preston senior scholarship was in the bag.

4. Campus was ninety minutes from home, too far to commute but close enough to come home and do laundry on the weekends.

It would be better to go there for so many reasons. So what if Auden was prancing around with her acceptance to *her* dream school? DeKinsey had a big, beautiful campus with another clock tower for me to fall in love with. Decent food in the cafeteria. Skilled professors. Most important, they wanted me. Things were going to be fine. They were.

No matter what happened.

No matter what happened.

My inbox dinged and

There.

It.

Was.

I grabbed Mom's arm. She dropped her magazine. "Well?"

I froze. "I can't do it."

"I can't, either."

We looked at each other.

"So now what?" I asked.

She reached across me and poked Dad. "James."

"One second... YES. Got you, you mouth turd!"

Mom thrust the laptop at Dad, who stared at her in confusion. "What?"

"It's Devon's letter from McCafferty."

"Oh. *Ohhhhhhh!*"

He clicked. "It says I need to log in."

"Just click the link. My password should be saved."

Dad clicked twice, then, his face giving nothing away, turned the screen toward me.

> Dear Miss Kearney,
>
> Congratulations! On behalf of the staff and faculty at McCafferty University, it is with great pleasure...

"I'm in." I sat stock-still while I waited for it to sink in. "Oh my God, I'm in!"

Mom screamed and threw her arms around me. Dad did two quick fist pumps and yelled out the biggest "YES" I'd ever heard. That broke the tension and we all collapsed in laughter. We laughed and laughed. It felt so good to feel joy again.

"Honey, this is wonderful," Mom cried. "Cancel all your plans—we're going to celebrate! Call Blair! Tell her to come with us."

"I'm so proud of you," Dad said, squeezing me. "Frankly, I'm not even surprised, but that doesn't make this moment less special. How are you feeling?"

"I'm in shock," I said.

They laughed again. But I wasn't kidding. Was this really happening?

The proof was right there. I couldn't see the stars right now—it was still daytime—but I knew they were out there. And now I was going to be able to catch them.

I turned to the sky and silently said *Thank you* to the universe.

Meanwhile, Dad was already crunching the numbers. "With your scholarships and what we have put away for you, we won't need to take out too much in loans to cover the rest of your undergraduate career."

"And I can always work."

Dad's forehead wrinkled. "Mom and I would rather you focus on your studies."

"In that case, I qualified for some student loans," I said quietly. "I filled out a FAFSA when I did my Common App."

Stunned, Mom and Dad looked at each other, then at me.

"Sorry not sorry, but your TurboTax password was super easy to crack." I pulled up a file, then turned the screen to Dad.

With a slight frown, he nodded and punched more numbers into the calculator on his phone. Then he and Mom looked at each other again. She gave him a slight nod.

"So, here's the deal, Pumpkin," Dad said. "Mom and I talked a lot since our chat in the fall, and we've already decided we're going to take out a loan for you. We've qualified for a private one with a great rate."

"You don't have to—"

"Save your direct loans for graduate school. Let us take care of you for now."

My breath caught. "So, this is real."

"This is real, Bun."

"McCafferty is a go?"

"McCafferty is a go," Dad confirmed. "Send in that acceptance and make us all proud."

Chapter 41

LATE APRIL, ASHTON FINALLY REPLIED TO THE THOUSAND letters I'd sent him. My eyes welled up when I saw the letter in the mailbox at the end of a craptastic Monday. I couldn't get to my room fast enough to read it.

Dear Devon,

How are you doing? I hope okay. I miss you all the time.

Thank you for writing so many letters. Now I have something good to read every night before I go to sleep.

You asked about my days. They wake us up every morning at six, even on the weekends. I get a ten-minute shower, and I have to use an electric shaver because they don't trust me with blades. Breakfast is okay on cereal days. Group therapy freaks me out. I sit with a bunch of other kids who are as fucked up as I am, and the leader picks on one of us every day. I had my worst day Thursday. I ended up in the quiet room, where they send us to freak out. For some reason, that moved me up a level, and that's why they finally gave me your letters.

I have a private therapy session every day. The therapist asks a bunch of really hard questions, and I think he gets off on making me cry. Every time I have a session I think was bad, he tells me to keep up the good work.

I can have visitors on Wednesdays and Sundays. I hope I'll see you soon.

I love you always,
Ash

★ · ● · ✕

Lucerne was a colonial-style brick building with fancy landscaping and lots of trees. The lobby tried to give off a semblance of comfort, with its big green chairs and dozens of plants, but I could taste the unease in the air. My hand shook when I signed in at the front desk. The receptionist led me to the common area where the patients visited with family members or friends. I tapped my foot while I waited for Ashton to appear.

I'd researched how to support someone after a suicide attempt, so I was ready. I was ready to be positive for him. Encourage him. Make plans with him. I was ready to be an ear whenever he needed me. Every single time he needed me.

When Ashton finally appeared, escorted by who I guessed was a social worker, I had to draw in a breath. He looked younger in his polo shirt and jeans. The lines were gone from around his mouth and eyes, and his hair was shaggy.

"Dev!" His face lit up, and I launched myself into his arms. There was no familiar waterfall scent this time, but he smelled clean, like a bar of pure white soap. I held tight because I couldn't believe I was touching him again, feeling his heart beating against me.

"You're here," he murmured into my hair.

"I got your letter Monday. I wanted to come that night."

"I'm so glad to see you." Already his fingers were twirling my curls. "Come on, let's sit over here."

He took my hand and led me to a quiet corner. We sat together on a squashy green love seat. For a few minutes, we regarded each other. Soaked each other in. It felt so perfect to have his eyes on me.

"You look good," I said.

He ruffled his soft waves. "I need a haircut."

"I kinda like the shagginess. Makes you look less intense."

He frowned thoughtfully. "I didn't realize my look was intense."

"Sometimes you didn't look quite so wound up. Mostly when you were sleeping. You actually look your age today."

"What, you're saying I looked old?" He smirked, so I knew he was teasing.

"Well, not exactly old. More like stressed out. Now you remind me of how you looked that summer." Except maybe more tired. Sadder.

He took a deep breath. "I hate that you saw what happened that day."

"Ashton, it's okay."

"It's not, really." He looked down. "I was really sick. I still am."

"But you're in here. Getting better."

"Trying to."

I wrapped my arms around his waist and snuggled against him. He rested his chin on my head and twirled my curls around and around his fingers.

"I miss you," I murmured, closing my eyes and sighing. I loved when he played with my hair. When he threaded his fingers through the spirals. Massaged my scalp. He never seemed to mind getting coconut oil all over his fingers if it meant getting to touch me that way.

I glanced around, taking in the families playing card games, the patients eating junk food, the counselors keeping a discreet watch over the whole scene.

"Tell me about some of these people," I said.

Ashton nodded in the direction of a stocky redhead with glasses. "That guy over there? That's my roommate, Luke. We don't talk much, and he's in a separate group from me, so I have no idea what he's in for."

"But you know about the people in your group?"

"What they share. We don't really get to talk outside of group."

"Why not?"

"Not allowed. Not allowed to be alone, either, really, especially if you're a suicide risk."

Suicide risk. He said it as if it were no big deal. As if it were the flu or something.

"My first week in here, they watched me all the time," he said. "I couldn't even go to the bathroom without an escort. I still can't have floss or mouthwash."

"You must hate that. Why?"

"I could hurt myself with the floss. And mouthwash has alcohol."

I sat back, astonished. "People get that desperate?"

"You'd be surprised." He gestured toward one of the attendants watching the room—a pale, college-aged, brown-haired guy wearing scrubs. "That's Brett. He was my escort. He's an intern."

"He looks nice."

Ashton grabbed a marker and started flipping it around. "I hate not having my freedom, and I hate being watched all the time. But I'm used to the routine now. It's good, in a way. They keep us so busy, I don't have time to think too much."

"Have your parents come to see you?"

"My mother came this morning. She ate lunch with me and brought me a bag of snacks." He sighed, his expression tired and sad. "She's trying."

"That's a good thing, right?"

"Yeah. I mean, it's going to take more than Cheetos and M&M's for us to be okay. But it's a start. As for my father... we're in group therapy. It's going as well as you'd expect." His face darkened. "I wish she would divorce him. But she's so worried about her image, and all that other WASP bullshit."

"But your family doesn't do the divorce thing, remember?"

He frowned, tapping his lips with the marker. "My mother can be the first, then. A trailblazer. Shaking things up."

We were quiet for a while. The chill from the air-conditioning blew right on me, and I wrapped my arms around myself.

"I got into McCafferty," I said.

He dropped the marker. "What? Holy shit, Dev! That's awesome." He sounded excited, but the light didn't reach his eyes.

"So I guess we'll see each other on campus next year?"

He shifted. "Maybe."

"What do you mean 'maybe'?"

"Dev," he said with his wry smile, "I'm a mess. Like, truly a mess."

I brushed his hair from his forehead. "A beautiful mess."

"Nothing beautiful about this. It's not romantic at all, Devon." He shook his head. "You shouldn't have to put up with it."

"I'm not *putting up* with it," I said, my voice quiet. "I'm here because I love you. This is part of loving you."

His expression turned serious. "Devon, you're heading to your dream school. Your life is about to become epic, and you should be focusing on that, not worrying about if I'm going to hurt myself." He chewed his lip. "A lot of times I feel guilty about dragging you back into my life."

"But you didn't drag me. I wanted you like you wanted me. I still do."

"And you're the best thing that's ever happened to me. God, I love you so much."

"So why does it feel like you're pushing me away?" I asked in a small voice.

Ashton picked his nails—since when did he do that?—then ran his hands through his hair. "I'm going to be in here a long time. My counselor thinks I can get better with a lot of work. He thinks we can make the Dark go away, but I don't know. I'm on a ton of medication right now, and I'll be on medication for the rest of my life. I'll probably have to go to therapy for the rest of my life, too."

"Okay."

"I don't want to force that on you," he said. "And I don't want to make you wait for me."

"You're not making me do anything."

"Aren't I, though?"

I looked him in the eye. "Sometimes I'm scared that I'm not strong enough to deal with"—I waved my hand around—"this. I don't know what it's like to want to take my life. I have no idea how to relate to you in that way. I worry that I'm going to do or say the wrong thing."

"No! God, no." He put his hand on my cheek. "You could never."

"After that day in the ER, I kept wondering how I could've kept you from taking all those pills."

He wiped away the tear racing down my face. "None of this was your fault, okay? It's my brain. I get so deep inside my head that I don't remember what's real. See, this is what I mean. This isn't the life you're meant for. I'm not worth it."

"Don't ever say that," I said fiercely. "You're everything to me."

He took a deep breath. His hands shook. Something strained came over his face, and the tension was suddenly rope thick. I could barely breathe.

"What if I let you go?" he asked. "You can go to college, date other people. Meet someone who's not messed up like me. You deserve that, Dev."

I grabbed his wrists. "There are two of us in this relationship, Ashton. I want to stay with you."

"But is that the best thing?"

"You can't go through what we did and throw it away."

"But that's just it," he said, his voice scarily calm. Steady. "You shouldn't have had to go through it."

"Yeah, but it happened, and we're here—"

"Devon, I want you to live a normal life."

My throat was stinging. "Well, stop it. I want to live *our* life. Together."

He shook his head and turned away.

"Don't," I said. "Do not shut me out. Don't you dare."

He turned back to me, his face flushed. "I look at you sitting here, and all I can think is that you can do so much better.

You're beautiful and incredible. There's a world out there waiting for you to conquer it, and I'm holding you back."

"Stop! I know things suck for you right now, but I'm here. I'm *right here*, Ashton."

"I just need some time. Okay? We both do."

I tried to control my breathing but the air got stuck in my throat, choking me. Burning me. "I can't believe you're doing this. You promised you weren't going to leave again."

He leaned his forehead against mine. "I love you with all my heart, Devon. But you gotta let me go."

I grabbed his wrists again. "No, dammit. I already told you *no*."

He kissed the top of my head. Then he stood and walked away.

Chapter 42

STUNNED.

Absolutely, positively stunned. There was no way he'd just broken up with me.

Somehow, I made my way out to my mother's car. I sat frozen in the driver's seat, not seeing anything. Not feeling anything.

Numb.

I had to stay numb. I couldn't let this destroy me. I couldn't let *him* destroy me. Not when I'd promised myself I would be stronger. Not when I'd promised myself I would be better.

Pain.

I pinched my thigh hard so I would stop focusing on my heart, which I thought was going to jump right out of my chest. I was shaking so much I couldn't get my seat belt to buckle. It would not go in. A sob caught in my throat, but I swallowed it back down. Because I wasn't going to do this. Not again. Never again.

Somehow, I got home. Mom sat in the living room, legs crossed, eyes closed. Meditating. Her calm face a complete contrast to the meteor storm inside me. I focused on her orange tank top. On her big gold hoop earrings. Her flawless brown skin. Anything to keep my mind off what had happened at Lucerne.

Her eyes fluttered open. "Hey, Bun. How'd it go?"

"Fine," I said with false brightness. "Great."

Her smile faded and was replaced with concern. She was gearing up for a big old heart-to-heart, but I could not do that right now. I needed to do something physical. Hard. Intense. Yoga wasn't going to be enough. I needed to run.

Ten minutes later, I was flying down my street. The trees were soft with their rosy pinks and cottony whites. Flowers were shyly poking colorful heads through the soil. Everything was coming to life around me.

But I was dying inside.

Sometimes, looking at stars didn't make me feel excited. Sometimes, stargazing made me feel small and insignificant. As if nothing I did or said on this Earth mattered in the long run because I was nothing but a tiny speck in the midst of billions of red giants and pulsars and galaxies and planets.

And I know it was clichéd to feel like that. But how could I not?

That night, I dragged my telescope out to the backyard and strained to see the stars through my tears. The technology was top-notch. Ashton had chosen well. But what did it matter when I couldn't stop shaking enough to even focus on the Big Dipper? So I gave up. I let myself feel small and insignificant, because this way, at least I had a real reason to be sad, instead of being pathetic and feeling sorry for myself. That night, I raged at the sky, at these stars that had let me down. Wishes didn't really come true, and the thing was that I'd always known better.

★ · ● · ✕

"What the King Kong fuck?" Blair exploded. "I'm going to fucking kill him if I see him."

"Don't do that," I said flatly. "Your going to prison isn't going to help anyone."

"He doesn't get to do this to you again, Devon," she said. "Not after everything you've done for him. You saved his life! And you were in that hospital every damned day. I was rooting for him, and he pulls this shit? I swear, I'm going to Lucerne to kick his ass for hurting you again."

"He asked his grandma about rings, Blair." My voice broke then.

She gave me a fierce hug. "I'm so sorry. You've been through so much with him. I really hoped you two would make it."

That didn't help, either. I clenched my fists and sobbed into my best friend's shoulder.

I had gone back to Lucerne the next visiting day, Sunday. When the attendant told me that Ashton wasn't able to see me, I'd nodded and walked out, my throat tight.

Okay. Fine. Whatever. I didn't need him. But if it had to be like that, I wanted the last word. After I got home, I pulled out stationery and chewed on my pen.

What I wanted to write:

You probably think I miss you. Well, I don't. I don't miss you at all.

I'm starving for you. I'm longing for you with every part of me, and it's tearing me apart that you're not here. Do you think about me half as much as I think about you? Wait, don't answer that. It would break my heart if you said no. Because I can't stop thinking about you.

I can't stand that you ended it. Ended us. We were amazing together. But right now, I hate you.

What I wrote instead:

> I shouldn't even be writing, but once upon a time, I told you everything. It's a hard habit to break. You were such a big part of my life, and now you aren't. You didn't give me a chance to say good-bye—again—so I guess I'm doing it now.
>
> So...this is it. Please take care of yourself.
>
> Love,
> Your Sunset Girl

I debated all evening whether to mail it. Finally, Monday morning at school, I put the letter in the mail drop. Now it was up to him to make the next move, and up to me not to obsess about it.

Time to move on.

Again.

Chapter 43

The weeks passed by in a blur of projects and exams and senior activities. College acceptances or not, the teachers continued to squeeze every drop of work out of us before we left this place for good. I was grateful for the demanding assignments because they distracted me so thoroughly. Graduation loomed, but I couldn't bring myself to get excited.

I was so over *everything*.

"Hey, I heard about Ashton," Auden said to me right after Mother's Day. She tugged one of my curls. "Is he all right?"

Leave it to her to be doubly annoying right now. Today had been long and exhausting, and I just wanted Calculus—and this day—to be over with. "Did you just touch my hair?"

"It's so silky," she said. "I didn't expect it to be that silky."

What. The. Hell.

"He's getting better," I said through clenched teeth. "And if you touch my hair again, I'll bite you."

She grinned. "I'm glad to hear he's better. You've been totally out of it, and it's no fun antagonizing you when you just sit there and take it."

I rolled my eyes. "Whatever. I beat you on yesterday's pop quiz, and you are still salty."

"Ha, listen to you, being all ghetto."

Whoa whoa whoa. Hold the phone. "What the hell, Auden?"

She poked my shoulder. "Don't tell me you're mad. It's not like you're really ghetto."

I took a deep breath to keep from smacking her, but I didn't erase the threat from my voice. "I'm not mad. I'm tired. I'm done."

She switched on her tablet. "Lighten up, Devon. You're being too sensitive. It was a joke."

A joke, my ass.

"Auden, why is that word even in your mouth? Is it because I'm Black?"

"Of course not! There are ghetto white people."

Inhale two... three... four.

Exhale two... three... four.

I could not make a scene right now. Because I was in a rich, white private school on a scholarship and going off on Auden, who was really very clueless and also really very wealthy, would not be good at all. Thank God the teacher started droning on about derivatives. Derivatives made sense. Derivatives had order. Just like me, on the outside. I could go on pretending that everything was fine, just fine.

During the days, I faked it pretty well. I smiled when I was supposed to smile, laughed at all the right jokes, participated in all the senior activities, and posed for a billion photos. I had everyone fooled. I was rocking this. Everything was great. Fan-fucking-tastic.

Night? Not so much. I literally ached, longing to hold Ashton again. Kiss him again. I wanted to hear his voice, stroke his hair, breathe in his waterfall scent. I hated that he was in that institution all alone and that I wasn't there to hold his hand when things got hard. I hated that he didn't want me there. But mostly, I hated that I missed him so much. I hated how weak it made me feel. And I hated that I couldn't control my feelings. Turn them off like a faucet. Then destroy the sink so they wouldn't come dripping out again.

Then there were the nightmares. Dream after dream of those texts of his flashing ominously, like strobe lights. Of me rushing to his room that day, only for it to be too late, only for him to be gone forever. I lost count of how often I jerked awake at the sound of my sobbing. Then stayed awake, soaking my pillow once I remembered that he was indeed alive, but still lost to me forever.

Because as the weeks went by, it became evident that he wasn't going to write me back. And one day it sank in. It was really and truly over. I hadn't even realized I'd been holding out for a change of heart. So this sucked.

Dad found me crying in bed that night. I tried to dry my face with the pillowcase, but he wasn't fooled. Not at all.

"Whatever it is, I can make it better," he said, hugging me tightly.

"No, Daddy. Not this," I choked out.

Mom sat on the other side of me and stroked my hair. My parents stayed with me for hours, comforting me with their quiet strength. And when the words came tumbling out, they listened, without judgment—only with love.

After Memorial Day, Mom and Dad sent me to therapy.

"I don't need a therapist. I'm fine," I told them. And I really was! I had finally stopped crying myself to sleep every night, and my appetite was halfway back to normal. I still missed Ashton, but I really was getting better.

"You've been through a lot," Dad said. "Ashton's suicide attempt was a serious situation, Pumpkin. And the breakup on top of that. You need to talk about stuff. Process it. Mom and I aren't equipped. We want you to see a professional."

They made me see the counselor for other reasons, too. "You need to find your way back to yourself," Mom said. "I know you think you're okay. But, Bun, you're not. You haven't been for a long time."

I hated Dr. Braun. I hated her bland office with its ugly tan rug and dull beige couch and blocky brown bookcases. I hated her clipboard and clicky pen, her sensible shoes, her boring khaki pants and white blouse. I hated her wavy brown hair and milk-white skin and mauve lipstick. I hated how she was always calm no matter how much I yelled. But mostly, I hated how she dug and dug and dug until I was sobbing in her office. She made me feel so weak, so pathetic because I loved Ashton so much. Because I apparently didn't love myself enough to realize that my relationship with him had become "codependent" and "unhealthy."

"Were you with him because you truly loved him, or because you felt like you needed to be with him so he wouldn't hurt himself?" she challenged, her beady eyes burning holes into mine.

"I loved him," I told her, my fists clenched. "I loved him before I knew about this stuff, and I love him now."

"You constantly redefined your boundaries for him. You were worried and stressed all the time over him. Do you think being codependent equals love? A good relationship?"

"What does that even mean?"

"Devon, on more than one occasion, you rearranged your life for him."

"But that's what people in relationships do. They make room so the other person can fit."

"Might you have been making an excessive amount of room, especially near the end?"

"I worried about him," I said in a low voice. "I still do."

"I know," she said gently. "And while it's normal to be concerned about your loved ones, this isn't healthy. Have you considered that it's better for you to not be with him? At least while he's healing?"

True, it was easier knowing he was at Lucerne, where he couldn't hurt himself. Knowing that professionals were looking after him, so I didn't have to feel responsible for making sure he was okay. But was it better? I didn't think so. I still thought about him constantly, and no matter what, I couldn't make myself stop loving him. I couldn't stop wishing he and I were back together.

"Do you ever feel like he's holding you back?" she asked, her voice even more gentle.

"I'm getting awesome grades. I'm going to college. I got scholarships. I'm okay."

"Are you sure?"

Why couldn't she understand? I hadn't been looking for love, but it came steamrolling in, and it changed me. But I was still the same Devon at the core. *Wasn't I?*

I crossed my arms. "I'm sure."

She studied me with her irritating calmness. As if she could see what I tried to hide, even from myself—especially from myself. Except I *wasn't* hiding anything, so why did she have to keep picking—*tearing*—into my soul?

"Stop!" I yelled. "Please stop it!"

"You're angry."

"I—" I started to protest, but then I clamped my mouth shut, clenching my jaw until it ached. She had it wrong. I wasn't angry. I was furious.

"Who are you angry at?"

"Him. Me. Everyone."

She watched me with that annoying thoughtful expression. "Why are you angry at yourself?"

I picked at the fringe on my gray T-shirt. "I should have known better than to fall in love with him again when he hurt me before."

She sighed and leaned back. "I wish you wouldn't beat yourself up over falling for him. In many ways, he sounds like a good person. And even if he wasn't—again, love plays by its own rules. *It's okay that you love him.*"

"Even when it hurts so much?"

She nodded. "Even then."

"Oh."

"You said you're angry at him. Tell me why."

"I don't know if I can." My throat hurt. It was hard to talk.

"Can you try?"

I nibbled my thumbnail. "I don't like being angry at him. He's sick."

She set her clipboard on her desk. "What do you want to say to him?"

I closed my eyes and let the anger settle into my bones. I let the hurt and rage I'd been trying to resist overcome me until the words flew out. "I don't know what I want to say, but I know I want to make him cry, like he made me cry." I dug my fingers into my jeans. "Sometimes I hate him. I hate him for hurting me; I hate him for not wanting to live for what we had, because it was beautiful. And I hate him because he won't let me be there for him. And those feelings are horrible, so I feel guilty on top of everything, and I hate him for making me feel *that*, too."

She held up her hand. "Hang on. This is not the time to be so judgmental of yourself, Devon. Earlier you told me that he made promises to you, that he was even making plans for your future together. Your feeling of betrayal is completely normal."

"But he's sick! I'm a terrible person for thinking these things."

"Feelings aren't good or bad," she said. "They just are. But how you handle them is what makes you a terrible person or not."

I managed to let out a small snort. "Thankfully, my brain is still working even though my emotions are a hot mess."

She glanced down at her clipboard. "You said you were angry at him for not wanting to live for what you and he had. Do you think he was selfish?"

I wrapped my arms around myself. "I think I could've helped him more."

"There's nothing you could have done to fix this. You said it yourself. He's sick. Only proper treatment—whatever that entails for him—can help him cope with his depression and suicidal ideation. You have to stop blaming yourself, especially when you did an amazing thing. By checking on him that day, you saved his life."

She crossed her legs, then tapped her clipboard. "Devon, I don't know Ashton other than from what you've told me, but I do know something about depression. You said you were deeply in love. In the meantime, he was fighting a constant war with himself and what his brain was telling him. I'm going to wager that he felt he didn't deserve what the two of you had together. That he didn't deserve you."

"Sometimes I wish he was normal," I blurted. "But I know I don't mean it, because I don't even know what *normal* is. His depression is a part of him. And I love *all* of him."

"You wish things could be easier."

"Yeah." I nibbled my fingernail. "Is that bad?"

"He needs a lot of help, way more than you're capable of giving him. That doesn't mean you can't be there for him, but I'd hate to see you neglecting your own life trying to save his."

"I worry about him. All the time. I don't think that's ever going away. I'd be okay with that if it meant I could have the rest of him, too. But now, all I have is the worry, and I'm pissed off that he made it like this. If I'm going to have all these feelings, I want everything else that comes with it."

"Except he took that choice away from you."

I nodded. "That's another reason I'm mad."

"And as I said, that's okay. But, Devon, try not to let the anger consume you. It won't bring him back, and it'll only hurt you."

I let out a long sigh. "So what should I do?"

"Focus on you. Whenever you start to think about him, turn it back to you. You can do that by journaling. Talking with your best friend, your parents. Don't keep your feelings bottled up. You have to process them so you can heal."

"Will I ever stop loving him so much?" I asked in a small voice.

She gave me a tissue and a sad smile. "He was your first love. He'll always have a special place in your heart. But one day you'll be able to move on. I promise."

"But what if I don't *want* to move on?" My voice, smaller still.

"Ultimately, only you can decide what's right for you. I do urge you to take care of yourself. Loving a person who has a severe mental illness is challenging at best. Devastating at worst, with every high and low in between." Her phone let out a tiny ding. "That's our time for today, but I'd like to see you next week. Will you come back?"

I nodded and gathered up my stuff. "Thank you, Dr. Braun."

"You're going to be all right. You know that, don't you?"

I paused, then nodded. "Yes."

Chapter 44

Graduation day. So bittersweet. On one hand, I was super excited to walk that stage and hold that diploma in my hand. The stars were waiting for me, and I was so close to catching them! But on the other hand, how could I say goodbye to a place that had been my second home for so long?

I stared in the mirror, putting the finishing touches on my hair. A million bobby pins to keep my graduation cap from tumbling to the ground. A few golden curls to frame my face. Then I slipped on a pair of sparkly earrings and smoothed my white sundress. Perfect.

Sugary breakfast scents wafted into my room, making my stomach grumble, so I headed to the kitchen.

Dad looked up from frying eggs and making cinnamon

toast. "There she is! The woman of the hour! Ready for your big day?"

"Totally."

"I'm so proud of you." Mom squeezed me. "You're graduating at the top of your class. Dream college sewn up, scholarships in place. You really are incredible, you know that?"

My cheeks grew warm with pleasure. "I guess I'm all right."

When we got to school, my parents took their seats in the courtyard while I met Blair in the staging area next to Campbell Hall. The scent of freshly cut grass tickled my nose, and a light breeze took the edge off an already boiling sun.

Blair grabbed my hands. "I still can't believe today is our last day of high school," she said. "Finally!"

I glanced up at Bishop Hall towering over me in all its glory. Any minute now, the bells would ring to signal the start of the ceremony. "I'm going to miss this place."

"Ugh. You would. I thought we'd never get through it. I'm so looking forward to summer. No homework. No rushing from class to class. Just long, lazy days with my best friend forever."

"Damn straight!" I grinned at her, but she was looking over my shoulder, her expression suddenly hard.

"What in the—?" I turned around and found myself looking right at Ashton. "Oh."

I hadn't seen him since that Ugly Day in April. His graduation gown flowed in the wind, but the cap sat on top of his head like a perch. He leaned against a tree, a thoughtful frown on his face. I wasn't prepared for the ache that rushed me as our gazes locked and held.

His lips parted as he gave me a slight nod, and I managed to nod back before turning to Blair. I needed to keep it together. I was the valedictorian, and I had a speech to give.

But ugh, really? Not so long ago, he and I had been naked in each other's arms, connected in the most intimate way possible. And today, I get a nod from across the courtyard?

"Want me to smack him?" Blair asked, her face pink and tight with irritation.

"Your violent tendencies are really starting to concern me."

"What can I say?" She shrugged. "He inspires rage. The Rat Bastard."

"Hey, Devon." Auden popped up and held her hand out to me. "It was iffy for a while there, but you earned that top spot fair and square. Congrats."

Leave it to her to bring up a time I'd rather forget. Thank God for makeup tests, extra credit, and the willpower to study until my eyeballs were raw. I didn't lose my straight-A status, although I came very close.

"Listen, I'm sorry about the 'ghetto' thing," she said. "I messed up. But I'm learning to be better."

I'd almost forgotten about that. But this was big of her. Auden never apologized for anything. "We're good. But keep learning."

"You got it. Sign my yearbook?" She thrust our final creation at me. They'd come out beautifully. Hunter green and gray, every page told of our legacy. From the Harvest Ball, to pop quizzes, to exams and meetings, to lifelong friends and people who changed us forever.

These Are Our Moments.

Damn right they were. Good and bad, painful and joyous. They were ours. They were mine.

I handed my yearbook to Auden and chewed on my pen as I thought of what to write in hers. What did one say to someone so annoying?

"Ahem." Dr. Steelwood cleared her throat. "Everyone please line up."

I shivered all over when the music blared. Elgar. "Pomp and Circumstance March in D Major, Op. 39, no. 1." We marched in to the slow, hopeful rhythm of the violins, filing into row after row of white wooden chairs. My face heated when I spotted my parents. They were shameless: Mom dancing in the aisle and snapping a billion pictures, Dad yelling *woooooo* like a frat boy. And I loved them for it.

The crowd roared as the top ten students marched across the stage. The brilliant sunshine kept my mind off my sweaty palms. I barely paid attention as we sang the school song, and I totally zoned out when the speeches began. I almost missed them calling my name, but I managed to make it up to the podium without incident and deliver my farewell speech without one flaw. The cheers that rose from the audience sent my heart soaring. The rest of the ceremony sped by in a blur, and then I had my diploma in my hands. We tossed our caps in the air and screamed. And just like that: High school was over. A chapter closed, and now I was waiting for the next one to open.

After the ceremony, we gathered in the field. Some people snapped photos, others signed yearbooks. My parents handed me a dozen pink roses—which would wreak havoc on my allergies, but I didn't care because I loved them so much—then captured a million photos of me.

Blair bounced over, hand in hand with Tyrell, her blue eyes twinkling. "We need pictures with our diplomas!"

I set my roses on the ground, and then Blair and I struck silly poses, grinning as the cameras clicked.

"Wait, one for Instagram!" Blair yelled, handing her phone to Tyrell, who snapped a million more pictures.

"Okay. I have to get going—my parents want to take me and Tyrell to a fancy lunch," Blair said, hugging me tightly. "I'll see you later at your party?"

"You'd better."

"We should get to the house," Mom said. "People are arriving for your party in an hour, and we've still got to pick up the cake."

"Okay." I started to walk with them, but then I remembered my flowers. "I need to get my roses."

"We'll meet you at the car," Dad called.

Preston Academy's courtyard was quiet now. The noon sun beat down on me, making me sweat. But I didn't mind. I'd take this over the dead of winter any day.

"Devon."

I froze. I knew that voice, except it wasn't icy. Not anymore. "Hello, Mrs. Edwards."

"Eleanor," she said. "Please call me Eleanor. And, Devon, I'd like to apologize to you."

It was all I could do to keep my mouth from dropping open. "Okay."

"I made many unfair judgments about you, and I was wrong for that. You're a kind person with a good heart, which is the only thing that should have ever mattered as far as I was concerned. Ashton is lucky to have you."

Is. Have. Present tense. Had he not told her he broke up with me? I had to admit that as much as I still missed him, it had been nice not having to deal with Edwards Family Drama.

I nodded stiffly. Because if she expected me to tell her she was forgiven, she had another think coming. Still, it must have taken a lot for her to admit this. I did give her credit for that.

"Congratulations on McCafferty," she said. "I know you will succeed there."

"How did—?"

"Endowment report. Remember?"

"Oh. Right." I gave her a small smile. "Thank you."

She squeezed my shoulder. "See you around."

Mind reeling, I headed back across the courtyard. White chairs were strewn haphazardly all over the lawn, along with crushed graduation programs and crumpled coffee cups. But no flowers. They weren't where I'd left them. I twirled around to look for them and crashed into something hard. No, not some*thing*. Some*one*.

"Whoa, sorry," Ashton said. He handed me the bouquet. "You all right?"

"Yeah," I choked out. "Fine."

I wasn't fine. My head was spinning because he was right

here and gazing at me with his intense look that made me lose all reason.

No, Devon, do not lose even a little bit of your reason.

"They sprung you, huh?" I tried to keep my voice light, but my heart was practically pirouetting out of my chest.

"Two weeks ago."

I gave in to looking at him. Drinking in his skin, which looked clear and healthy. His eyes, which were bright and deep. His hair, which was short and neat and thick. The dark shadows were gone, the lines faded. He was still skinny, though. He'd probably be a rail his entire life.

And he still took my breath away.

Would I ever stop having this reaction to him? Would I ever be able to look at him and feel nothing?

"You didn't come back to school," I said.

He shook his head. "I needed to take care of some stuff."

"How did you—" I gestured toward his diploma.

"Tutoring. Lots and *lots* of it. Basically, once I was well enough, all I did was study."

"Cool."

A crumpled program skittered across my feet.

"Can we talk?" he asked.

"You never wrote me back," I said.

He looked at the grass. "I did write you. I just never sent them." His voice lowered. "Didn't feel I had a right to."

More silence. God. How were we back to this awkwardness again?

My phone buzzed. A text from Mom:

Where r u?

"I need to meet my parents—"

"It won't take long."

I almost said okay, but then I remembered what Dr. Braun had said about me redefining my boundaries for him. My parents were waiting for me, and I needed to respect that. "I really have to go. But come to my house later. We're having my graduation party."

"You sure?"

I touched his hand. "I want you to."

I need you to. It's not fair how much I still need you when you were the one who said good-bye, but right now I don't care. I just want to be close to you.

He gave my hand a gentle squeeze. "I'll stop by."

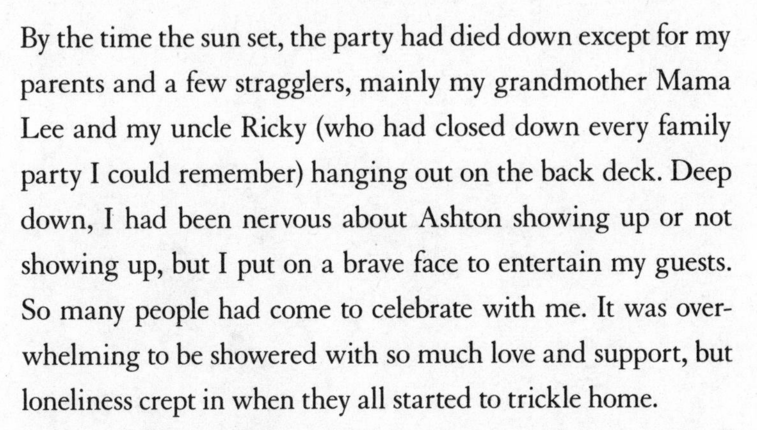

By the time the sun set, the party had died down except for my parents and a few stragglers, mainly my grandmother Mama Lee and my uncle Ricky (who had closed down every family party I could remember) hanging out on the back deck. Deep down, I had been nervous about Ashton showing up or not showing up, but I put on a brave face to entertain my guests. So many people had come to celebrate with me. It was overwhelming to be showered with so much love and support, but loneliness crept in when they all started to trickle home.

I curled up on our new porch swing, swatting mosquitoes and wiping beads of sweat from my forehead. I was sticky all over—from the heat, from the chocolate cake my parents had gotten custom-made for me, from all the line dancing with my family. "Electric Boogie." "Trans-Europe Express." Even "Boot Scootin' Boogie." It was one of those steamy nights where the air was so thick I may as well have been breathing in soup. I loved it.

When Ashton's car pulled up to the curb, I had to remind myself to breathe. By the time he stepped onto the porch, I was trembling all over. We looked at each other for a long time.

Then he pulled me close, and we stood there, clinging to each other as if the world would end if we let go. I buried my face in his shirt, but I refused to cry. He was never going to see a tear from me again.

NOW

"I CAN'T BELIEVE YOU BROUGHT YOUR TELESCOPE TO THE beach." Blair's voice came from behind me, the familiar lilt of affection rising and cresting with the waves. "You really are a nerd."

"This is the first time I've had one small enough to haul with me." I peered through the eyepiece again. "The sky is breathtaking out here."

"I'll take your word for it," she said. "Here, have some water."

I grabbed the bottle and drank deeply. "*Mmm.* I hadn't realized I was so thirsty."

She plopped down and dug red-painted toenails, which matched her skimpy red bikini, into the sand. "Sit with me. I want to talk to you."

With reluctance, I put the cover on the telescope lens and settled next to Blair. Buried my own (light-blue) toenails in the sand. Let the surf tickle my feet as it washed the sand away. "I've always loved this beach."

"It's really gorgeous here," Blair said. "And your cousin is awesome. So optimistic and happy. She's a complete gem."

"Well, it runs in the family. The gem part, I mean."

She poked my shoulder. "And you're a diamond, except when it comes to volleyball."

I buried my face in my hands. "Oh God."

She laughed, long, low, and rich. "What's up with you running away every time the ball comes toward you?"

"That bump thing hurts my forearms."

"You're such a wimp," she teased.

I shrugged. "I don't like balls flying at me."

She snorted. "You said *balls*."

"Oh my God. Why are you twelve inside?"

"You thought it was funny. Admit it."

"Okay, yeah, it was kinda funny."

"I'm going to miss this so much," she said. "Even though I'm excited to go to the Fashion & Design Institute."

"You're going to blow them away. I cannot wait to see what you come up with while you're there. And which free outfits you're going to design for me."

"Yes," she deadpanned. "Once you're a rich and famous astrophysicist, you can wear my clothes and everyone will want them. Free advertising for me!"

"Sounds like a win-win." I looked around with a content

sigh. "Summer in the Hamptons last year was awesome, but this place has my heart. Can't believe I almost let you-know-who ruin it for me."

Blair glanced at me, her eyebrow raised. "You needed time to heal. Nothing wrong with that."

"Maybe." I wrapped my arms around my knees. "What did you want to talk about?"

She pulled a bag of Doritos out of her tote. "We're talking about it now."

"Ashton?"

She offered the Doritos to me. "Do you miss him?"

"Of course." I grabbed a couple and started munching.

"I can tell. It's in your eyes."

"You've been gazing into my eyes? How romantic."

She poked me again. "I'm being serious."

I dragged my fingers through the wet sand. "I'm having a great summer, but I'm not going to lie. We made memories all over this place." My voice lowered. "I just want the real thing, too."

Blair pulled a joint out of her bag and lit it. Then she took a long drag, holding the smoke in longer than I thought was humanly possible. She blew out a series of smoke rings, coughed, and sipped her water. Her shoulders relaxed as it took hold.

"Better?" I asked, smirking.

"Oh yeah." She closed her eyes and smiled. Then she turned to me, blinking lazily. "So. Remember last week when I went to see Tyrell?"

"I kinda wish I didn't. You went into way too much detail about your reunion."

Her lips curved into the kind of smile that told stories and held secrets. Secrets involving whipped cream and...oh God, brain, stop.

She pulled an envelope out of her bag and tapped it. "I wasn't going to tell you, but I feel bad keeping things from you."

"What things?"

"I ran into Ashton."

I froze, my hand stuck in the sand.

"Do you want the lowdown?"

"I don't know. Do I?"

She rolled her eyes. "He wasn't with a girl, if that's what you're wondering."

"I wasn't—okay, I was." I couldn't even pretend with her. And my relief must have shown front and center on my face. "So? What's new?"

"He had a dog with him. Said his name was Buddy."

This meant a couple of things to me. First: Ashton must have been doing better if he took Buddy in. Second: Maybe he would stick around for a while. People who were planning to die by suicide didn't adopt pets, did they?

"Do you want a hit of this?" she asked.

I shook my head. "I'm good."

I wasn't good. Because now a million questions rushed through my head: Did he miss me? Did he think about me? Had he kissed another girl while I was spending the summer here? And what about those nights when the longing for more than kissing got to be too much? I went running on the beach. What did he do? Who did he turn to?

No. I refused to fall down that spiral. It wasn't my business, anyway.

"Does he seem happy?"

She tilted her head. "I mean, he doesn't seem *not* happy, but he looks better. If that makes sense."

"It makes perfect sense."

"How long's it been since you've seen him?" Blair asked.

I picked at the label on my water bottle. "Graduation night."

She stared at me. "Did you have sex with him?"

I nodded slowly. "Yeah. I thought I could handle it. I was wrong. So I told him I needed time off to think. Haven't talked to him since. But I'm still confused. And scared of how much I still love him."

Blair touched my shoulder. "You've been holding this in all this time? Why didn't you tell me?"

I breathed out a small laugh. "I was embarrassed. He hurt me *again*, and then I turned around and slept with him. Who does that?"

"A girl who's in love would do that. Devvy, you never have to be embarrassed with me."

I nodded and looked out at the rolling waves.

"Do you ever think about clearing the air?" Blair asked.

"Every single day. I just don't do it. I don't know what I want. Wait, that's not true. I still want him. But since I'm still so confused, I should just...*not* with him."

More smoke rings. "I get that, and I approve."

"School starts in two and a half weeks."

She rolled her eyes. "I know. You won't stop talking about how you're going to live in the dorms and join the Honor Society and study all the astronomy and physics and math forever and ever amen."

"I think he's going to be there."

She sighed. "It's a big campus, though, isn't it?"

"Not that big. Maybe we can have a fresh start."

She stared at me again, blinking those ridiculously long eyelashes. "You guys have way too much baggage for a fresh start."

I nodded again. "You're right."

Blair regarded me then, her dark hair blowing all around her face. Then she handed me the envelope. "He asked me to give this to you. I wasn't going to, just so you know."

I stroked the smooth, stiff envelope. "What changed your mind? I thought you hated him."

"I never hated him. I hated that he hurt you." She pointed to the envelope. "Are you going to open it?"

I slid my fingers under the flap and pulled out a photo. "Arcturus." In all his orangey-red glory. Standing out against his fellow Boötes constellation friends, a grand disk glowing among shimmery dots.

I let out a trembling breath, then stared out at the crashing waves. My eyes were blurring and I knew it wasn't from the sea spray. Or Blair's "herbal" refreshment.

"Told me he went out every night for two weeks, trying to get the perfect shot," she said. "He *begged* me to give it to you."

I studied the photo again. Perfect composition. Crystal

clear. He'd printed it on matte paper, which he'd once said was more professional than glossy. Eight by ten, the perfect size to frame and hang in my dorm room.

"I see the longing on your face when you're thinking about him." Blair's voice tugged me out of my thoughts. "It's like how I feel when I see a rare steak."

My head jerked up. "I don't want to *eat* him. God."

She stared at her joint, which barely had a single hit left. "I'm still not sure giving you that picture was the right choice. But I really want to believe you're stronger now."

Two summers ago, I'd sat in this same surf. The tide had carried the sand from under my toes. I'd had no idea that I was going to meet a boy who would change me in so many ways. I'd had no idea that I was going to fall deeply and relentlessly in love. I'd had no idea that my life would never be the same.

I'd never love anyone like I loved him. This I knew for sure. Maybe there was still a future for us, but it would take a lot of hard work to get there. That was okay. I wasn't afraid of hard work. I couldn't be, not with what McCafferty had in store for me.

But I was ready for McCafferty and its rigorous curriculum. Anything to push me toward my dream? I welcomed it with open arms. But was I ready and willing to do the hard work of being with Ashton? I knew I could handle it. Except there was this: I didn't want to be waiting around, wondering if and when he was going to break my heart again.

No matter how much I loved him.

I gazed at the sky, then at my photo of Arcturus. My red giant. I let myself fill with the star's strength one last time. Because now I needed to do things on my own. Make good choices. Be strong and smart and *ready*...for what was coming. For my dreams. For my life.

I was *so* ready.

I pulled out my phone. Scrolled to Ashton's name. The contact picture was the two of us on Christmas Day. Happy, radiant, excited. I smiled at the photo. Let out a long breath. Stroked the key pendant on my chain and relaxed. I didn't have to make a choice now. Because here was the thing: With or without him, no matter what happened, I was going to have an epic life.

AUTHOR'S NOTE

I WAS DIAGNOSED WITH DEPRESSION IN 2004. AFTER YEARS of wondering why my mood tended toward darkness, it was a relief to have a reason why. The diagnosis filled me with shame nonetheless. I struggled for years with taking my medication properly, with internalizing certain negative attitudes, with feeling as if I should be able fix it all myself.

Spoiler: I couldn't.

These days, with medication and therapy, I'm doing better. But even now, depression can sneak up on me and yank me back down into a hole I've been climbing out of for months or even years.

Sometimes it comes out of nowhere, taking over and making me so tired it's easier to give in than to fight it. Sometimes it's triggered by certain events. But all I care about is that it's here. Again. Pressing down on me like weights on my chest. Filling my brain until all I see is fog.

It lies and makes me think no one cares. That I have to do this all on my own. It tells me that I'm powerless. And the worst thing depression does is tell me that I'm unlovable.

I wanted to show my depressed character, Ashton, being loved—deeply.

Depression takes many forms for many people, but for me, the main constant is the lack of control I feel when it's taken over.

I wanted to write a book where my characters are taking control. Maybe they don't always get it right, but they try.

It's okay to keep trying. It's okay to keep learning. It's okay to get help.

We don't have to do this alone. There are resources out there. And it's always okay to turn to them.

Suicide Prevention

National Suicide Prevention Lifeline: suicidepreventionlifeline.org

In a crisis, call their free and 24/7 US hotline: 1-800-273-TALK (8255)

National Hopeline Network: 1-800-442-HOPE (4673)

American Association of Suicidology: suicidology.org

American Foundation for Suicide Prevention: afsp.org

Suicide Awareness Voices of Education: save.org

Suicide Prevention Resource Center: sprc.org

For Suicide Loss Survivors

Alliance of Hope for Suicide Loss Survivors: allianceofhope.org

American Association of Suicidology survivors page: suicidology.org/suicide-survivors/suicide-loss-survivors

Friends for Survival: friendsforsurvival.org

National Suicide Prevention Lifeline survivors page: suicidepreventionlifeline.org/help-yourself/loss-survivors

Understanding Mental Illness

Mental Health America: mentalhealthamerica.net

National Alliance on Mental Illness: nami.org

National Institute of Mental Health: nimh.nih.gov

ACKNOWLEDGMENTS

THE ROAD TO PUBLICATION IS LONG, AND FILLED WITH A LOT of ups and downs. Lots of feelings. Lots of hard work. Lots of *people.*

People like my agent, Caitie Flum, who told me she *dreamed about my characters.* I'd already known she was the right person—sensitive and fierce—to represent Devon's story, but that solidified it. Her vision for my book perfectly aligned with mine. Caitie, I must say we make a great team.

People like Kheryn Callender, who believed in me and in Devon's story, and who pushed for it to be out there. So grateful you took a chance on me.

People like my amazing editor, Nikki Garcia. She is a true rock star and a fierce editor, loyal and understanding, who knows just how much to push to get me to take risks and try new things. Nikki, every day, I'm happy and honored to work with you.

Thank goodness for organizations like We Need Diverse Books and POC in Pub, who continue to help pave the way for new stories and voices. You all laid the path, and I'm so happy I get to step onto it. I look forward to bringing others along with me.

Little, Brown Books for Young Readers has been my dream

publisher for years. They lived up to my expectations and more. My everlasting thanks to the editorial team for their hard work and thoughtful notes; the Novl team for their enthusiasm, incredible hugs, and excellent Instagram stories; my publicist, Katharine McAnarney, who is so chill and masterful; Lindsay Walter-Greaney, whose timeline work is worship-worthy; and the designer, Marcie Lawrence, who gave me the most perfect cover. I couldn't have dreamed up a better one!

I tried to give up writing many times. I am so glad I had an army of people behind me who refused to let me go through with it. Thank you to my critique partners: Rachel Foster—who refused to let me get away with anything; S. F. Henson—who was my cheerleader; and Regan McDonnell—whose notes always terrified me but were always spot on. Kody Keplinger, you saw a pretty early version of the manuscript and set me on the path to shaping it into an actual book. Thank you.

Thank goodness for #ChiYA—Samira Ahmed, Gloria Chao, Kat Cho, Lizzie Cook, and Anna Waggener. Yummy brunches, carpools, and delicious ice cream. Love you all.

Thank you to all the groups and group chats that have offered me support and love over the years: Black Fiction Squad, #SuperBlackGirlMagic, Kidlit Alliance, Novel19s, and Kidlit Authors of Color. You were there when I needed you, and for that I am grateful.

Dear Writing Weasels 2016, in a cold (to me) mansion in Scotland, you let me read my query and first chapter aloud. You encouraged me to keep going. Marieke Nijkamp, you have the best style, and I love how you move through the world. Fox

Benwell, you are perfect and I miss your restful nature. Dawn Kurtagich, you are as lovely as you are talented (Hint: That's a *lot*), and Cecilia Vinesse, I'll never be as cool as you are.

Rachel Strolle, you lovely, amazing person you! Your love for our books, and your tireless work to get them into the hands of people who want and need them, is not unappreciated or unnoticed. Thank you, thank you, thank you.

Jen aka The Book Avid, your voice is more important than you could ever know, and I'm so glad to know you.

#TeamCaitie! I feel like I found a group of sisters and brothers but we all write, too, and it's awesome!

Kendare Blake, you took a look at this book in its very, very, very early stages, and gave me feedback that made me want to keep going, keep improving, to get this out there. You're a true cheerleader, my friend.

Dearest Ivy Decker, you were one of my very first-ever online friends and my very first critique partner. You were one of the first people who took my writing seriously, who encouraged me to follow this dream. You've taught me so much over the years, not just about writing, but about life.

Mandy Hubbard...you've believed in me for fourteen years. You were with me from my very first baby steps into this industry, and I'm so glad you're with me now. Those hours-long AIM critique sessions finally paid off! Thank you for your incredible instincts and honest feedback. They helped mold me into the writer I am today.

Thank you to Chris Davis, for your encouragement when I tried this publishing thing the first time around.

Sarah Lisenbee...thank you for helping me stay sane on this journey, for keeping me grounded, and for your gentle encouragement. I'm so glad we have our Mondays.

Andy Green, you have been there for me so much for so many years. You are a true treasure, honestly. I mean, you believed in me so much that you once bought me a laptop! Finally, finally, I get to say, "Here is your book!"

Thank you to Wanda Lotus, for your support, for your love, and for inspiring me with your own creativity. Most important, thank you for *all* the attention!

Thank you to Adib Khorram, for always knowing. Just knowing. Your friendship is one of the best things that has come out of this book journey.

Thank you to my buttercup Jennifer Niven for your bright light. You are the Helen to my Gladys, my soul sister, my bestie. Here's to more European tours, plates of carpaccio, and quality time in the ABBA museum.

Rena Barron, you are my brainstorming partner, my rock, my safe space, my best friend. Words can't express how much you mean to me and how much I look up to you. Clown-face emojis forever!

Thank you, Lenora Kita, for never denying me the joy of reading and writing. For never making me turn out the light when I was reading under the covers (except that one Christmas Eve). For letting me dream. You're the best mommy a girl could ask for.

Thank you to Adam Selzer for putting up with me and my quirks, for indulging my Disney World obsession, and for building me my little writing nook, which is one of my favorite places in Chicago. This *is* the Good Place!

Thank you to Aidan Davis, for being the actual best son a mother could ever ask for. You're everything I wish I could be, but better. I still don't know how I got so lucky.

And finally... thank you, Dear Reader, for taking a chance on me, and on my words. I hope they've touched your heart, and I sincerely hope you come back for more.

Aaron Gang

Ronni Davis

lives in Chicago, where she copyedits everything from TV commercials to billboards by day, and writes contemporary teen novels about brown girls falling in love by night. You can visit her at ronnidavis.com, and follow her on Twitter and Instagram at @lilrongal.